PRAISE FOR JE

"Jennifer Jaynes writes a smart and twisty ~~thriller that's guaranteed~~ to keep you reading well past bedtime . . . I am anxiously awaiting the next book."

—Gregg Olsen, *Wall Street Journal* bestselling author of
A Wicked Snow

"Jennifer Jaynes serves up pulse-pounding suspense with a large helping of heart . . . She's an author to be reckoned with."

—J. Carson Black, *New York Times* bestselling author of
Darkness on the Edge of Town

THE STRANGER INSIDE

OTHER TITLES BY JENNIFER JAYNES

Strangers Series

Never Smile at Strangers

Ugly Young Thing

Don't Say a Word

THE STRANGER INSIDE

JENNIFER JAYNES

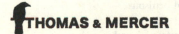

Text copyright © 2017 by Jennifer Jaynes
All rights reserved.

Published by Thomas & Mercer, Seattle

www.apub.com

Amazon, the Amazon logo, and Thomas & Mercer are trademarks of Amazon.com, Inc., or its affiliates.

ISBN-13: 9781477817919
ISBN-10: 1477817913

Cover design by Edward Bettison

Printed in the United States of America

For Mark Klein.
Thank you for believing in me all of these years.

Long dark hair, big bright eyes . . .
The type of girl that I despise . . .
At the count of three, or maybe two . . .
I will have a surprise for you.

PROLOGUE

AN ICY BLAST of wind roared through the quiet night, sending a beer bottle jangling across the concrete and a shiver sliding down the young college student's back. Exhaling loudly, she almost laughed at herself for being so creeped out.

Almost.

But she had the sinking suspicion someone was watching her, and with every step the sensation only grew stronger. What's more, it wasn't the first time. She'd had the feeling before. A week ago, she could have sworn she'd seen someone watching her through her small bathroom window. But when she'd told her friends about it, they hadn't taken her seriously. They'd just laughed it off, then quickly buried their noses back in their smartphones. And because they'd doubted her, it had been so easy for her to doubt herself.

She pulled her wool coat tighter around her body, suddenly wishing she didn't live off campus. She rented a ground-floor studio apartment from an older couple who lived in the top two floors of a three-level townhouse. At first she'd been hesitant to live in the same house as the couple, but her space was totally separate and she had her own side door. And the place had been a steal.

Her mother hadn't been very happy about her living alone. She'd seen too many horror stories about kidnappings and murders of young women on the evening news. The girl had seen the same stories on her own social media news feeds, but it hadn't been enough to scare her off from walking by herself at night.

Kidnappings . . . murders . . . those were the types of tragedies that happened to other girls. Not girls you actually knew, much less yourself.

Four nights a week after her classes ended, she took care of an elderly woman with Alzheimer's. She prepared food for her and read to her until the woman's son came home from work. And when he did, she normally called her boyfriend, and he walked her home. But they'd been arguing tonight. So tonight she was walking home alone.

Up ahead of her was the alleyway, a poorly lit four-block residential stretch she had to walk through to get to her apartment. She walked faster, the muted lights from inside the townhomes that lined the alley casting long shadows at her feet.

The stretch was usually teeming with college students—either walking home from class or heading out for a night of fun. But tonight it was deserted, silent except for the wind rushing through the skeletal trees. Most of the students had already left for Thanksgiving break.

Inhaling a combination of icy air and spicy wood smoke from nearby chimneys, she entered the dark alleyway. But she froze when she thought she heard footsteps.

She whirled around.

No one was there.

She frowned and started walking again, even faster. "You're letting your imagination get the best of you," she whispered to herself. When a gust of wind blew her long, dark hair forward, she didn't bother to brush it out of her face. She kept forging her way closer to her apartment. "Two blocks to go," she whispered through chattering teeth. "You've got this."

Without slowing, she dug her keys out of her backpack and fumbled for the sharpest one, tucking it between her fingers and fist.

If someone tried anything, she'd stab them.

The gate to her apartment building finally came into sight. The warm, yellow light above her door glowed like a beacon, but it still seemed a million miles away. There were still so many dark corners between her and the wrought iron gate that her landlord had instructed her to always close and lock once she was safely in for the night.

She heard it again. This time she was sure it was footsteps.

Whipping around, she peered into the darkness again—and this time she saw someone. A person about three yards away, wearing a hooded jacket and moving toward her.

"Um, hey," she called, walking backward.

Still moving.

"Pretty dark out tonight, isn't it?"

The person didn't answer, and the space between them started to close in.

Or was she just imagining it?

But some primitive part of her kicked in, telling her she wasn't imagining it at all. That this was bad. Very bad.

A bolt of terror shooting through her, she broke into a sprint. Her legs burned as she raced toward the gate. *Just one more block*, she told herself, her eyes brimming with tears.

A few seconds later, she grabbed the gate's cold metal handle and, in one swift movement, threw it open. It screeched against the concrete, and she dashed toward her apartment door. When she got there, she heard the metal squeal of someone opening the gate behind her, and the keys fell from her hand to the concrete.

Oh my God.

"Help! Please help! Somebody!" she tried to scream, but her throat was closing up on her, so her pleas were no louder than a whisper. She retrieved the keys, then fumbled to find the right one.

Hurry, hurry!

Sweat sprang up on the nape of her neck as she flipped through the keys: the key to her parents' house, one for her mother's car, for her father's car, for her PE locker. Finally finding the one that opened her apartment door, she jammed it into the lock.

When the lock turned over, she shoved her apartment door open and felt a soothing curtain of warm air caress her face. She could also smell the savory aroma of a hot dinner wafting down from the floor above.

As she scrambled to get inside, a hand shot out of the darkness and clamped down hard against her mouth.

CHAPTER 1

A STUBBORN RAY of sun weaseled itself into mystery writer Diane Christie's bedroom window and shone brittle morning light across her face. She stirred out of a restless sleep, an all-too-familiar feeling filling her stomach.

Something is very wrong.

At the thought, adrenaline flooded her veins. *Stop it*, she murmured to herself, her eyes still closed. Forcing the thought away, she pulled her thick down comforter closer to her body and turned to her side.

She'd been feeling the same curl of dread in the pit of her stomach every morning for over a year. Memories flashed into her mind, a recounting of the all-too-brief moment when her life seemed to be looking up: the six-week period when her rocky marriage seemed to be getting better, her five-year-old daughter adored her, and the adoption agency called and said they had the perfect baby for her. A little boy who had been abandoned by his mother at a hospital.

But the season had been short-lived, and before long her marriage had crumbled all over again. Now her husband was dead, and her daughter, who'd just turned nineteen, showed nothing for her but contempt and disdain.

She couldn't do anything for her husband now, but she wanted desperately to repair her relationship with her daughter. It had been an uphill battle over the years, but the last thing she would do was give up on one of her kids. She would do anything for them. And more than anything, she wanted her family to finally come together and feel whole. To feel as though, for once, they were all on the same team, the same side.

She inhaled the briny sea air that wafted in through her bedroom window and tried to relax her mind. Today was the day before Thanksgiving . . . exactly a year since she and her sixteen-year-old son, Josh, had moved to the small coastal town of Fog Harbor, Massachusetts, to escape what had happened back in New Jersey and be closer to her daughter, Alexa.

Fog Harbor had been very good to them. The house and community had been everything their landlord, Mr. Davidson, had promised it would be. Their rental was clean, large, and sunny. And even better, the neighborhood was quiet, the people were friendly, and the area was safe.

Her alarm clock sounded. She switched it off and swung her legs out of bed, her bare feet sinking into the carpet's lush pile. She went to her bedroom window that she had left cracked open the previous night and peered out at the harbor. She gazed out at the jewels of light that sparkled on the surface of the dark blue water.

The fishing boats had long left for the morning, and only sailboats now floated in the distance. She placed her palm on the cold glass of the window and let the calming scent of the sea loosen the knots in her shoulders.

But then her eyes caught a flash of color in the yard and her heart sped up. A man in a long leather coat was walking the property line. It took her a moment to realize it was her landlord. Before she could duck out of sight, she saw his eyes flicker up to the window and zero in on her. A smile spread across his face.

Sighing, she opened the window wider and chilly winter air rushed into her bedroom. "Good morning, Mr. Davidson," she called.

"How's my favorite mystery writer this morning?" he asked cheerily, rising on his tiptoes, then rocking back onto the hard winter ground. The man was never in a bad mood—or else he never let on that he was. He was an older gentleman, rail thin and friendly, and owned several rental properties in the area. He was also an avid mystery reader. When she'd filled out the rental application and he'd discovered who she was, he'd told her he'd read every book she'd ever written.

"No complaints. And you?"

"Great as always," he said. Still smiling, he pointed to the binder in his hand. "Just doing the usual monthly rounds, checking out my properties. Didn't mean to disturb you none. Did I wake you?"

"No, I was up."

"Oh, good."

The wind picked up outside, racing through the barren trees that bordered the yard and whipping through Mr. Davidson's gray hair.

"Well, if you don't need anything, I should go and get my day started," Diane said.

"Yes ma'am! Write me another one of your fantastic books, will you? And make the next one extra scary!"

Diane returned his smile. "I'll try and do that."

She slid the window closed and glanced at the clock on the bedside table: 7:47 a.m. She grabbed her phone and texted Alexa, asking if she was planning to come to Thanksgiving dinner. She'd called already and had sent two texts. But, as was typical, she'd gotten no answer.

She threw on her robe and tied it tight against her slender frame, then headed to the kitchen to pour a cup of coffee. But as she passed her son's bedroom, she heard a cough.

She froze in her tracks.

Josh had been expected at the high school by eight a.m. sharp for a makeup exam. They'd discussed this last night. Had he overslept *again*?

She knocked on the door. "Josh? *Please* tell me you're not in there."

She was answered by two more coughs, then a muffled "I'm not in here."

She opened the door to find not her son but a lump beneath the covers. "Are you feeling okay?" Josh had been diagnosed with an autoimmune disease called pulmonary sarcoidosis shortly after they'd adopted him at eighteen months old. And because of everything he'd been through medically, she couldn't help but be a little panicked any-time he exhibited symptoms of becoming ill again.

"Relax, Mom. I'm fine," he croaked.

"Are you sure?"

"Yes."

"Then up. Now. You can't be late again."

"I'm up. I'm up," Josh protested from beneath the covers.

"You can't blow this exam. You're doing *so* well this semester."

Josh surfaced, his dark hair unkempt and his eyes tired half-moons. "Don't worry. I've got it in the bag."

❖❖❖

WHEN DIANE STEPPED into the kitchen, coffee was already brew-ing. She poured a cup, then made Josh a quick sandwich to take with him.

She licked mayonnaise off the butter knife and set it in the sink, then flipped on the small, under-the-cabinet TV just as Josh clumped into the kitchen. As she pulled some stationery out of a cabinet to start her grocery list, she was distracted by the local news anchor:

". . . a report that a University of New Cambridge student was found murdered this morning. The student's body was discovered just over an hour ago by the property owner of the basement apartment she'd been renting—"

Oh my God.

A surge of adrenaline shot through her. "What the—?" Alexa attended the University of New Cambridge.

"Holy crap," Josh said a few feet away.

Diane swung around to face the television. The coverage continued at the crime scene, where a bundled-up reporter was interviewing onlookers. Tiny spikes of fear crawled up Diane's arms as she tried to simultaneously focus on the reporter's words and scan the scene in the background to see if anything looked familiar.

"Relax, Mom. It wasn't her. See?" Josh said, stepping forward and pointing at the screen. "That's not her apartment complex. It's a townhouse."

Josh was right. The crime scene was a townhome . . . *not* the apartment building where her daughter was leasing a studio apartment. She sank into a chair at the kitchen table to watch the rest of the report, her heart still drumming in her chest. When it was over, she glanced at her son. "Maybe I should drive you to school this morning."

"Seriously? That happened in New Cambridge . . . that's, like, ten miles away. Besides, I'm a big boy. I'll be fine."

Diane contemplated her son's words and realized he was right. Trying to ignore her instinct to be overprotective, she mustered a smile.

"You're right." She got up and followed him to the front door. "Good luck today."

Josh shrugged. "Luck? With this brain, luck's got nothing to do with it."

Diane smiled at her son, marveling at how quickly he was growing up. He'd been born with an innate sense of confidence and was much more laid-back than she or Alexa. Perhaps a little too laid-back at times, especially when it came to time management, but overall, she'd take the laxness over her near-constant state of anxiety anytime.

A few minutes later she watched him disappear around the corner in his Jeep. She stepped back into the house, grabbed her phone, and called Alexa again. As the phone rang, she finished her coffee and poured a second cup, then returned to the television set to watch for more news coverage. But now they were airing a dog food commercial.

Most of the time when Diane called Alexa, she didn't answer. She had better luck texting her, but even then, Alexa didn't respond 95 percent of the time. Alexa was angry with Diane—she had been since she was five years old. Although Alexa wouldn't admit it, Diane suspected much of the anger had to do with her adopting Josh, who was three years Alexa's junior.

After all, Alexa had gone from a seemingly happy and loving five-year-old girl to a melancholy, painfully reserved, and rather awkward child shortly after they had brought Josh home as a foster child and learned that Josh would require frequent hospitalizations . . . which meant long stints away from home for Diane.

And long stints away from Alexa.

"Dammit, Alexa," she said, again getting a computerized voice for her daughter's outgoing voice message. "For once, just answer," she said to the phone.

After a few minutes and no reply from Alexa, she poured her coffee into a to-go cup and bundled up. She was driving to New Cambridge to make sure her daughter was okay.

CHAPTER 2

LATER THAT AFTERNOON Diane flipped off her desk lamp, and her office became a gloomy gray, the cloud cover outside making it appear much later than it was.

She'd been working on the same scene all day, writing and rewriting it only to trash the entire thing. She'd been too worried about Alexa to fully concentrate. When she'd driven to Alexa's apartment that morning, her daughter's car hadn't been parked in its assigned spot. She'd still knocked, then driven around campus for thirty minutes, hoping to catch sight of her.

But she hadn't had any luck.

Again, she told herself not to freak out. Her daughter's silence was far from unusual.

She walked downstairs and pulled on a coat, then stepped out onto the deck. She stared up at the dark clouds that drifted in packs across the sky, and made a conscious effort to breathe deeply and calm her mind for a little while. As she breathed, she listened to the rowboats knocking into the piers and tried to think of nothing else, but it was impossible.

In thirty minutes she was expected at the crisis center where she volunteered once a week. She didn't have the energy for it tonight but she knew she couldn't bail. The holidays were by far the center's busiest time of year.

A few minutes later, and no calmer than before, she gave up. As she turned to go back inside, the pungent odor of ozone zinged her nose. The telltale scent of impending rain.

A storm was on the horizon.

❖❖❖

WHEN DIANE STEPPED inside the small crisis center half an hour later, she was greeted with a rush of warm air and two even warmer smiles.

Lance, a Fog Harbor policeman and fellow volunteer she often shared shifts with, walked up to her with a Styrofoam cup of steaming coffee. "Just the way you like it," he said with a wink. "Piping hot."

She smiled. "Aw. You know me too well."

Lance was in his late twenties, about ten years Diane's junior. Chiseled face, closely cropped brown hair, blue-eyed, and fit, he had the look of a man one would expect to see on movie screens or magazine covers. Not in a police uniform, and especially not in a small coastal town hardly anyone outside of Massachusetts had ever heard of. He was wearing his uniform now, crisply pressed, his walkie-talkie secured in its holster on his shoulder.

Lance had recently lost a brother to suicide and had been volunteering at the hotline ever since. Aside from his reputation for being a playboy—which Diane didn't know for sure was truly deserved—he seemed to be decent. For Lance, flirting just seemed to be a pastime. Maybe even a coping mechanism.

Over the months he'd flirted with Diane off and on. Just playful flirting, nothing overt, but still Diane was careful. She didn't want to give him the wrong impression. She'd learned there was a fine line between friendship with a man and something more, and a romantic relationship, or even an affair, was out of the question. After what she'd been through with her late husband, she was done with men.

Diane set down her purse in her cubicle, then, cupping the warm Styrofoam coffee cup between her hands, returned to the main area where Lance and the shift supervisor, Mary Kate, sat at a large, round table. "How are the phones tonight?"

"Slammed like always," Mary Kate said with a thick Boston accent.

The crisis center took calls for a large portion of eastern Essex County, encompassing over sixty square miles and serving close to two hundred thousand people, and it was rare for the phones to be quiet. As if proving that what Mary Kate said was true, a phone rang. One of the volunteers in the back quickly picked it up.

Mary Kate was the shift supervisor during most of Diane's shifts. She practically lived there. She was around Diane's age, but trauma had weathered her and she looked much older. She'd been at the hotline for two years, since her thirteen-year-old daughter committed suicide after being cyberbullied by some girls from her school.

All the volunteers had their stories. Most were cringeworthy, tragic.

Over the last several months, Diane, Lance, and Mary Kate had become more than acquaintances . . . maybe even friends. During shifts with few calls—a rarity, but it happened—they would have some downtime and the chance to talk. And something about sharing the type of job they had at the crisis center created an instant connection. The type Diane would imagine most victims of tragedies would likely forge.

Lance and Mary Kate were the first adults Diane had regularly spoken to in years, aside from her best friend, Ellie, back in New Jersey. But she and Ellie, although close, hadn't had the chance to see a lot of each other in person over the years. Ellie and her husband did everything together. And Diane was always so busy with the kids and her work. They'd been friends in spirit more than anything.

Diane had a long roster of repeat callers at the center. People who she'd managed to help in the past. Most of them were people who were desperate for encouragement. For a little hope. A listening ear. Women called from inside their closets after being knocked around and worse. High-powered men called after losing their jobs. Depressed teens searched for someone who would tell them that it was all going to be okay. Even young children called in, reporting abuse to their mothers or themselves.

Mary Kate's forehead creased. "You hear about the murder in New Cambridge?"

"Yeah, how terrible," Diane said. "What do they know so far?"

"College sophomore," Mary Kate said.

Lance sipped from his coffee cup and set it down. "Strangled in her apartment."

A chill crept up Diane's back. "God, that's awful. Do they know who did it?"

Lance shook his head.

"Was it a break-in?" Diane asked.

"As far as I understand, no signs of forced entry," Lance said.

"Boyfriend?"

Lance stared at her. "You working the case, Detective?"

Diane smiled. "Sorry."

"Or is it the mystery writer coming out, maybe?" He winked. "Yes. There was a boyfriend in the picture. He's at the station now in New Cambridge. Friends reported that they'd been fighting yesterday."

"I see," Diane said, relieved at the possibility that the murder might have been a crime of passion instead of a dangerous predator roaming the campus. "Have they released the victim's name?"

"Not yet. Last I heard they were in the process of locating her next of kin."

Diane nodded. She checked her phone again. No missed texts.

Dammit, Alexa. If you're getting these texts and aren't answering me . . .

Diane often wondered if Alexa *wanted* her to worry. It was definitely possible. But maybe she just didn't have her phone on her. Or she was still in class. Or maybe she'd even taken a trip to Boston. Weeks ago, Alexa had mentioned taking the occasional trip there with friends. But her daughter's story hadn't rung true. Alexa had never been very social—in fact, she'd always been socially awkward, even painfully so. And Diane had a difficult time believing she'd changed much in that regard over the last several months.

She'd contemplated driving back to Alexa's apartment again but had resisted the urge. Now she was wondering if she'd made the right decision.

"Diane?" Lance asked.

Diane looked up to find Lance staring at her. "Sorry, did you say something?"

"I asked if you were okay. Your daughter goes to New Cambridge, right?"

She managed a tight smile. "Oh, I'm fine. I've just had a tough time getting a hold of her today. But that's a teenager for you, right?" She tried to laugh, but the sound got stuck in her throat.

Lance's eyes narrowed a little. "Well, if you need to talk, call me." He handed her a sticky note with his number on it. She stared at the handwriting. Chicken scratch, like many men, but ultimately readable.

"My shift at the station starts in ten minutes, so I better get out of here," he said. "See you tomorrow? Five o'clock, right?"

"I'm sorry?"

"Thanksgiving dinner."

Thanksgiving dinner. She'd nearly forgotten. She'd invited both Lance and Mary Kate because neither had family close by. She'd wanted to be kind, but now that she was stressing over the murder at the college and Alexa, she regretted the decision. "Yes." She smiled. "Five o'clock. Let me write down the address."

"That's okay. You live out on Beacon Street, right?"

She blinked at him, then nodded. "How did you know?"

"It's a small town. I've seen your minivan parked out front. The gray Cape Cod, right?"

"Yes, that's it. The gray Cape Cod."

❦❦❦

"THIS IS SALLY. How can I help you?" Diane said twenty minutes later, using her alias. For privacy reasons, all the volunteers were required to use them.

The other end of the line was silent. She waited several seconds, then repeated herself. "This is Sally. How can I help you?"

More silence.

Silence wasn't uncommon when someone phoned in. Most callers were reluctant to talk, at least at first. Calling was often a last-ditch effort of desperation. Several didn't know what to say. Some were embarrassed. And many doubted they could actually be helped.

"Can I do something to help you?" she asked.

A robotic voice shattered the silence. "I was hoping it would be you . . . *Sally.*"

A cold flush swept over Diane's skin, and she leaned forward in her chair. The person was using some type of a voice changer. It made her flesh crawl, but she stayed composed. "Do I know you?"

The line was quiet again.

Diane watched Mary Kate walk to the small station at the back of the room and pour a cup of coffee.

"Have we spoken before?" Diane asked.

The caller ignored her question. "Did you hear about the murder?"

"Yes. I did," Diane answered.

The mechanical voice continued. "How did it make you feel?"

"It made me feel sad," Diane said. She turned the conversation back to the caller. "And you? How did it make you feel?"

16

"Horrible," said the caller. "A little . . . crazy even. I can't stop thinking about it."

"I can understand."

"How painful it must have been. To die that way. Not able to breathe. And so very scared."

Diane heard what sounded like muffled sobbing on the other end of the line.

Who's crying? she wondered, goose bumps breaking out along her arms.

The caller?

Or . . . someone else?

"Yes. It . . . must have been horrible," she said.

"But you know what would be even worse?" the person asked.

Diane's pulse thrummed in her ears as she waited for the caller to go on.

"What would be far worse is . . . if Katie wasn't the only one. But the first of many."

The caller had said the name *Katie*. Had they even released the victim's name yet? According to Lance just twenty minutes ago, they hadn't. Diane grabbed a pen and yellow legal notepad.

She looked up and saw Mary Kate sipping coffee and staring at her. The supervisor lifted her eyebrows in question.

Diane jotted down the name *Katie* and returned her attention to the phone call.

The caller was breathing heavily now but wasn't saying anything.

"If you have information, you should call nine-one-one," Diane said. "We're a crisis hotline, not the police."

"I don't want the police. I'm having a crisis."

"A crisis about the murder?"

"Yes." The person had spoken the word so softly she had barely heard it.

Diane's pulse sprinted. Was this person confessing to the murder? Or at least to having some knowledge about what had happened? She tried to think back to her forty-hour training, but her brain was slamming into a wall.

Maybe she should ask more questions. Try to get more details. "I'm not so sure I understand why . . . why you think I can help you. Do you just need to talk? For me to listen?"

The caller was quiet.

"Are you sure we haven't spoken before?"

The caller didn't answer.

"We must have. You said you were glad it was me who answered, right?"

"I did," the caller said, quietly. "I was glad it was you because—" She heard the sobbing again on the end of the line. "Because I'm afraid you're the only one who can stop it."

CHAPTER 3

HER WIPERS LASHING across her windshield, Diane drove to the grocery store, every nerve ending on edge.

I'm afraid you're the only one who can stop it.

What the hell had *that* meant?

She'd filed a report with Mary Kate before she left the center—and although Mary Kate had assured her she'd send it through the proper channels, the supervisor also felt pretty certain the caller was just some lonely attention seeker. Someone who got off on shocking strangers. Callers did that sometimes—especially around the holidays. As much as Diane wanted to believe her supervisor was right, she wasn't yet convinced.

"Siri, call Alexa," Diane said into her phone. It was the seventh time she'd tried to reach her daughter since that morning, not including the drive to her apartment.

And again, no answer.

Staring out at the swollen Atlantic, she wanted to hurl the phone against the windshield, frustrated at her daughter for ignoring her all day, but instead she tossed it on the passenger seat. She flipped on the radio, hoping to hear coverage of the murder to see if the victim's name had been released yet, but they were airing a countdown of popular love songs from the eighties.

A few minutes later, she pulled into the parking lot of Brookmart, then hurried through the automatic doors, praying that Wayne, the kind-but-helpful-to-the-point-of-sometimes-being-horribly-annoying store manager, had already gone home for the day.

But as soon as the bright fluorescent lighting of the store hit her eyes, she spotted him with his ever-present clipboard, chatting with a young cashier. Before she could grab a cart and duck out of sight, his eyes flickered to her, and he rushed over to greet her.

"Well, hello, Diane." He smiled cheerily. His full cheeks were splotched with pink, and Diane noticed he'd recently touched up his roots to match the unnaturally lemony yellow of the rest of his hair. "I was wondering if you were going to stop in for Thanksgiving supplies."

Diane smiled tightly. "Hi, Wayne."

"You waited until the very last minute, did you?"

"Yes, I'm afraid I did."

He grabbed a shopping cart. "That's okay. What do you need? I'll help."

Diane sighed, surrendering to the fact that Wayne was going to shop with her, and handed him her list. He read it quickly, then stuffed it in his pocket. "We'll get you all set up."

He pushed the cart toward the meat section and motioned for her to follow. As a crime writer, Diane knew she tended to view the world with a darker lens. As a result, she constantly saw suspicious people wherever she went, especially suspicious men. And in her first several months in Fog Harbor she had been unsure how to feel about Wayne and the undue attention he showed her. But after a while she realized that he was harmless.

These days she rarely minded Wayne's company. In fact, sometimes she even embraced it. After all, it was like having a personal shopper and food expert at her disposal, free of charge. She also felt he was just being genuinely kind. But tonight her mind was like taut wire, and she couldn't follow his small talk.

Diane spotted the frozen turkeys, but Wayne shook his head. "Don't even think about it," he said, bringing the cart to a halt. "Wait right here." He disappeared through the swinging doors of the butcher section.

Diane was too anxious to stand and wait, so she decided to grab the potatoes and some saline for Josh's breathing treatments. Since he'd been coughing earlier, she was going to insist he do a treatment tonight. Although he hated doing them, if early symptoms weren't immediately addressed, he ran the risk of landing in the hospital with a respiratory infection.

She hurried through the displays, looking for the potatoes, and found them stacked impressively in a small tower. As she absentmindedly replayed the conversation at the crisis center again, she grabbed a potato and, almost in slow motion, the tower began to tumble.

It took her a moment to realize what was happening. When she finally did, she reached out to stop the avalanche. But she was too late. Spuds toppled over each other and onto the floor. In a matter of seconds—which seemed like eternity—the entire tower of potatoes was scattered everywhere.

Diane stood in the middle of the chaos, holding what she realized must have been a cornerstone potato. She stared incredulously at the disaster at her feet and couldn't help herself.

She began to laugh.

Hard . . . uncontrolled laughter. She didn't know if it was the potatoes or the stress of not talking with Alexa yet or her experience with the caller that afternoon—a combination of all three, she supposed—but she couldn't stop.

"Do this much?" a deep, gravelly voice behind her asked.

Diane spun around to see a tall, incredibly handsome man with dark, tousled hair.

"Is that your MO? Terrorize supermarkets late at night? Destroy their artful potato displays?" he asked, a smile playing on his lips. He knelt and picked up some of the strays.

She wiped away the tears her laughter had brought on. "I guess I wasn't paying attention. Today's just been . . ."

He pointed to a domed security camera nestled in the corner of the ceiling. "If you're really quick, you can probably still make a run for it." He smiled, revealing perfect teeth.

Her stomach fluttered, which surprised her. She hadn't had that type of reaction to a man for a very long time.

"I'm only joking," he said.

"Of course."

"It could've happened to anyone."

"Yeah, sure. Anyone," she agreed, wiping at her eyes again and realizing she felt a little calmer.

He offered his hand. "I'm Rick."

Diane took it. It was big, warm. Strong. "Diane."

He studied her face. "Has anyone ever told you—"

"Yes." She nodded, knowing what he was going to say. "Diane Lane, except with lighter hair, right? I get it all the time." She couldn't count the number of times over the years that complete strangers had come up to her asking if she was the actress. And the fact that they shared a first name just added to the confusion. Not that she minded the comparison. Diane Lane was clearly a knockout.

"But a younger version," he added.

"Well, not by much."

"I mean, seriously. The likeness is incredible."

"So I hear."

She knelt down to help pick up the potatoes. As she did, she stole a glance at his shopping cart. Fruit, vegetables, bread, pasta, beer, potato chips, paper towels, razor blades. She noticed the absence of diapers, tampons, or women's toiletries.

He was definitely a bachelor.

And she realized that pleased her.

"I appreciate the help," she said, then heard footsteps approach from around the corner.

"What the Sam Hill?" Wayne said, rushing over. "I can't leave you alone for a second." He surveyed the disaster, his mouth agape, his hands pressed against his generous hips.

"Wayne. I'm *so* sorry. I just grabbed one and . . ."

Wayne peered down at Diane and his face softened. "Oh, hon. It's just produce," he said. "They don't break. Don't worry about it. C'mon. Off that floor." His small hand was clammy as he helped her up.

After she was standing, Wayne eyed Rick as though noticing him for the first time. "Wayne, this is . . . I'm sorry, it was Rick, right?"

"Yes ma'am."

"Rick, this is Wayne. He's the—"

"I'm the store manager here," Wayne interrupted, proudly extending his hand. His gaze shifted between the two. "Do you two know one another?"

"No. We just met," Rick said.

Wayne glanced from one to the other again and nodded. He fixed his attention on Diane. "Well, if you want to get out of here before Thanksgiving, we really need to get to the rest of your list."

Diane nodded and looked at Rick. "Thanks again for the help."

Rick smiled. "Don't mention it. Maybe I'll see you around. Happy Thanksgiving."

After her shopping was done, Wayne walked Diane back to her minivan, rattling off cooking tips for the turkey. The sky had blackened considerably since she'd been in the store, but thankfully, the rain had let up.

A foghorn moaned in the distance as Wayne opened the back hatch of her silver Honda Odyssey and slid the paper grocery bags in. Diane had long since learned not to try to help load the groceries into her minivan. Wayne wouldn't have it.

After the last bag was tucked neatly in the back of her vehicle, Wayne closed the hatchback and looked at her. He frowned. "That guy in the store. Have you seen him before?"

"No," Diane said, staring down at her iPhone, searching for a new call or text.

"Probably a drifter . . . working winter boat prep at the fishing yard," Wayne said. "Here today, gone tomorrow. You know how that goes."

No, she didn't. "Yeah," she said. "Probably."

"You hear about the murder at the college?" Wayne asked. He shook his head. "Tragic."

"Yeah," Diane agreed. "It is."

"My buddy is with the police department in New Cambridge," Wayne said. "From what he tells me, they have no clue who did it yet. Might be the boyfriend, but they're not so sure . . . it could have been anyone, so it would pay to be careful. Because you never know what people are capable of," he continued. "You just don't know."

CHAPTER 4

GROCERIES IN HAND, Diane pushed open the front door and was met with a whoosh of warm air and the fresh scent of floral laundry soap.

Was someone doing laundry?

She heard Josh cough from somewhere deeper in the house, then speak to someone. She walked into the living room and saw him sitting in his gaming chair with his gaming headset on. Next to him, on the couch, with a matching headset, was his friend Bruce. A familiar game was on the big-screen television. An oddly lifelike soldier was holding a semiautomatic weapon and heading into an old building, three other soldiers trailing him.

"No, seriously, man. What would you do if that happened to you?" Josh was saying into his mic, talking to a player online. A moment later: "What do you mean, you've never thought about it? Do you ever think about anything but that girlfriend of yours, dude? Seriously, what's in that head of yours? Marshmallow fluff?" He laughed.

It sounded to Diane like he was having another one of his philosophical conversations. One of his many lifeboat scenarios in which he'd ask "What if—this?" "What if—that?" questions. It was one of his many interesting quirks. Both he and Alexa had more than their share of fun idiosyncrasies that Diane had really enjoyed over the years, but these days Alexa kept her walls erected too high and too thick for Diane to even see hers.

Josh said into the mic: "Dude! A little help here, maybe?"

Bruce noticed Diane in the doorway. "Hi, Mrs. Christie," he said, then kicked Josh's chair to let him know she was there.

Josh turned and grinned. "Hey, Mom."

"Hi, sweetie. Hi, Bruce."

Bruce smiled, then his attention went back to the television set.

"How was your test?" Diane asked Josh.

"Easy peasy. I'd be surprised if I didn't score a hundred."

Diane rustled his thick, dark hair. "Great job." She looked at Bruce. "Are you guys hungry? I can make you a snack."

"No, thank you, Mrs. Christie. I have to be home in a few minutes."

At first Diane had worried about pulling Josh out of his high school in New Jersey and relocating him to Fog Harbor, but Josh's life was more active than ever since making the move. He quickly made friends with Bruce and a few other guys, all well-mannered kids from middle-class working families. Their parents seemed to be nice people with similar values. Josh often also played games online with some of his childhood friends back in New Jersey, and now a lot of his friends in Fog Harbor and his childhood buddies knew one another.

"You need help with those?" Josh asked, eyeing the groceries.

"No, I'm fine. Finish your game."

She set the grocery bags on the counter, then went to retrieve the rest. When everything was in the house, she locked up, then went to the laundry room and flipped on the light. She placed her hand on the dryer.

Sure enough.

It was warm.

It had been used recently.

Josh didn't do his own wash, so did that mean Alexa had been by the house? It was the only time Alexa ever came by. To do her laundry.

Josh appeared in the doorway with an apple. "I'm driving Bruce home. I'll be back in a few minutes."

"Hey, have you heard from your sister today?"

"Yeah. She just left," he said, biting into the apple. "Washed a bunch of laundry. She said to tell you to quit blowing up her phone. She'll probably be by for Thanksgiving dinner, but she—"

"Makes no promises," Diane finished, blowing out a heavy sigh, feeling an equal mixture of relief and frustration. Noncommittal, distant. Summed up her daughter to a tee.

Hell, why can't Alexa just answer one of my texts?

Really? Is that too much to ask?

If she had, the day wouldn't have been nearly as stressful. But Alexa was headstrong, the most stubborn person Diane had ever known.

She placed a kettle on the stove and turned on the burner, hoping a cup of chamomile tea would help unfurl the knot in her stomach, just enough so that it didn't ache to breathe. "I must've texted her twenty times today, and she didn't answer."

Josh stared at her. "And that surprises you why?"

He had a point.

"Did she seem okay?" Diane asked. "When she was here?"

Josh shrugged. "Yeah, I mean, I guess so. Why?"

"Just with the murder at the college and all."

He seemed to think about it, then shrugged again. "She seemed the same as always to me."

●●●

AN HOUR LATER, after she'd brined the turkey and prepped the stuffing and sweet potato pie for the next afternoon, Diane trudged up the staircase with a glass of pinot noir.

Screw chamomile tea.

She needed something stronger.

Even though she now knew Alexa was safe, the strange call that afternoon still had her feeling on edge.

She ran a bath and undressed. Once in, she stuck her foot beneath the stream of hot water, letting it rush between her toes. Steam drifting over the bathtub, she brought her wineglass to her lips and let the tang of red wine hit her tongue. Wine had become part of her survival kit over the last year. Wine, warm baths, the ocean. Aside from her kids, those were all she needed to feel satisfied . . . which was exactly what she told herself when she found herself replaying her run-in with the guy in the supermarket.

But Frank used to make her stomach flutter, too . . . in the early days, when he still tried. Back when they enjoyed late-night dinners in Manhattan. Making love until the wee hours of Sunday morning and sleeping until Sunday afternoon. Only leaving the bed to grab dough-nuts and coffee, then doing it all over again. Impromptu trips to the beach. Long, sensual showers together. But it hadn't lasted. Before long, he'd become distant.

Frank had become a stranger . . . living inside her home.

More memories of Frank flashed into her mind. Terrible ones.

The children's high-pitched screams.

Her own screams muffled into her pillow once the kids fell asleep.

She quickly shoved the memories away.

Fifteen minutes later, she rose from the warm, sudsy water of her bath, dried off, and slipped into a cotton nightgown, feeling almost as anxious as she had before. Neither the bath nor the wine seemed to have helped enough.

Desperate to be well rested for her dinner guests the next afternoon and to calm her frayed nerves, she reached into her medicine cabinet for her sleeping pills . . . a surefire way to get some deep sleep.

But when she opened the prescription bottle, she noticed something odd. The container was half-empty. She frowned. Why would some of her pills be missing?

She double-checked the date she'd had the prescription filled. A little over a week ago. She shook the pills onto a folded washcloth and counted them, then she did the math. Yes, twenty of them were definitely unaccounted for . . . and now that she put some thought into it, she remembered thinking some pills had been missing the previous month, too.

Had one of the kids taken them? Or one of the guys that Josh had over sometimes? After all, who else could it have been? Her landlord, Mr. Davidson, had a key to the house, but the idea of him sneaking in unannounced to steal her sleeping pills was a bit of a stretch.

"Good night," Josh called from her bedroom door.

Carrying the prescription bottle, she walked to the bathroom doorway. "Josh? You wouldn't know what happened to my sleeping pills, would you?"

He stared at the pill bottle in her hand. "No, what do you mean?"

"Some are missing."

"That's weird. But no, I didn't take any."

❖❖❖

DIANE WASHED A sleeping pill down with a cup of tap water, then climbed into bed and burrowed beneath her heavy down comforter.

Usually her comforter and satin sheets felt like heaven against her exposed skin, but tonight she was too unnerved to feel any comfort. She kept hearing the caller's robotic voice.

She was also feeling uneasy about the pills. Was it possible one of the kids had a drug problem and she didn't know about it? She'd seen no sign of deceit when she'd asked Josh about them.

A wave of loneliness washed over her as she listened to the persistent *Drip! Drip! Drip!* of the tub's leaky faucet—and she found herself longing for the days when she used to snuggle with her children. There was nothing like cuddling with their warm, little bodies. Listening to their rhythmic breathing as they slept. She missed bonding with her children like that. Being so close physically.

And with Alexa, also emotionally. In many respects, her daughter and she seemed like mere strangers now.

The season with Alexa and Josh being so young and small hadn't lasted long enough. And now they were rapidly approaching adulthood. She still couldn't quite believe it.

After several minutes, she gave up on sleep, powered on her iPad, and did what she'd wanted to do all evening but hadn't because she had long ago vowed to keep her mind murder-free in the evenings.

After researching and writing about murder all day, almost every day, her mind desperately needed a break from the darkness. But tonight she couldn't help it. She pulled up a browser to see if there'd been any updates on the murder in New Cambridge.

She saw that they had released the victim's name: Katie Worth. The caller had called her Katie. He'd already known her name. She frowned, wondering what time the girl's name had been released. She checked the time stamps on the three articles she found. All had been posted online at eight p.m. or later.

She grabbed her iPhone and found Lance's name in her contact list and shot him a text.

DIANE: Do you know what time they announced the murder victim's name?

As she waited for Lance's reply, she read a bio of the girl. She was a sophomore at the college. A talented artist from Vermont who was riding a full scholarship.

She searched around some more and found the victim's Facebook page. Her timeline was already full of RIP posts from friends. Someone had also set up a group page by the name *RIP Katie Worth!* And another person had already set up a GoFundMe account for her funeral expenses.

She clicked on one of the girl's photo albums and studied the pictures, especially the most recent ones, which were mainly of Katie and her boyfriend, a handsome, college-aged boy. In the photos, they looked happy together—and had taken at least fifty selfies in the last few months alone. Photos on the campus grounds, in what appeared to be a bar, on the coast, in an apartment or dorm room.

Her phone chimed, letting her know she had a text.

LANCE: Doing murder mystery research, Beautiful? ;)

DIANE: Something like that.

LANCE: IDK when they released it, but I can find out.

DIANE: Thanks. That would be great.

LANCE: Give me a few.

DIANE: K.

As she waited, she flipped through the rest of the girl's Facebook photos, then scrolled through her status updates. Her last status update read:

KATIE: See you soon, Mom and Dad! Can't wait to be back home!

The girl's last online words tugged at Diane's heartstrings. When the girl had written that update, she'd had no idea that she'd never see home *or* her parents again.

Diane was still scrolling, learning more about the girl, when her eyelids grew heavy. *Thank God.* The sleeping pill was finally kicking in. She powered off her iPad, switched off her bedside lamp, and pushed deeper beneath the covers.

A moment later, she felt her body jerk as sleep claimed her. She turned onto her side and burrowed her face into her satiny pillow.

Her phone chimed again, alerting her to a new text. She reluctantly crawled through the fog of sleep and fumbled around for her phone. When she found it, she saw that Lance had replied.

LANCE: They released the vic's name a little b4 8 tonight. Why? Inquiring minds want to know. :)

In a sleep-induced haze, Diane slowly did the math. She'd received the anonymous call around five o'clock . . . which was three hours before the victim's name had been released.

The realization jolted her awake again.

How had the caller already known the victim's name?

CHAPTER 5

HE SAT IN front of his laptop, a muscle in his left temple twitching.

He pulled up his Facebook account and brought up her profile: Jill MacDonald. Just looking at her profile photo made him ache with anticipation.

Like most of the others, Jill had long, glossy dark hair, light eyes, and creamy young skin . . . impressive breasts that often spilled out of the tops she wore in the photos she posted. She also had few cares in the world and absolutely no regard for personal security.

All he had to do was follow her online to learn everything he needed to know about her life. Where she was going to be for the day, who she was with, when she'd return.

She was careless.

Oh, so careless.

With his finger, he traced her face on the screen. Some days he watched a forty-six-second-long video of her that was taken at Disney World with her family over and over again, wanting to memorize her every feature, how she squinted and pursed her lips when she was trying to look sexy. The way she twirled her hair. The way so many of her teeth, including her molars, showed when she laughed.

But tonight his mind ached, and he knew her voice would only scrape at his already bruised brain. So he stared at her photos instead and fantasized, running a scenario through his head. One that he hadn't been able to stop thinking about since his high with Katie had vanished.

Which had happened much too quickly.

As far as Jill knew, he was her age, six foot one, single, with dark, longish hair, an early college graduate who had recently moved into the area from Southern California to just take it easy for a while. And it had been simple to find photos online to prove it. He'd found some, compliments of a guy in Australia named Chad.

Before reaching out to Jill with a friend request, he had studied her interests lists and made sure they shared at least a few groups. He'd also engaged her in a few online threads . . . and she had happily engaged him back.

Yesterday he'd posted a photo of Australian Chad with a new Labrador puppy. A chubby yellow bundle of boundless energy with a bright pink tongue. That had gotten him twenty-five likes from his online "friends." And one of those likes came from beautiful Jill.

He didn't talk much about himself on social media. He just listened, which was fine, because she mostly loved to talk about herself anyway. In fact, she couldn't seem to get enough of it. Obviously no one had warned her about online predators. Either that or she hadn't taken the warning seriously.

But she *definitely* should have.

He sat back and replayed his conversation with Sally. He remembered her soft, caring voice. She'd genuinely wanted to help him, hadn't she?

Of course she had.

And he wondered if she could.

He snapped his laptop closed and popped open a can of soda. He let it fizz on the tip of his tongue for a moment while he watched his goldfish swim in lazy circles in its little round bowl. He set the soda down, picked up a small container, and added a pinch of powdered food to its water.

The fish attacked the food, gobbling up every morsel. When it was done, it turned toward him again, staring, its fins pinwheeling as it swam in place. He and the fish stared at one another for a long moment.

He felt bad for the animal. It was going nowhere. Trapped in such a small bowl. He'd felt like that once. But not anymore.

Now he could venture out of his bowl anytime he wanted to.

CHAPTER 6

HER EYES CLENCHED tight, Alexa Christie lay curled up beneath a heap of blankets and freshly washed clothes and fantasized about killing herself. Clearly her happy pills were not doing their job.

Not only did she feel incredibly *un*happy, a horrible emptiness had formed in her middle, making her feel hollow. Even worse were the oceans of tears buried deep inside her chest. And the sensation just continued to intensify because she was unable to cry.

The tears just kept building, building, building. Hurting . . . hurting . . . aching to the point she felt crazy. All her life she'd felt like a dark cloud was hovering over her to some extent, but only in the last year had it begun to overpower her.

She gazed at the sleeping pills she'd taken from her mother's medicine cabinet and wondered if they were enough to send her to sleep forever. She wished she could climb into a black hole—some dark, quiet place where she could curl up and not have to worry about interacting with anyone. A place free of pain. Somewhere no one would have expectations of her.

She could just see it on social media if she went through with it. Some people would call her a coward. Others would take up for her, saying that people just didn't understand how horrible depression could be.

How it could just swallow someone whole.

Like it was doing to her now.

But then after about two minutes, everyone would stop talking about her—and forget that she'd even existed at all.

Not that she really cared.

She just wanted the pain to go away.

She wondered if this was how her father had felt before he decided to—

God, she didn't want to think about him right now.

She sat up on her mattress and scanned the open-plan area of her almost-claustrophobic three-hundred-square-foot studio apartment and grimaced. Her roommate Trish's side of the apartment was tidy and organized . . . while hers was a disaster of clothes, blankets, dirty dishes, and glassware.

The cheapo doctor that she'd visited off campus said it would take over a week, maybe even two, for the new antidepressant to kick in. It was the third he'd prescribed her over the last six months. And so far, like the other two, it had done nothing to help.

Nada, zippo.

In fact, lately she hadn't only felt just as depressed, but she was dealing with some really gnarly symptoms she'd never had before, like swollen fingers and ankles. Her dreams were also scarier than usual.

At least the sleeping pills, while they lasted, helped her bypass the pain and the weird dreams. But taking two sleeping pills at a time bought her twelve hours of relief at most, leaving her emotionally raw for at least another twelve long, miserable hours every day.

Then there had been the sleepwalking incident. She wasn't sure what to blame *that* on—the new antidepressant or the sleeping pills. Two mornings earlier, she'd woken and found herself in her car. The engine had been running and she'd been parked in front of a pier a few blocks from her apartment. She'd been freezing, her teeth chattering so hard they had ached for an entire day. She had no memory of how she'd gotten there, but it was obvious she'd driven herself.

She knew good and well that she could've easily killed herself . . . or someone else . . . driving in that condition, and she was frightened it could happen again. But she couldn't stop taking the pills. She needed them to fix her. She needed relief.

She turned on her side and sighed. Her mother had been blowing up her phone all day. She'd even stopped by and knocked on her door. A loud, persistent knock that had nearly split Alexa's brain in two—but she hadn't had the energy to get out of bed.

Thankfully she had parked her car a block away because some asshat had been in her spot when she'd last driven home. If she hadn't, her mother would probably still be there now. Alexa hated the way her mother hovered and worried over her. And she hated that she needed to pee right now.

She really didn't want to get up.

She felt around for her phone and found it by her left leg. She picked it up and looked at the time.

Christ.

She didn't have very long to get dressed for Thanksgiving dinner. She stood up and felt lightheaded, colorful circles blooming in front of her eyes. She blinked hard, and they rearranged themselves, then finally vanished.

She trudged across the apartment to her tiny bathroom with the stained linoleum tiles. As she reached the doorway her big toe caught on a break in the cheap flooring, and she lurched forward. "Gah!"

Tears sprang to her eyes.

"Good one, *Grace*," she muttered, fully aware that grace was one of several traits she'd never possessed. But then she realized the pain had actually felt good. So did the few tears she was finally able to release.

After using the bathroom, she went to the mirror and frowned at the image staring back at her. Her gray-blue eyes looked dull and lifeless, like those of a beached fish, and her shoulder-length blonde hair hung unwashed and limp. She ran her fingers through it and it stuck up every which way.

She moved back into the main area of the apartment, to the full-length mirror. She peeled off her nightgown and stared at her image in only a pair of white granny panties, which were at least a size too big for her and pooched out on her behind.

She groaned.

Looking had been a mistake.

She shook her head. There was no way she was going anywhere.

Screw Thanksgiving.

It was too much work.

She turned to crawl back beneath the covers when she heard a key turn in the lock. Before she could think or move, the apartment door burst open.

●●●

"UM, DID I . . . *walk in on something?*" her roommate, Trish, asked, the southern twang in her voice reminding Alexa of warm maple syrup. Trish's eyes darted around the room, then quickly landed back on Alexa.

Blood rushed to Alexa's cheeks and she crossed her arms against her small, bare breasts. "What do you mean?"

"I just thought maybe there was a guy in here or something."

A guy? Yeah, right, Alexa thought.

"Just never seen you prance around the place half-naked before," Trish said and set her things down. "Nice panties, by the way."

Alexa turned away from her roommate and began rooting around for something she could wear to her mother's house. She didn't want to go to Thanksgiving dinner, but now that Trish was there, she *had* to go, because she'd invited her. She had been hoping Trish would flake, but apparently she wasn't going to. Plus her stomach was rumbling, and she had no food left in the apartment and no money to buy any. She'd already blown through the monthly check her mother had given her for expenses like food.

"Damn, girl. You empty out your whole closet on your mattress?" Trish went to Alexa's side of the room and dug through the huge pile of clothes. She pulled a blue dress off the floor that Alexa's mother had bought her a few years back. It was something Alexa wouldn't be caught dead in. It even still had tags on it. "Ooh, this is nice," Trish said. "Mind if I try it on?"

"Knock yourself out."

Trish slid out of her workout clothes, letting them fall to the floor. Alexa caught the girl's reflection in the mirror and narrowed her eyes. Trish had a rocking body. Perfect curves, smooth, even skin, concave stomach. It wasn't fair. She thought about her mattress again. Burrowing beneath the covers.

Trish pulled the dress over her head and smoothed it out. She went to the mirror. "You sure it's okay that I come to Thanksgiving dinner with y'all?" Trish asked, studying the fit of the dress. "I mean, I know I kind of invited myself."

You totally *invited yourself.*

"It's fine."

"And you checked with your mom?"

"Yes."

"And she was cool with it?"

"Thrilled."

The truth was, Alexa never had asked her mother.

"Want me to help you with your hair?" Trish asked.

"No."

"Are you sure? Because seriously . . . it looks like it was caught in a blender. Just sayin'."

Not bothering to answer, Alexa pulled a hair tie from her wrist and gathered her hair into it. Then she went to the bathroom to rummage for a few bobby pins.

Listening to Trish going about her business on her side of the tiny apartment, Alexa wondered again why she'd decided to share such a small space. She hated having a roommate, especially one like Trish. Being around her was like having all of her many shortcomings constantly thrown in her face. It was exactly like being around her mother.

Alexa had always been a bit of a mess. Not pretty enough. Not thin enough. Her stomach stuck out a little no matter how much she starved herself. She wasn't tidy or organized. She was terrible socially. Almost everything that came out of her mouth was wrong. She was the spitting opposite of Trish in every way she could imagine.

But Alexa had needed the money. And it was only temporary. Trish needed the place for just four weeks and was rarely even there. Plus, despite the fact that Trish made her feel awful about herself, Alexa kind of liked her . . . sometimes.

The screen on her phone lit up. It was her brother.

JOSH: U better show up today. And try 2 be on time for once, k?

If she'd had the energy, she would've rolled her eyes. Instead, she tossed her phone on her mattress and reached for a black sweater that was balled up in the corner next to her window.

It was clean enough . . . and the color would suit her mood.

◆◆◆

DARK CLOUDS HUNG low in the sky as Alexa and Trish walked the block to Alexa's car. When they reached it, Alexa half hoped it wouldn't start.

But when she plopped down on the chilly vinyl seat, stuck the key in the ignition, and gave it a turn, the car roared to life. Groaning, she threw her purse into the backseat and reached for her seat belt.

She shivered as she drove down the residential street. When she made a right a block later, she was surprised to see two police cars parked in front of a row of townhouses. Yellow crime scene tape was strewn across one of the yards and a tall, black iron fence.

Trish stopped typing into her phone. "Gawd, it still gives me the creeps thinking about her," she said, quietly. "I mean, it happened so close to us."

"What are you talking about?" Alexa asked.

"Katie Worth."

"Who's Katie Worth?"

Alexa felt Trish's eyes on her. "You're kidding, right? Don't tell me you didn't hear."

Aside from going to her mother's to do some laundry and, well, driving in her car in the middle of the night two nights ago, Alexa had pretty much just slept away most of the past five days. Trish was the only living, breathing human being she'd seen or even had heard from. Well, except for her brother when she'd been at her mother's. But when she'd seen him, he'd had a friend at the house and barely even acknowledged her.

"What happened?" Alexa asked, slowing the car even more.

"She was murdered."

Blood thrummed at Alexa's temples. "Wha-at?"

"They found her strangled to death in that townhouse." She pointed at the building that was surrounded by police tape.

Alexa stared as they drove past. The yellow police tape snapped loudly in the wind, suddenly bringing back memories from New Jersey that she didn't want to recall. She squeezed her eyes shut, hoping to push a vision out of her head . . . a vision she never, ever wanted to see again.

"Watch out! Alexa!" Trish yelled.

Alexa opened her eyes and slammed her foot down on the brake, making the car lurch and her head nearly hit the steering wheel. A girl their age wearing a sweat suit stood a foot in front of the car and flipped them the bird.

Catching her breath, Alexa gave her the finger back and pressed the accelerator.

"OMG! Did you just close your eyes while you were driving?" Trish asked.

"No."

"Yes, you did!"

Alexa could feel the heat of Trish's stare again. Then her passenger straightened and started furiously thumbing something on her phone. Probably tweeting about what just happened. She wouldn't be surprised if she had been the laughingstock of Trish's Twitter profile since she'd moved in with her.

Alexa hated social media. She used her accounts only to spy on others, not to post everything she ate or the brand of toilet paper she used . . . maybe she was a loser, but at least she wasn't a narcissist.

The car was silent until they reached Fog Harbor. As soon as they rolled onto her mother's pebbled driveway, Alexa felt her mood get even blacker. Something she had thought was impossible. She parked the car and killed the engine. It shuddered to a standstill.

Just get through this and get back to the apartment, Alexa thought to herself.

And score more sleeping pills.

She reached to pick up her purse and noticed a paper coffee cup lying on the back floorboard—and she had an idea. Something that might make dinner more palatable. She picked it up, and brushed it off to make sure it was still usable.

It was.

She grabbed it and headed inside.

CHAPTER 7

DIANE SAT BUNDLED up on the crisp winter grass and stared out at the cold, dark water of the harbor. She shivered as she tossed pieces of torn bread and watched a flock of five mallard ducks compete for them.

While the rest of Fog Harbor's ducks had likely flown south for the winter, this handful of stragglers had stayed behind for some reason. Probably because she fed them so well.

She'd woken early that morning and had spent the last several hours cooking and cleaning her house top to bottom, preparing for Alexa, Mary Kate, and Lance. Now she was trying to relax as she watched the ducks angle for the bread. The largest male duck ruffled his feathers and quacked loudly, irritated with the female for snapping up the last few scraps.

"Now, don't fight. There's plenty for everyone," Diane said.

There were four males, each proudly displaying his glossy green head. But it was the plain brown duck, the female, that was her favorite. She was smaller than the others but just as aggressive, if not more. She was also the more trusting of the bunch. The only one who would take bread directly from Diane's hand. Diane wondered if she felt well, though, today. Although she still took her share of the bread, she didn't seem to be moving as fast as usual.

She let her thoughts drift back to last night. She'd called Lance, convinced that the anonymous caller at the crisis center was Katie Worth's murderer. After all, how could he possibly have known the girl's name hours before police released the information?

But Lance had tried to calm her fear by telling her plenty of people could've known the victim's name before it was released to the public: landlord, neighbors, friends. As soon as the first police cruiser had shown up and the place had been roped off with police tape, word had probably begun spreading. And when it came to murder, word had a way of spreading faster than wildfire.

Lance said he'd talk to Mary Kate about the crisis center's policy on these types of calls, then based on what he learned, he might talk with someone at the New Cambridge police department, if Mary Kate hadn't already. But he sounded skeptical. She knew he believed the caller was simply someone looking for attention, just as Mary Kate had . . . and nothing she had said during their conversation had convinced him otherwise.

Diane held the last of the bread out to the little brown duck. It walked up to her and quickly pecked it off her palm.

"She must be your favorite," said a male voice behind her.

Startled, she whirled around.

It was Lance.

"I'm sorry. Did I frighten you?" he asked.

"Oh, it's okay," she said, her pulse racing. "I'm just a little jumpy today."

"That call yesterday still bugging you?" he asked, reaching out to help her off the ground.

"No. I mean, yeah," she said. "Maybe a little. It was that voice disguiser. Well, and the things he said, of course. It was all just very creepy." A gust of wind blew her hair from her face and she shivered again. "But you know what? Let's not talk about any of that today. Let's just enjoy the holiday."

"Got it." He smiled.

"Come on. Let's get out of the cold."

She led the way to her back door and he followed.

❖❖❖

INSIDE THE HOUSE, the rich, savory scents of Thanksgiving dinner wafted through the kitchen: turkey, stuffing, potatoes, sweet potato pie.

Diane slid a tray of asparagus into the oven and uncorked the bottle of wine Lance had brought over. "I told you not to bring anything," she said.

"Yeah. Like I was going to show up empty-handed. Besides, it's just a bottle someone gave me. I didn't have time to get to the store after my shift last night."

She wasn't sure she believed him. It was an Andrew Will Sorella, a high-quality cabernet. A favorite of hers. She took a good look at Lance and smiled. "You look nice." And he did. He was dressed in a stylish green sweater and pressed tan slacks and looked very much like he had walked right out of a J.Crew catalogue.

"You do, too. But of course you always look beautiful," he said. "Thanks again for the invite."

"Well, I couldn't have you sitting home alone with a Hungry-Man turkey dinner and this nice bottle of cabernet, could I?"

Josh walked into the kitchen and poked around at the different dishes. "How much longer?"

He reached for a serving spoon and Diane slapped his hand away.

"Not until Mary Kate and Alexa get here." She looked at Lance. "I assume you met my son."

Lance smiled at Josh. "Oh, yeah. Me and Josh . . . we go way back. I think we met . . . when was it?"

Josh looked at Lance, confused.

Lance snapped his fingers. "I remember. It was when you answered the front door. About five minutes ago."

Josh smiled politely, but Diane knew he thought the joke was corny. Silence filled the room. "Do something to your wrist?" Lance asked, looking down at the blue brace on Josh's right arm. From carpal tunnel syndrome to repetitive thumb injuries, gaming had taken a toll on her son over the years, but thankfully the braces seemed to do the job, when he remembered to wear them.

"It's for a gaming injury," Diane said.

"Gaming injury? Like video games?"

Diane nodded. "He plays a lot, especially in the winter. And he gets repetitive wrist and thumb injuries. In fact, a lot of the kids do."

"Wow. That's pretty hard-core."

"Yes, it is."

Diane's iPhone chimed. She glanced at it and saw it was a message from Mary Kate. She set her spoon down.

> MARY KATE: So sorry for the late notice, but I won't be able to make it today. I feel awful. I think it's the flu.

Oh no, Diane thought, realizing how awkward the dynamic would be without Mary Kate's presence. Now it would just be her, the kids . . . and Lance. Alexa would certainly wonder if he was a date, and she would probably have a field day with it. She just hoped Lance had the tact to not flirt with her in front of the kids. Playful flirting or not. It would just confuse them.

> DIANE: I'm so sorry to hear that. Hope you feel better soon and have a Happy Thanksgiving anyway!

Lance shrugged off his coat, and Diane took it for him. "Mary Kate's not coming. She thinks she has the flu."

"That sucks."

She went to the closet in the foyer and hung up his coat, then returned to the oven and checked the asparagus. "I guess now we're just waiting on my daughter to show. It shouldn't be long."

Josh laughed. "Seriously? Wait on Alexa and we might not eat until *next* Thanksgiving."

"Uh, Josh? That's like calling the kettle black," Diane said. But Josh was right. Alexa wasn't always just late, they were lucky if she even showed up.

She poured wine into two glasses. "Let's give her another ten minutes. If she doesn't show by then, we eat. For now, here's a drink," she said, passing a glass to Lance. She picked up her own. "Cheers."

"To getting to know each other better," Lance said.

Not too much better, Diane thought, smiling. She clinked her wineglass to his and hoped that dinner wouldn't be awkward.

Josh lifted his glass of water. "And to eating very soon."

Diane clinked his glass. "We'll eat soon enough."

Josh groaned.

❦❦❦

TEN MINUTES LATER and no word from Alexa, Diane sighed and decided to start Thanksgiving dinner without her. Just as she was uncovering the last bowl and arranging it on the table, she heard the front door open and the sound of footfalls in the foyer.

Relieved Alexa had shown, Diane wiped her hands on a dish towel. But when the footfalls reached the dining room, she found herself staring at not her daughter but a stunning brunette she'd never seen before.

"Hi," the girl said with a southern drawl, smiling. "You must be Alexa's mom. I'm Trish."

Trish? Diane stared into the girl's striking ice-blue eyes as she tried to process the situation. Who was Trish? And where was Alexa?

"I think Alexa ran to the bathroom," Trish said. Then the smile fell from her face and her eyes widened. "Oh Gawd. She didn't tell you I was coming, did she?"

This was a friend of Alexa's? Diane was surprised. Alexa had never brought friends to the house. Not even as a young girl. So maybe she *had* been telling the truth when she said she took trips to Boston with friends. Maybe she was doing better socially now, after all.

"Oh, she probably told me and I just forgot," Diane said with a smile. "Either way, we're very happy to have you."

Diane introduced Trish to Josh and Lance, showed her to Mary Kate's seat, and took her coat. "So, have you and Alexa known each other long?" she asked.

"Just a couple of weeks. I'm rooming with her until my new apartment is ready."

"Rooming? Like roommates?" Diane asked, again surprised.

"Yes, ma'am."

"But that's such a tiny space."

Trish laughed. "Yeah, it's pretty cozy."

The girl had a good temperament. Diane already knew she was going to like her. Even better, her daughter had a friend. One she was close enough with to bring over for Thanksgiving dinner.

CHAPTER 8

ALEXA WAITED UNTIL Trish stepped into the dining room, then she made a beeline for the kitchen. As she'd suspected, she found plenty of wine on the kitchen island—four bottles total. She swiped one, along with a corkscrew, and hurried to the small half bath.

Once she uncorked the bottle and filled the paper coffee cup to the top, she snapped on the cup's lid, tucked the bottle under some towels in the cabinet beneath the sink, then headed to the formal living room.

She walked in. Sitting at the table were her brother, her mother, Trish, and—her stomach did a little flip-flop—some guy.

And he was *model* hot.

Like seriously, he was *smoking.*

He reminded her of Paul Walker from the cheesy Fast and Furious movies that Josh had watched over the years back in New Jersey. She swallowed hard, the fact that he was there making her even more nervous.

Her mother smiled at her, looking just as stunning as ever. Her long, golden-brown hair was up in a messy bun, her white sweater hung perfectly on her slender frame, and her skin had the luminance and elasticity of someone half her age. Next to her mother she'd always felt like an ugly duckling. It was frustrating. Sometimes downright infuriating.

"There you are. Come sit down," her mother said, patting the spot next to Trish. "We were just getting to know your friend."

Okay, *friend* was a stretch. The only reason Trish was there was because she'd invited herself. And Alexa knew she should've said no . . . but she was terrible at that kind of thing. Actually she was pretty terrible at most things, which really sucked.

"Here. Let me throw that away for you," her mother said, reaching for Alexa's coffee cup full of wine.

"No, thanks," Alexa said, jerking the cup away a little too fast.

"But it has to be awful cold by now. And I just made a fresh pot."

Alexa shot her mother a look. "Really, I'm fine."

Her mother sat back down. "Lance, this is my daughter, Alexa."

Lance reached across the table to shake Alexa's hand. She accepted it and felt her cheeks flush.

Lance turned to her mother. "She's just as pretty as you."

Alexa blinked and noticed an odd look cross her mother's face. She definitely looked more uncomfortable than pleased.

For the first several minutes of dinner, everyone passed around dishes, filled their plates, ate, and talked about random stuff. The unseasonably rainy weather. The dumb video games Josh was into. Trish's boring family back in Podunk, southern Georgia.

Alexa quietly sipped her wine from the paper coffee cup, enjoying the bloom of heat as it slid down her throat, and wondered if Lance really thought she was pretty.

Or if he was just trying to be polite.

She tried not to stare at him, but it was hard. She noticed he looked very relaxed at her mother's house, kind of like he was at home. She narrowed her eyes, wondering how many times he'd been here before.

How good *friends* he and her mother were.

Men and her mother had always been like moths to a flickering porch light. It was gross, and it pissed her off. Even though she certainly didn't look like it, her mother was almost two decades older than she was, so why did Alexa always feel like they were competing? *Why do some women have it so easy while others didn't?* she wondered for the millionth time. Seriously. It wasn't fair.

She took another sip of her wine, listening to Josh doing his annoying what-would-you-do-in-this-really-freaky-situation thing he'd started doing a couple of years ago, where he'd ask dorky questions. But Lance and Trish seemed really into it.

Alexa tuned out the conversation. The dark cloud that had been hovering over her head for as long as she could remember seemed to have backed off a little, thanks to the wine. She stared down at her mashed potatoes and daydreamed about kissing a guy like Lance.

"So, what about you, Diane?" Lance asked. "Red or blue pill?"

"Yeah, Mom. Red or blue?" Josh said, eating a spoonful of stuffing.

Alexa watched her mother set her wineglass down. "I'm sorry. I must not have been following. Red or blue what?"

"Pills," Josh said. "Haven't you seen *The Matrix*?"

"Just bits and pieces, but I never really followed it. What's the difference between the two pills?"

"The blue pill is like a sedative," Lance said. "It allows you to continue to live in ignorance. Protected from all of the ugliness in the world."

"But the red pill allows you to see the truth," Josh said around another bite of food.

"The truth about what?" her mother asked.

"Everything. Including stuff you don't want to know," Lance said. "So you have to ask yourself." He held his palms out as though weighing the two. "Do I want to know the scary truth or do I want to live peacefully in ignorance, even though to do so, I'm basically just buying into a big, fat lie?"

Diane raised her eyebrows. "Hmm. Heavy stuff. I might need to think about this one."

As the other four stupidly contemplated red and blue pills, Alexa wondered if she dared sneak up to her mother's bathroom to grab more sleeping pills. It would be risky but totally worth it if she didn't get caught. Besides, she was going to need more—and soon.

After the stupid red pill–blue pill debate began to lag, Josh started in with another one. "Here's one you guys'll like. There are five people underground and they need to get out quick. A fire is spreading, and the only way they can get out is through a manhole. But a really overweight guy tries to get out first and gets stuck. And he's like *really* stuck. You try to help him get unstuck, but he won't budge. You are the only person who can save the people underground. They're screaming, and if you don't help them, they'll be dead in five minutes. But the only way you can save them is you have to take an axe and hack up this guy so you can unstick him and pull him out . . . you know, in, like, pieces. What would you do? Would you hack him up to save the four other people?" Josh asked.

What a seriously messed-up question, Alexa thought.

"Oh my Gawd!" Trish said. "That's horrible. Of course not!"

"So you're saying you'd just stand around and let four people burn to death?" Josh asked.

"Well, I certainly wouldn't hack some guy up. Ew!" Trish said.

"How about you, Mom?" Josh asked.

The crease between her mother's brows deepened. "Where do you get these awful questions?"

Josh shrugged. "Bruce asked me that one. It made me think a little."

"No, I don't think I'd have the heart to hack him up," Diane said.

"No?"

"No."

"Well, what if Alexa and me . . . what if *we* were two of the four people who were about to burn to death? Would you do it then?"

Alexa put her fork down. "C'mon, Josh. That's disgusting. Can't you see we're trying to eat?"

"Oh, sorry, princess," Josh said.

Alexa shot him a look. "Bite me."

"Kids," their mother warned.

The room was silent.

"You have to give it to him . . . the question does make you think," Lance said.

"Can you pass the stuffing?" Josh asked, his dumb question clearly already forgotten. Alexa watched him shovel stuffing onto his plate and take a huge bite. She'd never seen anyone eat as much as her brother yet manage to remain a beanpole. It made her jealous.

But it wasn't the only reason she was jealous of Josh.

Alexa took another helping of mashed potatoes. She poured some white gravy into the middle of them, making a volcano, and started poking at it with her fork.

"Oh, wait. I almost forgot. Guess what *I* finished this morning?" Lance said, wiping his mouth with a napkin. "*Deep in the Darkness*. It was seriously incredible, Diane," he said. "I couldn't put it down."

Alexa rolled her eyes.

Trish's eyes brightened. "*Deep in the Darkness?*" she asked, her voice rising an octave. "I've read that! It's like one of my favorite books of all time!"

"Yeah?" Lance pointed at Diane. "Well, you know she wrote it, right?"

Trish's fork clinked loudly against her plate. Her jaw dropped, and she covered her mouth with her hands. "Oh my Gawd!" she squealed. "You're . . . you're Diane Christie! Oh my Gawwd! I *knew* you were somebody!"

Still slack-jawed, she turned to Alexa. "Why didn't you tell me your mom was Diane Christie?"

"It's hardly a big deal."

"Oh, stop! Your mom's amazing!"

Alexa watched her mother smile at Trish the way she usually smiled when someone recognized her from her books. A little uncomfortably. "Thanks, Trish. That's so nice to hear."

"Wow. Just wow," Trish said. "My mind is *blown*."

Alexa rolled her eyes. "Jeez, why don't you two get a room?"

Lance laughed and almost choked on his wine.

Alexa stared at him. Wow. She didn't usually get laughs with her sarcasm, just blank stares . . . or in her mother's case, disappointed looks . . . which always made Alexa feel a little like an ass.

But Lance thought she was funny. She liked that. He caught her staring at him and grinned. Did she see a flicker of interest?

"I've read all of your books!" Trish was saying. "*All* of them. And *Deep in the Darkness* was seriously my absolute favorite!"

Alexa took another sip of her wine. Why did people think it was such a big deal that her mother was a writer? Seriously—how hard was it to string together a few pages of words? It wasn't like she was a rocket scientist or something.

Her eyes flitted back to Lance, his gaze locking with hers. He grinned at her, sending every nerve ending in her body sparking to life. She shifted a little in her seat.

Maybe he *was* interested in her.

Was that even possible?

She drank more wine.

"Did I mention that Lance is a police officer?" her mother said.

"Really?" Trish said.

Alexa watched Trish bat her ridiculously long eyelashes at him. It was obvious that she thought Lance was hot, too. What girl wouldn't? But it made Alexa feel sick to her stomach. If Trish was interested in Lance, Alexa knew she'd have no chance. Girls like Alexa *always* lived in the shadow of girls like Trish. The ugly duckling landing the hot guy was just something that happened in the movies. It *never* happened in real life.

Josh excused himself to go to the bathroom. When he passed her, he leaned close and whispered into her ear: "That must be some coffee."

Alexa shot him an icy look.

"Oh, wait. So if you're a cop, you know all about Katie Worth, don't you?" Trish asked Lance, referring to the murdered girl.

"Not much more than you'd see on the news," Lance said, wiping his mouth with a napkin. "I'm with Fog Harbor PD."

"We passed her townhouse this morning on our way here," Trish said. "It was pretty creepy."

The memory of her father that dreadful morning appeared in Alexa's head for the second time that day. She winced.

"Did you girls know her?" her mother asked.

"I don't think so," Trish said. "I looked at all of her pictures on the Internet, and she didn't look familiar."

"Alexa?"

Alexa shrugged. She didn't even know what the girl had looked like.

"Who would've thought in New Cambridge. Where everyone looks so *normal*," Trish said.

"Normal?" Lance said, chuckling. "Something people need to understand is that the most notorious killers appeared very normal.

56

The worst monsters are masters at blending in. I'm serious. People are capable of things you could never even imagine."

"I'm afraid he's right," Alexa's mother said, standing.

As Alexa watched her disappear into the kitchen, the room swayed a little. She blinked, and the room swayed again.

Oh, no.

Her mother walked back into the room with a pitcher of tea, and Alexa saw two of her and two of the pitcher.

"Sorry, everyone," her mother said. "Murder talk is off limits. Starting now. Let's just enjoy the holiday. Light, happy discussion only, please."

Josh laughed as he walked back to his chair. "Says the woman made famous by writing novels about serial killers."

CHAPTER 9

DIANE SIPPED TEA and halfheartedly listened to Trish talk about her family back in Georgia. Both of her children had excused themselves minutes earlier.

Well, Josh had, at least. Alexa had simply walked out, her gait fantastically crooked, grasping that paper coffee cup of hers like it was a security blanket. There had clearly been something in it other than coffee, and after doing an inventory of the wine, Diane had a good idea what. She also remembered the missing pills and was pretty certain she'd found the culprit.

Diane had watched as her daughter's countenance and mood changed throughout the night. She'd arrived in true Alexa fashion: stiff, uptight, defensive. But as the evening progressed, her posture had relaxed, then her speech. Then her ears, nose, and cheeks had grown cherry red before leaving the table.

She'd also noticed how Alexa's glassy gaze had wandered to Lance all night . . . and how, as the night grew later, those gazes lingered. The few times Lance had spoken directly to Alexa, her face had even lit up. Diane hadn't seen Alexa light up like that in years.

She'd also noticed that Lance seemed to pay special attention to Alexa. But it was innocent, wasn't it?

"Diane?" Lance interrupted her thoughts.

"Huh? Oh. I'm sorry."

"Writing another novel in your head?"

Trish laughed. A little too hard.

Diane peered at the clock on the wall. It was nearly nine o'clock. "Yes. A bedtime story," she replied. "Sorry. It's been a long day."

Lance set his napkin on his plate. "Well, at least let me help with the dishes."

"Me, too," Trish said. Then she looked confused. "Anyone know where Alexa is?"

Josh yelled from the living room. "She's in here. On the couch, snoring like an old man."

"Should I wake her?" Trish asked Diane. "She's kind of my ride."

"No. Let her sleep. I can give you a ride home," Lance offered.

"Are you sure?" Trish asked.

"It's no problem."

"A police escort home? How can I turn that down? That's . . . so sweet of you," Trish said.

Diane scraped scraps into the garbage as she listened to the conversation. She should be grateful Lance was offering to give Alexa's new friend a ride home. He was her friend. A policeman. A nice guy. So why didn't she trust him? Was it the talk at the crisis center about him being a playboy?

"I'll get my coat," Trish said.

Lance turned to Diane and opened his arms to hug her good-bye. She wiped her hands dry on a dish towel, then gave him a friendly embrace. She stiffened when he drew her in a little tighter. He held her for a moment, then pulled back and gazed into her eyes. "Thank you so much for inviting me. I can't tell you how great it was to spend Thanksgiving with all of you."

"It was great having you," Diane said. She smiled tightly and waited for him to release her.

But he didn't.

Instead, his forehead creased and he leaned in, as if getting ready to kiss her, and she jerked away. A reflexive move.

His eyes flashed and his Adam's apple bobbed. He let go of her, straightened, and began zipping up his coat.

She'd embarrassed him.

He offered her a tight smile, and she smiled back. They were silent in the foyer for a long moment until Trish reappeared.

A few minutes later, Diane watched Trish climb into Lance's van. She locked the front door, then turned toward the sound of her snoring daughter in the next room.

❖❖❖

THE FIRE IN the fireplace had burned itself out and was now just glowing embers. Diane went to where Alexa lay on the couch and removed her shoes, adjusted the blanket on top of her, and added a second blanket.

She studied her daughter. Her mouth was parted and she was snoring softly. Now that she was asleep, the near-constant furrow between her eyes had smoothed out. She took in Alexa's fine, feminine features and imagined how much happier she might be if she didn't have such a hard attitude and permanent scowl on her face. But Alexa had been through a lot. Diane not being around as much as she should have been during a pivotal time of her life. Witnessing firsthand what her father had done.

She'd wanted both of her children to go to therapy after their father died. Josh had for a few months, but Alexa had refused. And Alexa was the one who had needed it most. Although things tended to bounce off

Josh's back, they didn't with Alexa. She took everything hard, seemingly unable to let anything go.

Diane now wished she'd been able to do everything the parenting books had advised her to do back then. She'd done her best, but it had been incredibly difficult to be consistent. She'd involved Alexa as much as she could with Josh's care, frequently rewarded her with compliments and surprises for being such a good big sister, and even sought out a highly reputed child psychologist for her.

But Alexa just became angrier . . . and nothing Diane did changed that fact. She'd tried so hard. But ultimately failed. She'd just been so overwhelmed and mentally and emotionally fatigued, caring for a chronically sick child.

She gently brushed blonde wisps out of her daughter's face and realized it was the first time she'd touched her in a long time without Alexa shrinking away.

Josh strode through the room, snapping Diane back to the present. "She's a lot nicer like that, isn't she?" he said, pointing to a sleeping Alexa.

Returning her attention to her daughter, Diane thought again of how Alexa carried herself during dinner: hunched over, bored, and completely miserable—well, until she was under the influence. How she'd fixed her with ice-cold stares throughout the night. It was like she listened to every conversation just so she could find reasons to hate it.

Diane went to the kitchen to find Josh filling his plate with more turkey and cranberry sauce. She was careful to keep her voice low in case Alexa woke. "Do you think Alexa's okay?"

"Okay or *sober*?"

"Well, I know she's not *sober*," Diane said, not quite sure how she was going to broach the drinking with her daughter, since she didn't seem to have any leverage with her. "She just seems so unhappy."

"Don't tell me you just noticed."

"Yeah, well . . . I guess maybe I thought she'd grow out of it at some point." Diane smiled wearily at her son. "So . . . what did you think about Lance?"

He made a face. "Eh," he said. "He was okay, I guess."

"Just okay?" Diane had thought Lance had been a big hit with all three of the kids. Had there been something in particular about Lance that had rubbed her son the wrong way? If so, she wanted to know.

"Yeah. Some of his jokes were a little dorky. And Alexa kept making goo-goo eyes at him all night. *That* was pretty gross."

"Yeah. I noticed that."

Josh filled a glass with milk. "He kind of creeped me out a little, too."

"Really?"

Josh nodded.

"In what way?"

"He just didn't seem very genuine. He seemed kind of, I don't know, slimy. Maybe it was how he looked at Alexa a few times. I didn't like it."

So it hadn't only been her. Josh had sensed something, too.

"But whatever. I could be wrong." Josh drained half of his milk and wiped his mouth. Then he stared at her as though he had more to say.

"What is it?" she asked. "Something else about Lance? If so, I want you to tell me."

"No. About Alexa."

Alexa? She nodded for him to go on.

"You know that thing they say?" he said. "You know, if you love something, let it go?"

Diane nodded.

Josh's brown eyes were steady on hers. He was being serious for a change. "Mom, you try too hard with her. And you just keep banging your head against the wall, trying to get her to be different. Why don't you just try leaving her alone for a while?"

Diane was surprised to hear her sixteen-year-old say that. Her therapist had said the same thing to her with different words. Her best friend, Ellie, too. While she appreciated everyone's concern, she couldn't fathom just standing around passively when her daughter might need her. Maybe Alexa's anger . . . her reclusive nature . . . were cries for help? Also, if she didn't rebuild their relationship before Alexa graduated, she could easily move off somewhere, and then they would never have a chance. This was her last shot. She was frightened of not being there for her daughter. Of losing her for good.

She mustered a smile. Josh reached out and hugged her tightly. "I love you, Mom," he said. She breathed in his scent: cologne-scented hair product and fabric softener . . . and her eyes filled with tears.

After Josh returned to his room, Diane found a checkbook and made out a check to Alexa—something to supplement the monthly allowance Diane gave her to pay her expenses. Alexa never mentioned the extra money, but she never turned it down, either. And Diane had a burning need to help her daughter.

Any way she could.

She went back to the living room, stuck the check into Alexa's purse, then sat next to her on the couch again. She tucked some loose hair behind her ear and whispered: "I'm so sorry I wasn't a better mom to you, sweetheart. But I'm *really* trying now. Please . . . let me in again."

❋❋❋

A FEW MINUTES later, in bed, Diane let herself remember her late husband. She'd been only twenty-one when she married Frank—not much older than Alexa was now. At the time she'd been an emergency room nurse, moonlighting as an aspiring writer. And while she really enjoyed her nursing work, she enjoyed her writing even more. Less than a year after marrying, Frank had asked her to quit her job as a nurse. To just be a housewife. To attend to him and the house only.

She'd agreed, and she'd molded herself into what she thought he would like best, because at the time pleasing Frank had been the ultimate goal. She'd been taken by his good looks, his charm, his success—he was a partner of a privately owned chemical company. Enamored of Frank and the bright new world he promised, she did everything he asked of her: She quit her job. She cut her long hair into a stylish bob and lightened it until it was the shade of a caramel candy. Everything was all about Frank, Frank, Frank . . . until Alexa arrived, and it suddenly wasn't.

When Alexa showed up, Frank didn't even try to hide his jealousy—and he cheated on Diane for the first time when Alexa was just ten days old. In the beginning, Diane had forgiven him because she'd desperately wanted her family to be whole. But after the third affair she changed her priorities . . . and Frank was no longer one of them. Her daughter was, as well as building a successful writing career that would make her self-sufficient.

She threw herself into taking care of her daughter and her career. She worked on her books during Alexa's naps and late into the evening hours after her daughter was asleep. She wrote and rewrote every manuscript until it shone, then she hired freelance editors to poke holes in plots. Many nights she fell asleep with her daughter in one arm and a writing book in the other. When she was happy with her manuscripts, she found a cover designer to create intriguing covers that rivaled the ones that the big publishing houses in New York were producing—then she uploaded her books to Amazon . . . and crossed her fingers.

In her first few months, she sold maybe one or two of each title a week. Some weeks she sold nothing. But she didn't let the lack of sales discourage her. She kept writing—and by the twenty-first month of having her books available, the tide suddenly turned and she began to sell an average of fifty copies per day, then hundreds . . . some days even thousands.

She kept writing and publishing, and before she knew it she had agents contacting her, offering representation, and a big New York publisher extending a seven-figure deal for her first three books.

Seeing her success changed something within Frank. He became soft again.

Well, soft*er*.

He was nicer and more pleasant to be around. It was as though he suddenly valued her more. He suggested counseling, so they tried it. And for several weeks, things seemed to improve. She thought that maybe she could be happy with him again.

She and Frank applied to adopt a baby. Since she'd been adopted herself, adopting a child had always been one of Diane's dreams. A few months after filling out the first of the applications, she received a phone call about Josh. He'd been found abandoned in a hospital waiting room, sitting in a chair in only a T-shirt and a diaper. He'd had a backpack in his lap that contained a sippy cup and a picture of him with a woman, presumably his biological mother. But bringing Josh home hurt her relationship with her daughter; it also drove another stake through her already-faltering marriage. At home, Frank spent most of his time in his office.

He spent little time with the kids and even less time with her. He came and went as he pleased. After the first few years, they were just coexisting, but she didn't leave him because she wanted her kids to have two parents in the household. She told herself she was content with just her kids and her career, even when the lonely years added up to more than a decade.

The night before she discovered Frank's body, he'd walked into the bedroom as she'd been reading in bed. He lay down on his stomach at the foot of the bed, which was uncharacteristic of him. He'd smiled at her; again, uncharacteristic.

In their last years together, the smiles had been rare. Yes, she'd seen him smile at his colleagues, his clients, at her when they were at a holiday office party and he was trying to impress his colleagues. But rarely when they were alone at home.

"What's going on?" she asked, watching him stare at her from across the bed.

"Nothing," he said and kept smiling. And to her surprise, it hadn't looked disingenuous. It had looked real. He'd actually looked relaxed for once. It had brought her back to their first year of marriage for a moment. Back when he was less rigid and more charming, actually fun to be around.

After lying there quietly for a few minutes—awkward ones for her—he rose, walked over to her side of the bed, and kissed her on the cheek. That night, he didn't come to bed. That in itself hadn't raised any warning flags. But when she woke up the next morning, she had the sudden, inexplicable sense something was very wrong.

She got up and walked to the window to see if his car was still parked in the driveway.

It was.

She opened their bedroom door and went down the hallway. But when she grasped the doorknob to his office, her hand froze. She took a deep breath, then slowly she opened the door. The first thing she saw were the toes of his socks hanging in front of her.

And his feet were still in them.

Her eyes reluctantly traveled upward, and she saw that he was still wearing his khakis from the evening before. The same green polo shirt. His neck was in a noose, and he was hanging from a rafter. She clamped her hands over her mouth to silence her screams.

Oh, God, Frank! No, no, no!

The kids! She had to get him down. She pushed the office door shut . . . too hard, and she jumped when it slammed. Her stomach roiling, she climbed atop Frank's office chair and struggled with his body. But she couldn't keep him still enough, and the wheels of his office chair kept sliding across the floor.

That's when she heard something in the doorway. She turned and saw the office door was open—and Alexa, her face ashen, in the doorway.

"Dad—wha-at?"

Then came the ear-piercing screams. The screams Diane could still vividly hear all these months later.

As Diane scrambled around the desk to get to her daughter, she saw Josh standing behind Alexa, peering in, tears streaming down his face. Diane yanked the door closed behind her and crumpled to the hallway floor, taking her children with her. It was at least another five minutes before Alexa would stop screaming.

CHAPTER 10

THE SUN WAS in its death throes the next evening as he watched Jill MacDonald carry her grocery bags back to her apartment, the branches above her casting jagged shadows on her path. She was taking a shortcut through the woods from the supermarket.

He followed her, his fists balled up at his sides. His brain felt swollen and on the verge of exploding. The anger trapped inside was too large for its small confines. It needed a release—and it needed it now.

As a cloud floated in front of the sun, darkening the sky, Jill stopped, set the grocery bags down, and rubbed her arms. Two yards behind her, he kept walking. His boot came down hard on a twig and it snapped in two.

He watched her head turn and her eyes find him. As their eyes connected, a shudder of pleasure crawled up his back.

Yes, we're alone.

Does that frighten you?

He could imagine the thoughts flashing through her mind. *Is he the guy who killed Katie Worth?*

Why, yes. Yes, I am, he answered in his head.

She quickly looked away, picked up her bags, and started walking again. But she was walking much faster now.

He walked faster, too.

He had woken earlier that day with fire in his stomach and had needed this tonight. To strike some terror into her . . . to extinguish some of his own. And it was working. He felt alive, his senses heightened at smelling her fear.

He walked even faster.

He wasn't concerned that he'd been seen. If she tried to describe him, she would only remember the black hood, have a general idea of his height. If they could find him on the basis of that, they deserved to catch him. But he knew that the police were slow when it came to finding people like him. Investigations were nothing at all like they were portrayed on television.

When she glanced over her shoulder again, he was much closer. Only a little more than a yard separated them. She threw her groceries to the ground and sprinted toward the apartments ahead. A can rolled out of one of the plastic bags and off the pathway, into the dead grass.

His hands now relaxed, he stopped and picked it up: SpaghettiOs. He watched as she topped the hill ahead and ran beneath the lights of the parking lot that wrapped around the apartment complex.

Smiling, he stretched his arms above his head and turned around. He'd done what he'd set out to do for now—relieved some of the tension.

Besides, he'd see her again soon.

CHAPTER 11

FIVE NIGHTS LATER, Diane pulled into the parking lot at Brookmart and parked.

She'd just left the crisis center, where she'd been intercepted by two pleasant, plainclothed police detectives, Chavez and Johnson, who were working Katie Worth's murder case. They'd spent thirty minutes in the back office with her, asking her questions: "We understand the caller's voice was altered, but do your best to tell us what it sounded like . . . Any idea of the gender of the caller? Did the person state one way or the other? How long did the call last? Can you confirm what time it came in? As accurately as you can, tell us what this person told you. Start at the beginning if you can. What were you doing before the call came in? What did you do when the call ended?"

She'd answered as best she could but was afraid she hadn't been able to give them much more than what she'd provided in the statement she'd given Mary Kate the evening of the call.

After the detectives left, she'd asked Mary Kate if the caller had phoned again, but she'd said he hadn't. She also asked if the lines had been tapped, but Mary Kate was unable to say. Crisis center policy was to insulate volunteers from that type of information. It was for their protection.

Diane had answered phones for the next three hours and had been relieved when Lance hadn't shown for his shift. His attempted kiss on Thanksgiving evening had been awkward, to say the least. Maybe he wasn't as troubled by it as she was. Or . . . maybe it was the reason he hadn't shown up at the crisis center. Doubtful, yes, but entirely possible.

Just as she was switching off the ignition, she heard two local deejays talking about the murder. She sat in the car and listened intently for a few minutes, waiting to see if there were new developments.

She'd read every article that had been written about the girl and had visited her social media accounts many times in the last several days, so she was fairly up-to-date with what was going on with the investigation. At least the information that was being shared with the public. Once she realized the deejays were just rehashing the same information again, she flipped the radio off. She would stick with her rule. No thinking about murder tonight. Real or fictitious.

Inside Brookmart, she maneuvered her cart through the aisles, quickly finding what she needed. Luckily, Wayne wasn't anywhere in sight. The store was also pretty empty. Probably why the Top 40 music from the PA system seemed a bit louder than normal. It was so loud she almost didn't hear her phone ring.

She tried to pull it from her coat pocket to catch it in time, but as she did, the phone slipped from her hand and landed on the tiled floor with a sickening thud.

Shit! Shit! Shit!

She picked it up and turned it over. The glass was shattered. She pressed the phone's home button but nothing happened. Just a blank screen.

It was ruined.

Sighing, she tossed the damaged phone in her purse and grabbed the remaining items on her list.

It was sprinkling out when she left Brookmart. She hurried to her car, realizing she'd never noticed before how poorly lit the parking lot was at night. Probably because she was almost always chaperoned by Wayne. By the time she loaded the groceries into her backseat, the rain had started coming down in sheets.

She fell into the driver's seat and pulled her hair from her face. Her wet clothes clung to her chilled skin. She turned the heat up as high as it would go.

The wipers couldn't keep up with the torrent of rain, and Diane drove slowly, squinting to see the road in front of her. She was reaching to change the radio station when suddenly she heard a loud *bang!* and the car began to slide across the road. She gripped the steering wheel tightly and eased on the brake, managing to gain control and get her car over to the shoulder.

Just great. A flat.

It was dark, pouring, she had a flat . . . and her phone was broken, so there was no way to reach anyone.

A sideways rain drummed against the window as she squinted into the storm, trying to get her bearings, then a pair of headlights in her rearview mirror caught her attention. They sat higher, like they belonged to a truck.

As the vehicle eased up behind her, she pressed the master lock button on the driver's door, and all the locks clicked into place. She kept her eyes glued to the truck behind her. The headlights were so bright she couldn't make out much else. She squinted to see if she could see any movement in the dark, but she couldn't.

She almost jumped out of her skin when she heard tapping on her driver's-side window. But when she saw who it was, she let out a sigh of relief. It was the man she'd met at the grocery store the night she'd been doing her Thanksgiving shopping.

She lowered her window—just a little. He leaned forward. "Fancy meeting you here," he said, his teeth gleaming white against the dark night.

Diane groaned. "I think I have a flat."

The man looked back at it. "Yeah, it certainly looks that way. And a pretty bad one. You have a jack?"

Diane nodded. "In the back."

"A spare?"

"Also in the back."

"Pop it open and I'll fix it for you."

"Are you sure? You'll get soaked."

He took a step back to display his already-soaked clothes and boots. "It's a little late to be worried about that. Don't you think?"

As he worked, she found herself worrying about Josh. Maybe he'd been the one who had called earlier when she'd dropped her phone. Maybe he'd needed something. She always answered immediately when her kids called or texted, so it was likely he was getting worried now.

A loud slam made her jump. She looked in the rearview mirror to see he had shut the back hatch and was walking back to the driver's-side door. She lowered the window . . . again just a little.

"You should be good now. But you're riding on the spare, so I'd take her into a garage tomorrow to get a proper tire."

"Thank you so much . . . um . . ."

He stared at her, a smile playing on his lips. "You don't remember my name, do you?"

"I'm not good with names. Sorry."

"It's Rick." He smiled at her. *That smile.* Despite not wanting it to, it gave her butterflies.

"I can't thank you enough, Rick."

"You're very welcome. Glad I could help."

Lightning streaked across the sky, illuminating his handsome face. "I think that's my cue to get out of this weather," he said. He brought his hand to the window and slipped a folded piece of paper through. "My bill. Whenever you get a chance."

He grinned again and jogged back to his truck.

Diane raised her window and unfolded the paper. His name and phone number were written in clear, crisp letters and numbers.

Meticulous handwriting.

She felt herself blush.

❖❖❖

AN HOUR LATER, after ordering a new phone, cleaning a little, and getting ready for bed, Diane lay on the couch at home and tried not to think of Rick. Instead, she watched Josh as he channel surfed (something he could do for hours), remembering back to when he was little.

"Would you stop looking at me like that?" Josh said, smirking, his eyes still on the screen.

"How'd you know?" she asked.

"Sixth sense."

She glanced at the television. Something caught her eye on channel four as he whizzed by it. "Hey, go back. And turn it up," she said. It was the local news. The caption BOYFRIEND CLEARED IN MURDER INVESTIGATION was splashed across the bottom of the screen in large red letters.

A female anchor was reporting from a news desk, and they were showing the college campus in the background. "Police have cleared Caleb Donaldson, the boyfriend of murdered University of New Cambridge student Katie Worth. He had been the lead suspect in the case," the anchor was saying.

Diane's gut twisted at the realization the killer was still at large.

"I knew he didn't do it," Josh muttered.

"Why do you say that?"

"He just . . . I don't know. He just doesn't look like the type who would kill someone."

In Diane's line of work, she had learned that public faces rarely reflected private misdeeds. And she was surprised she hadn't done a good job of teaching Josh that. "You know better than that. Don't you?" she said, staring at him. "You know that murderers come in all colors, shapes, and sizes. And most of them look completely normal, just like this guy," she said, pointing at Caleb Donaldson's image, which was now filling the screen. "That's why you need to always be careful. With *everyone*."

"Tell that to Alexa, not me. I'm a dude. Stuff like that only happens to girls."

"You never know," she said.

Josh rolled his eyes. "Thanks for being a ray of sunshine, Mom. You sound like your cop friend from Thanksgiving."

"Good," Diane said. "Because what he said was spot-on."

A few minutes later, Diane crawled into bed with her iPad. She powered it on and pulled up Katie Worth's Facebook profile for the third or fourth time. She enlarged the girl's profile photo again and studied it. The girl had been a beauty. Gleaming, long dark hair. Serious blue eyes framed by thick lashes. And dead at nineteen.

How tragic when she had so many more promising years ahead of her. The girl's parents had to be beside themselves with grief.

She couldn't even imagine . . . didn't *want* to imagine.

After a few minutes she powered off the iPad and set it on her bedside table, then turned on her side. As she waited for her sleeping pill to kick in and for sleep to claim her, she stared vacantly at the shadows dancing across the walls of her bedroom but could see nothing but images of the dead girl.

CHAPTER 12

THE NEXT AFTERNOON, after finishing her writing for the day, Diane checked her reviews on Amazon and was surprised to see fifteen new ones. All were pretty good, all four or five stars, except one. It was a rare one-star review. She pulled it up and groaned as she recognized the handle of the longtime reviewer, writewellorquit777—a troll who had reviewed every single one of her books over the last six years. While she'd grown numb to most bad reviews—it came with the job—this troll got under her skin because it almost seemed personal.

She read less than half of the review, then shut down her browser and went to her office window. The sun had begun its downward slide below the horizon, and the boats had already begun their return for the night.

Her best friend would be arriving soon for a weekend stay. She tried to get excited about the visit. She'd missed Ellie and was happy to see her again. But she'd woken up with the now-familiar foreboding sensation in her stomach.

Something's very wrong.

The feeling this morning had been especially strong and had haunted her all day.

Josh was driving back from the airport with Ellie right now. His driving alone to the airport had made her nervous, but he was only going to Hyannis. It wasn't like he would be dealing with Boston traffic.

Diane went back to her computer and searched for any new developments on the Katie Worth murder investigation. Any new leads. It still bothered her that the boyfriend had been cleared. She hadn't wanted to think there was a predator somewhere around the college. She wondered what was going on behind the scenes. What information, if any, the police weren't yet sharing . . . or if they had found any new leads.

Hearing the crunch of tires on the gravel driveway, she closed her laptop and headed out into the hallway. Just as she hit the bottom of the staircase, the front door opened and the whirlwind that was Ellie burst into the house, the scent of her perfume blowing in with her.

The scent immediately took Diane back to her college days. Studying for exams in the wee hours of the night with lots of potato chips, soda, and NoDoz. Blasting Prince songs as they got ready for long nights out at college bars. The only care she'd had in the world back then was passing her nursing clinicals—and she'd always done so with flying colors.

Diane hugged her old friend and noticed her hair already smelled of the salty sea air. Knowing Ellie, she'd probably had Josh ride in the wintry Massachusetts weather with the windows down.

"Oh my God, it's so good to see you!" Ellie said, holding Diane tight. Ellie pulled away and studied her. "You are such a sight for jet-lagged eyes."

Diane smiled. It was good to see Ellie, too. When she looked at Ellie, she saw home . . . whatever that was. It was the same way she felt when she looked at her kids.

Ellie was an attractive woman; solid, strong . . . but right now her face looked drawn. She also looked much thinner, and not in a good way. "Are you okay? You look terrible," Diane said.

Ellie laughed. "I was *wondering* why I missed you so much. It's that way with words you have."

Although she looked exhausted, Ellie was as stylish as always. A powder-blue winter vest, tight designer jeans, and a form-fitting T-shirt clearly showed off her well-toned figure. She pushed her long, wavy blonde hair off her shoulders and smiled at Diane.

Josh dragged in what was clearly a very heavy overstuffed suitcase. Ellie looked back at him and laughed. "Oh, you sweet thing. I would have got that. You shouldn't have to pay the price for my inability to pack light."

"It's no problem," Josh groaned. "I'll take it upstairs."

Ellie turned to Diane. "So are all the men in this town as dashing as this one?"

"If that's what you came here for, you may be sorely disappointed," Diane said.

"I bet you haven't even looked. Where are the bars around here?"

Josh laughed. "Uh, you're asking the wrong person."

He was right. She didn't go out much. And "not much" meant "not ever."

Josh reached the top step with the luggage. "There's a bar on Main Street."

Diane shot him a puzzled look.

Josh shrugged. "What? It's called The Bar. It wasn't too tough to figure out what the place was."

Ellie clapped her hands. "The Bar! It sounds divine. So why are we standing here? Let's get this party started, sister."

"Now?"

Ellie shrugged. "Why not? It's after five."

"You're serious?"

"Dead serious."

Diane smiled. Some things never changed . . . and she found that comforting right now. "You've been traveling for five hours. Don't you want to rest? Freshen up?"

Ellie waved her hands over her body. "Sorry, babe. But this is about as fresh as it gets. And I'll rest when I'm dead. Right now I need a drink."

"I have wine in the kitchen. We could sit—"

"Not the same," Ellie interrupted. "It goes down better when some hot bartender serves it to me."

Ellie climbed the stairs and gave Josh a hug. "What about you, kid? Got any plans tonight?"

Josh shook his head. "So you're available to be our driver. Drop us off and then pick us up when we are ready to turn in?"

"Sure. I can do that," Josh said.

Ellie smiled. When Ellie smiled, Diane couldn't help but think of the cat that swallowed the canary. She always seemed to be up to something—and she often was. "Because your mom and I . . . are going to get hammered tonight."

Josh snorted. His eyes went from Ellie to Diane, back to Ellie again. "Mom? Hammered? Yeah. Good luck with that."

❖❖❖

THE BAR HAD an old tavern feel with dark wood floors and Early American decor. Two TVs, one on either side of the long bar, were broadcasting a college basketball game while classic rock played just loud enough that you could still talk over it. There was a Christmas tree in the corner by the hall that led to the bathrooms, and Christmas lights and garlands strung across the back wall of the bar.

A small group of college boys crowded around one end of the bar, cheering on the game. Diane and Ellie grabbed two bar stools at the other end of the bar. Ellie got the robust bartender's attention and ordered two Sam Adamses and two bowls of clam chowder. She winked at Diane. "When in Rome . . ."

Diane situated her purse on her lap, feeling completely out of her element, which she found to be a combination of uncomfortable and exciting. It had been forever since she'd done the bar scene. The bartender brought over the bottles of beer, and Ellie handed one to Diane.

"To new beginnings *again*," said Ellie.

They clinked the bottles in a toast. Diane took a sip of the brown ale, enjoying the smooth, malty taste as it slid down her throat.

She noticed some of the college kids studying her and Ellie. She knew what they must have been thinking: two desperate cougars hoping to snag some young guys. Ellie glanced at them and then back at Diane with that trademark mischievous smile of hers, and Diane realized that the kids were probably half right.

"Still enjoying it out here?" Ellie asked.

"Yeah. It's been a really great move for Josh."

"I'm talking about you," Ellie said. "Are *you* enjoying it? You matter, too, you know."

Ellie didn't have kids. She didn't know what it was like. If her kids weren't happy, she couldn't be. Not wholly. "Yeah, I do. I love my new home. Being so close to the ocean."

Ellie raised her eyebrows. "And . . ."

Diane laughed. "No. I haven't met anyone."

"Don't wait too long. In this market, we have an expiration date, you know."

"Spending time with the kids and writing are the only things I'm concerned about. If another man never appeared in my life again, it would be too soon."

"Jesus, you don't mean that."

"I do."

Ellie shook her head. "You just need to get out more. You'll see what you're missing."

"Hey, I have fun. I have everything I need."

"Sure you do."

A waitress came by with their food, and Ellie asked to be seated at a table. Once there, Ellie ordered two more beers. When the waitress left, Ellie asked, "Dare I ask about Queen Alexa?" Ellie had been calling Alexa that since she was eight.

Diane sighed. "She's . . . still Alexa. Still angry and unhappy. And of course things have only gotten worse since Frank's suicide. She says she's okay, but I don't think she is."

She decided to fill Ellie in. She needed another sounding board. She'd been too busy to Skype with her therapist back in New Jersey for a month now, and she really needed to vent. When she was done, Ellie stared at her. "I feel for Alexa. No child should *ever* have to deal with the suicide of a parent. Much less *see* them, the way she saw Frank." She shook her head. "That . . . must have been just horrible."

Tears pricking her eyes, Diane stirred her drink. Took a long sip.

Ellie placed a hand on one of Diane's. It was soft, reassuring. "But still," Ellie continued, "it doesn't excuse her behavior toward you. You try so hard to please everyone. You always have. No matter the cost to you."

"That's not true."

"Yes, it is. First, rest in peace, Frank," Ellie said, glancing up at the ceiling, "but you were in a loveless marriage. But you stayed . . . for him and the kids. So that no one got hurt. Even though you were miserable.

"Frank didn't deserve you. He was looking for a pair of tits and a smile who would cater to his every whim, and he couldn't handle it when you turned out to be so much more."

Diane had to grin at that one. "'Pair of tits and a smile'?"

Ellie continued. "Then you have a teenage daughter who steps all over you. And always has. She uses you as a meal ticket and treats you like crap. And now she's stealing from you."

Diane's smile vanished.

"Don't look at me like that. I'm on your team. Look, what I'm saying is that you're an amazing woman, Diane. You deserve better than what you accept. You're so beautiful, intelligent, and talented, and kind, and . . . patient. Hell, you're *too* patient. You've always taken excellent care of the kids, but you've never taken even decent care of yourself. It's always been about someone else. But now that he's . . . *out of the picture* . . . and your kids are practically grown, live a little. Focus on you for once. You need someone in your life. Even if it's temporary. Everyone needs a companion."

Diane drank more of her beer. She set the bottle down on the bar. "I've missed you, Ellie," Diane said, cutting her off. "But now that I've vented, let's move on to happy things tonight, okay?"

"One last thing, then I'm done, okay?"

Diane nodded.

"You teach people how to treat you. You do. You need to think about that when it comes to Alexa. I know how much you love her. Don't think for a second that I don't. And because I love you, I love her, too. But think about what you've taught her, and if you want to continue doing it. Think about it, and you might decide that I'm right about this."

❋❋❋

AN HOUR LATER, with the help of a third beer and more enjoyable conversation, Diane was starting to feel a lightness in her chest that she hadn't felt for a long time.

Even the nagging feeling that something was very wrong had vanished for now. Ellie had been right. Going out had been a good idea.

She hadn't known how badly she needed it. To just get out, step outside of her daily life for a few hours.

While they'd talked, the bar around them had livened up. There were easily a dozen more people. Mainly men getting off work. A few couples. A group of three younger women at a table next to them.

A few minutes earlier, Ellie had confided that her husband, Ted, had left her for a younger woman, and they were getting a divorce. Diane had had no idea. But then again, she and Ellie hadn't talked much over the phone during the last year—and she had the feeling Ellie was embarrassed about it. Apparently they'd split five months ago.

They talked about life and starting over in the middle of it. They reminisced about old times. Ellie was in the middle of telling Diane about some young guy she'd been seeing at her office when she stopped midsentence and straightened in her seat.

Diane turned to see what had caught her attention and was struck by a jolt of excitement.

It was Rick from the supermarket and her tire blowout.

❦❦❦

RICK WAS SOAKED . . . again . . . and Diane realized it was a look that worked very well for him.

Their eyes met, and he walked up to their table and smiled at her. "Well, hello, Diane. Small world."

"Small town."

"Yeah, well . . . I guess that, too."

Ellie narrowed her eyes. "You guys know each other?" she asked, throwing Diane an accusatory smile. "You were holding out on me."

"Not really. We just . . ."

"Run into each other sometimes," Rick finished.

Diane scanned Rick's wet clothes. "I believe you were wet the last time I saw you."

"Wait. Was that supposed to be your line or mine?" Rick asked.

Ellie spit out her beer and bent over the table, laughing.

Diane smiled. "Hold on. I'm pretty sure that's not what I meant."

Rick held out his beer and winked at Diane. "I think I'm going to walk away, dry off a bit, come back, and start over. Okay?"

When Rick returned a few minutes later, she and Ellie invited him to sit with them. He accepted, and the three of them drank and talked and laughed for hours.

Diane realized she was enjoying herself even more with Rick at the table. She felt invigorated. Hopeful, even. For what, she wasn't sure. But it felt damn good to relax and just have fun for once.

Not to worry . . . about *anything*.

There was no denying there was chemistry between her and Rick. And the more she was around him, the more she was attracted to him.

She noticed two of the three younger women at the table next to them glancing over at Rick throughout the night. She saw him scan their table once, but his attention hadn't lingered. It had snapped right back to her and Ellie.

Well, to her, actually.

She learned Rick had recently moved to Fog Harbor and was working on the docks, doing a few odd handyman jobs, just as Wayne from the supermarket had suspected. After much coercing from Ellie, he also explained that he had just completed two tours of duty in Iraq as a Marine sniper—something he didn't seem completely comfortable talking about.

After he changed the subject for a second time, Diane nudged Ellie so she would stop prying. Ellie had been working at a pace of two beers to Diane's one and had lost all ability to read social cues. Not that she paid that much attention to social cues when sober.

As they talked, Diane suddenly noticed Rick's gaze flicker in the direction of the bar, and his expression grew serious. He took a long pull of his beer. She turned to see what he was looking at. It was the

TV above the bar, which had cut away from the game for a news teaser. The sound was turned down, but she recognized Katie Worth's photo.

"Am I missing something?" Ellie asked. "Why the serious faces?"

"A student was murdered at the university," Diane said.

"Which university? The one Alexa goes to?"

Diane nodded.

"Oh my God!" Ellie gasped. "What happened?"

"Let's not talk about that tonight. I'll fill you in tomorrow."

While Diane tried to push thoughts of the girl's murder to the back of her mind, Rick excused himself to go to the restroom.

When he was out of earshot, Ellie, clearly having no trouble forgetting about the murdered girl, fanned herself dramatically. "Oh, my stars. He's *gorgeous!*"

"He is."

"Why haven't you two hooked up? He's obviously interested."

"You think so?"

"He couldn't be more obvious if he was holding a sign."

Ellie motioned to the waitress and ordered a round of shots. Then she picked up her beer for another toast. "Tonight you're saying yes to possibilities," Ellie said. Her face turned serious. "And that's an order."

"To saying yes to possibilities," Diane agreed and clinked Ellie's bottle.

Diane took a sip from her beer and vowed she'd take a chance. That is, if Rick gave her another one.

After all, what was the worst that could happen?

CHAPTER 13

ALEXA PUSHED PAST Josh into the foyer. She had managed to miss most of the downpour, but Josh was soaking wet.

"Next time, call a tow truck," he blurted between gasps of air. "And, for the record, 'down the street' is very different than five blocks away."

Alexa dropped her duffel bag and grabbed a towel from the downstairs bathroom. She tossed it to Josh. "Relax. It's not like it was uphill or anything."

"Oh, right. So next time you break down, you push and I'll steer."

Alexa watched her brother grumble his way upstairs, then she picked up the duffel bag and retreated to the laundry room.

When Josh had told her that Ellie was in town and that she and their mother were going out, Alexa had decided to seize the opportunity to do her laundry and, more importantly, try to get more sleeping pills. But five blocks from her mother's house, her car had stalled and wouldn't start again.

Lucky for her, Josh had been home and helped her push her car to the house. But now that they were at her mother's, she wasn't sure what to do next. It was probably too late for an auto shop to be open. Plus, it wasn't like she had the money to get her car repaired anyway. She would have to wait to talk with her mother. Which meant she would also have to face Ellie, something she would rather avoid.

After starting a load of laundry, Alexa sneaked upstairs. Josh's bedroom door was cracked. He was either still changing or had already been sucked into one of his dumb video games. She tiptoed past his door and into her mother's bathroom.

Her hand shook as she opened her mother's medicine cabinet and looked through the various toiletries. Makeup, aspirin, floss, toothpaste.

Where were the pills?

They were always on the first shelf, all the way to the left. But they weren't there now. That was weird. Her mother always had a place for everything. And *this* was where she kept those pills.

"Damn," she muttered. Had her mother noticed pills missing and hidden them?

Lightning flashed outside and thunder rattled the windows as she checked all of her mother's bureau drawers and the drawers of her wardrobe.

No pills in sight.

She tried to lift the top from her mother's jewelry box, but it was locked. She hurried back to the bathroom and hunted for a bobby pin, something she'd been using for years to open her mother's jewelry box . . . as well as a few other items she'd found locked in the house. But when she had the jewelry box open, there were no pills in sight.

Crap.

She peeled off her wet clothes and dressed in a pair of her mother's sweats and a T-shirt and, desperate for a fix of some kind, hurried down to the half bathroom, looking for the wine bottle she'd stashed. But it wasn't there either.

Crap!

She should've known, given the fanatic her mother was about cleaning.

She went to the kitchen to see if she could find more wine. She rooted around and finally discovered two bottles in the back of the pantry. She grabbed one, found a corkscrew, and pulled the cork out. Then she poured a glass and gulped down several sips.

As she drank, she walked around the kitchen, moving things because she knew it would bug the crap out of her mother. She moved the kitchen scissors to a different drawer. The can opener, a spatula, a component to her mother's blender from the second drawer to the fourth. She opened the refrigerator and moved some items to different shelves. She envisioned her mother trying to find everything . . . and felt a little glow of satisfaction.

"What are you doing?"

Alexa jumped. Josh was standing in the kitchen doorway, wearing pajamas. "Christ. You scared the crap out of me!"

"What are you doing with the olive oil?"

"What does it look like I'm doing? Putting it away."

"Except it doesn't go in the bread box, nut job." He looked at the wineglass in her hand. Then the open bottle of wine on the kitchen island. "You got into Mom's wine?"

She took another long pull of the wine, swallowed, and winced. "I'm saving her from herself."

"Yeah, okay. And what am I supposed to say when she asks where her wine went?"

Alexa shrugged. "Why do you have to say anything? Are you in charge of the wine?"

A jagged streak of lightning lit up the sky outside. The wind picked up outside and pressed against the kitchen window.

"I want some," Josh said.

Alexa smiled and grabbed a glass from the cabinet and poured him some. Josh pulled out the popcorn maker and the popcorn, and they drank wine in silence as the popcorn popped. Soon the kitchen smelled like their old kitchen back in New Jersey. They'd popped a lot of popcorn in that house.

When the popcorn was done, Josh poured it into two bowls, then they went up to his bedroom. Josh plopped onto a beanbag chair and started flipping channels, settling on an episode of *The Walking Dead*.

Alexa set the wine bottle on his nightstand and poured herself another glass. "Want more?" she asked, offering the bottle to Josh.

"I better not. Mom and Ellie are going to call me when they're ready to come home. I'm their designated driver."

Alexa rolled her eyes. Her mother could somehow even ruin a good time when she wasn't around. She sat on Josh's bed and stared up at his license plate collection. There were like forty of them now. She remembered when he'd started collecting them as a kid . . . and had gotten his first two.

Josh started coughing, and soon it turned into a fit. He stood, went to the window, and opened it.

"Want a breathing treatment?" she asked. Hearing him cough always scared her a little because she knew how easily he could end up in the hospital.

He shook his head, his coughing fit apparently over, and he sat back down. She studied her brother as he watched the television. He seemed okay now, but he hadn't always been. When he was younger, he was in the hospital a lot. Like a dozen times; maybe more. And he'd almost died twice of pneumonia.

It hit her that it was this time of year that he'd come and lived with them when he was a toddler and she was five. When he arrived, *everything* had changed for her—and not in good ways. She'd always been jealous of him . . . and had wanted desperately to hate him, like she hated her mother because Josh was the child her mother spent all her time with. The one who had always been on her mind. Alexa had felt like an afterthought.

She remembered years ago finding, tucked in her mother's desk drawer, several letters Josh had written to her in crayon. One letter she remembered vividly had said:

Thank yu forr saveing me and leting me be yur sun.
love josh.

She'd taken it and crumpled it up, then thrown it in the kitchen wastebasket. She'd actually crumpled a lot of letters over the years. Taken a lot of things that hadn't been hers to take.

She wasn't proud of it.

She'd been insecure.

She was *still* insecure. She knew that. She'd been a little monster . . . the black sheep, and he'd been the golden child. She hated that it was that way. She would have given anything to be the golden child, but sadly, that hadn't been the hand she'd been dealt.

Josh's phone dinged. He picked it up and looked at the screen, then he quickly thumbed something on the keyboard before setting it down. He downed the rest of his wine, then reached to pour more.

"Thought you were designated driver."

"Mom just texted. She found a ride." He poured more wine, then his eyes swung back to his program.

Alexa tried to figure out what to do with the open wine bottle now that her mother would be home soon. Surely she would notice it was missing.

"So . . . why do you hate Mom so much?" Josh asked, his eyes still glued to the television.

The bluntness of the question startled her. "Who said I hate her?"

He looked at her and rolled his eyes. "It's not like it's obvious or anything," he said. "So, why?"

Alexa wasn't sure what to say.

"Mom does her best, Alexa," he said. "Besides, you had Dad."

Alexa grunted. As though that was a fair trade-off. Anytime she'd been home alone with her father, he would just set out a loaf of bread, a knife, peanut butter and jelly, and a cup of water, then retreat to his office with barely a word between them.

Being with him was even lonelier than being by herself.

"Dad? Yeah, right. He was as involved with my life as a freaking shoe."

"Well, at least he didn't hate you."

"What? Dad didn't *hate* you."

"Yes, he did. He never wanted me around. He treated me like I didn't even exist."

"Josh, he treated *everyone* like they didn't exist."

Josh seemed to think about that. "Maybe." He stared at the wall in front of him. ". . . and then he suddenly goes and offs himself like that. In the house. Couldn't care less that Mom would have to find him."

"Or one of us," Alexa mumbled. She twitched, her mind going back to that morning. Seeing her father hanging there. Suspended from the beam in the ceiling, his neck limp inside the noose—she tried to shake the image, but it was one she could never fully get rid of, no matter how hard she tried.

"I mean, what kind of tool does that?"

"I don't know," Alexa answered, wondering for the millionth time how her father could just abandon them like that. Not that he was around much while he was alive, but still. She remembered shortly before his suicide how just out of nowhere he'd surprised her by telling her that she was one of the best things that had ever happened to him. Guess she wasn't great enough, though, if he was still willing to do what he did.

"So . . . are you mad at me, too?" Josh asked.

She frowned. "What? Of course not," she said. *I'm not mad at you . . . I'm mad at them. Mom and Dad. But mostly Mom, because I never expected much more from him.* But hearing the words inside her head,

Alexa realized she sounded a little ridiculous. After all, what choice had her mother had? If she hadn't taken care of Josh, who would have? It wasn't like she could just return him to the adoption people because he was defective.

"You might want to stop playing victim. You're not the only one who hasn't had the perfect life, in case you didn't notice."

Victim? She felt herself bristle. "What are you *talking* about?" she snapped.

"Seriously? Don't play dumb," Josh said and reached for the wine bottle. But she snatched it away before he could wrap his hand around it.

"Maybe you shouldn't drink anymore," she said. "It's turning you into an angry drunk."

"Like you?" He glared at her. "Besides, I only had one glass."

"It looks like that's all you needed."

"Fine, whatever." He jumped up and pulled a floor fan out of his closet and plugged it in, then went to his window and opened it. He opened a desk drawer and pulled some things out, including a bottle of Febreze, a cigarette lighter, and something that surprisingly looked like a—

"Oh my God. Is that a joint?"

Josh? Drugs? Seriously?

Their mother would have puppies, especially with all the issues he'd had with his lungs.

Not bothering to answer her, he lit the joint and took a hit. She pulled a blanket off the bed, hugged it close to her body, and watched him.

It was childish, but she wished her mother knew about the marijuana. That she knew Josh wasn't so perfect after all. Wasn't so freaking golden.

"Life hasn't exactly been a cakewalk being me, either. Being so sick that I felt like I could die. Knowing I was making all of you guys miserable. And on top of that, knowing my *other* mother thought so highly of me that she was okay with throwing me away like a piece of trash."

Alexa remembered the story of how he'd been abandoned, and how no one had ever heard from her again.

He once told her he couldn't remember anything about her, and she was curious how that would feel. She knew that he used to keep a picture of her in the top drawer of his nightstand. She wondered if it was still there. She would have to look sometime. But for now she remained silent.

Josh stared out the window and a chilly breeze rustled his hair. "Mom loves you and would do anything for you. So stop whining and bitching and trying to make her life miserable. It's not cool, and you know it."

Alexa flinched. She blinked away tears.

Josh took another hit and coughed, then, still standing at the window, started watching *The Walking Dead* again. Alexa stared at the screen, trying to process what he had just said. Okay, so maybe she *had* been a complete ass about everything. *Had* been feeling sorry for herself. *Had* been selfish.

Like *really* selfish.

And yes, he'd gone through a hell of a lot more than she had. But he was stronger than she was. It made her wonder how some people became so strong while others became . . . well, like her.

She *was* an ass. A loser . . . but she didn't want to be. Not anymore. She stared at him and suddenly wondered what had just happened between them. If they were still okay.

A lump forming in her throat, she grabbed the wine and both wineglasses and fled to the kitchen.

CHAPTER 14

THE SECOND DIANE slid into Rick's truck, her pulse quickened. She was worried she had made a mistake. She was also suddenly feeling much drunker than she had felt in the bar.

She knew better than to get into a vehicle with someone she didn't know. Yes, she'd had a great time talking with Rick tonight . . . and yes, he'd come to her rescue when her tire blew out, and even with the potatoes at Brookmart, but still, he really was no better than a stranger. But everything had happened so fast, and before she knew it, Ellie had dragged her out of the bar and literally pushed her into the truck.

Ellie had reasoned that Rick had only had two beers the entire night. So why call Josh when they had a designated driver right there with them? Besides, it was late on a weekend night, when people were bound to be drinking and driving. There was no sense having her son out on the road, Ellie had said. And it all had sounded good to her—when they were still in the bar.

While Rick seemed safe and was certainly charming, Diane knew that's what they always said about the most notorious of serial killers. She thought of how charming everyone said Ted Bundy had been.

They'd said the same about Paul John Knowles, Charles Schmid, and Tiago Henrique Gomes da Rocha, as well as others.

Ellie climbed in after her, and Rick shut the passenger door, then walked around the vehicle and slid into the driver's seat. Their eyes met in the dim light of the truck's interior, and he winked at her. Ellie jammed her hip into Diane's to get her to move over. This forced Diane's left thigh against his right leg. A bolt of electricity surged through her, making her feel like a teenager again.

In the enclosed space of the truck, she also noticed his cologne for the first time. It was musky, masculine, sexy. She decided to deconstruct the scents rather than continue to think suspicious thoughts: pepper, sandalwood, lavender, musk . . . clean, strong, definitely masculine.

They pulled out of the parking lot, and the truck hissed over the soaked asphalt. As they drove, she checked out the truck's interior. Everything was incredibly clean. The vehicle appeared new and smelled of leather and pine needles, although she saw no needles anywhere on the floorboard.

She peered out the windshield. For once, the sky was clear enough to see the stars. "You'll want to take a right up here," Diane instructed, her words slurring slightly.

Dammit.

"Okay."

He's going to ignore the turn, she thought, revisiting one of the murder mysteries she'd written and the hundreds she'd read. *He'll drive us to a cabin in the woods.*

Do terrible things—

Rick slowed and turned onto the street as instructed. "We're right here," Diane said, relieved, pointing to her house. Suddenly the truck seemed to tilt to the left. She gripped the dashboard to brace herself.

"You okay?" Rick asked.

Ellie chuckled. "I told you I'd get you hammered."

Dammit. I am *drunk.*

Diane blinked a couple of times and nodded to her friend. Then she noticed Alexa's Subaru parked on the street and groaned. She'd forgotten that Josh had texted her about Alexa's car breaking down.

Rick pulled the truck beside Josh's Jeep in the driveway.

"It's early still," Ellie said. "You should come in for a nightcap."

Diane opened her mouth to protest, but Rick responded first. "Thanks, but I'll take a rain check," he said. "I have an early morning tomorrow."

Diane was relieved she didn't have to retract Ellie's invitation. She was going to have to talk to Ellie about being too trusting. Or was it simply being reckless? Either way, she should know better.

Ellie started to open the passenger door.

"No ma'am. Stay here," Rick instructed and climbed out of the truck. He walked around to the other side and opened the door, helping Ellie out. Then he held his hand out to Diane. Her heart pounded in her chest as she took it. "Thanks again for the ride," she said, feeling woozy.

"So about that rain check. How about tomorrow night?" Rick asked.

"Oh. I don't—" she started. "Ellie's in town for the weekend, and . . ."

"She would love to," Ellie said from somewhere behind her. "What time?"

Rick's eyes were locked on hers. "Seven p.m. good?"

"Seven p.m. sounds great," Ellie said and grabbed Diane's keys from her hand. Diane watched as her friend made her way to the front door, weaving a little.

"Sorry to put you on the spot there," Rick said, "but if that's what it takes to get a date with you, it was worth it."

Blood warmed Diane's cheeks. "Seven p.m. would be great."

Rick's lips curved into a smile. And she felt her stomach do a little flip.

❂❂❂

ALEXA HAD JUST hidden the opened bottle of wine and washed and dried the wineglasses and returned them to the cabinet when she heard a car pull up.

Then she heard someone fumbling with the lock on the front door, and she heard Ellie's voice mumbling something about not being able to find the right key.

Alexa opened the door to find Ellie hunched over, fumbling with her mom's key ring. Ellie looked up and smiled at Alexa. "Oh, hello there, Maleficent. I was just trying to find the right key," she said, her words tumbling into one another.

Alexa rolled her eyes as Ellie brushed past her and walked into the foyer. Then Alexa turned back to the front porch to see a man walking her mother inside. When they reached the bottom of the porch, Alexa got a good look at the guy. Tall, dark hair. Her mother's age. But who was he? And how did her mother know all of these men all of a sudden? She didn't pick this guy up at a bar, did she?

She stared as they made their way up the front porch steps. Her mother said bye to the guy, then turned toward the door. "Oh, hi, Alexa," she said, slurring her words. She gave her a weird smile and pushed past her.

Mom's drunk, too? Seriously?

Alexa had never seen her mother drunk before. What the hell was going on?

Alexa's eyes narrowed as she studied the man.

"Hi, I'm Rick," he said, his eyes flickering past her, into the foyer behind her. He offered his hand.

But she kept her hands firmly on her hips and shot him what she hoped was a frosty look.

He stepped down from the porch. "Make sure to take good care of her, okay?" he said, then he walked back to his truck. He looked back before getting in.

After the truck was out of sight, Alexa walked back into the house. Her mother was halfway up the stairs and Ellie was on the couch, sitting back with her eyes closed, babbling something about not knowing a girl had been murdered at her college. About how sad it was.

Josh grabbed an afghan and laid it over Ellie. "Thanks, sweetheart," she said. Then her eyes found Alexa. "You need to be nicer to your mother," she mumbled.

"And you need to mind your business," Alexa snapped.

Alexa followed Josh up the steps and stood in the doorway of her mother's bedroom. Their mother was sprawled out, already asleep on her bed, and Josh was taking off her shoes. Alexa was leaving to go back downstairs when Josh asked her to cover their mother with a blanket while he got some water to put on her nightstand.

Alexa begrudgingly obliged. She covered her mother, then sat beside her on the bed and studied her. Even though she was practically passed-out drunk, she still managed to look beautiful. It was infuriating. She stared at her mother, realizing for the first time how slight and frail she was—and she noticed the skin on the back of her hand looked to be thinning. The image of her getting older made Alexa's stomach hurt a little.

Alexa realized it was the perfect time for her to do something she'd wanted to do for years. She leaned down, pushed the hair out of her mother's face, and whispered quietly in her ear, "I hate you."

She straightened and looked at her mother again. She had thought it would feel good to finally tell her mother what she'd never had the guts to say. But she didn't feel good. In fact, she felt as though the air had been knocked out of her lungs, and her mouth tasted bitter. She realized maybe she probably didn't hate her mother as much as she thought she did.

She was confused. She didn't like the idea of *not* hating her mother. She was the reason Alexa and Josh had just gotten into an argument. After all, if she hadn't made Alexa feel so worthless while she was growing up, hadn't chosen Josh over her, Josh, who wasn't even her *real* kid, maybe her mind wouldn't be such a wreck now and she'd be a more decent person. Maybe.

She tried it again.

"I hate you," she said more loudly.

The words still didn't feel right . . . or good. In fact, now she felt a little sick to her stomach.

"What did you just say to her?" Josh asked.

Crap!

Alexa leaped off the bed. She hadn't heard him come back into the room. "I was just telling her good night," she spat. Then she hurried out the bedroom door.

CHAPTER 15

IT WAS LATE. He stood in the woods behind Jill MacDonald's apartment complex and waited—wondering what she would see the moment when she passed to the other side.

Is there another side?

Or is everything just . . . black?

With a shudder, he wondered what he would see when he, himself, passed—and whether he would know soon.

Tonight felt all wrong, much too soon. He was going against his instincts, but he had no choice. He was becoming unhinged. He'd woken with a dull roar inside his swollen brain and an unscratchable itch inside his skull that was driving him crazy. The longer he'd been awake, the more he'd felt disconnected from reality. And now the roaring was so intense inside his head, he felt as though he was wedged between two freight trains.

Some college guy was inside her apartment with her now, but he'd watched her enough to know that she never let them stay the night—and it was already very late.

He paced the woods, back and forth, back and forth, his eyes flickering back to her apartment window every now and then. He knew he should leave, but he didn't want to wait.

Couldn't wait.

The wind chilling his face, he wondered again what she was going to look like when she was frightened. Not for just a moment, but as whole minutes ticked by. And he tried to concentrate on the vision.

A few minutes later the apartment door creaked open. His heart kicked into high gear as he watched Jill and the guy walk to his red Toyota Yaris. As they lingered at the boy's vehicle, their backs to him, he slipped through the unlocked door to her apartment.

The TV was on and the apartment smelled of musk . . . the unmistakable scent of sex . . . and french fries. There was a grease-stained fast food bag on the table. An open burger wrapper with crumbs, a wedge of onion and lettuce, and a pool of ketchup. There was also an empty bottle of rotgut wine . . . the kind you could buy from a corner gas station.

He stepped into the bathroom and quietly pulled back the frilly pink shower curtain and waited.

This would be the last one—at least for a while, he'd promised himself. So he was going to make it really good.

Five minutes later, he heard her walk back into the apartment. She closed the door behind her, twisted the dead bolt home, and slid the chain lock into place.

Keeping the bad guys out.

Good girl.

His brain buzzed as she moved through the apartment. He listened to the sound of a microwave door being opened, slammed shut, then turned on. A minute later he smelled a new aroma . . . something sweet . . . and he heard the clink of a spoon in a bowl. He listened, waiting patiently for the right time.

He was leaning against the shower wall when she flipped on the bathroom light. The faucet at the sink squeaked on and the pipes shuddered inside the wall behind him. Then he listened to her brush her teeth. A few minutes later, the bathroom darkened again, and the sound of her footsteps receded.

A few minutes later, when the apartment became totally still, he realized it was finally time.

His pulse drumming in his throat, he pulled back the shower curtain and stepped out onto the tiled bathroom floor. In the hallway, only a lone lamp lit the apartment in dull, yellow light. Just enough for him to navigate the small area.

As he neared the doorway to her bedroom, the roaring started again. Wasting no time, he flipped on the light and watched her jolt upright in bed. She blinked owlishly at him, her mouth agape.

He wanted her to see him.

Needed her to see him.

He cocked his head and watched as her face twisted through an array of expressions: surprise, realization . . . then, yes, finally fear. He stormed toward her just as she was opening her mouth to scream—and slapped his hand against it tightly.

"You don't recognize me, do you?" he asked.

She thrashed around, her small fists connecting with his head. But he couldn't feel any pain. Just adrenaline . . . and an insane amount of pleasure.

When it was over, the droning in his brain had receded and was quiet again, and his body tingled. A much-needed calm swept through him. He breathed in deeply. He felt . . . okay, *right* . . . for once.

He sat, watching her for a while, pretending she was just sleeping. It was always easier for him, after the fact, once his need had passed, to think of them that way. Then he snapped a few photos of her with her iPhone.

An hour later, he slipped out of the apartment and disappeared into the quiet woods with her phone in a coat pocket, making his way back to his vehicle—and he replayed it all over again.

Yes, she had looked beautiful frightened.

CHAPTER 16

THE NEXT MORNING Alexa sat in the passenger seat of her mother's minivan as they drove from the auto shop to the supermarket. Her head pounded from all the alcohol the night before, and she felt on edge.

Silence hung between them as they drove through town. Usually her mother filled in the gaps of silence with words. But not this morning. Alexa squirmed in her seat, wondering what her mother was thinking. Had she heard what she had whispered in her ear last night?

That she hated her?

Is that why she was so quiet?

Blood pounded in her ears as she wondered if it was possible. But if she heard it, surely she would have said something by now, right? At least then Alexa could tell her she hadn't meant it. Because oddly enough, she hadn't. It had taken saying it out loud for her to realize something she'd believed for years wasn't even true. She was still trying to wrap her hungover mind around it.

Her mother had told her that the mechanic said her car needed a new fuel pump. That it wasn't a big deal, but they wouldn't be able to install it until the next day.

She wondered how much a fuel pump cost and wished she could pay for it herself. But it was hard enough just getting out of bed every day to go to school. That's why she was flunking all of her courses. She hadn't been to class in weeks.

When she'd woken, her brain felt agitated, and different noises were bugging the crap out of her. She'd taken a double dose of her new antidepressant, hoping it would help, and planned to make a doctor's appointment on Monday. Maybe see if he would prescribe something different or maybe something to go with this one. One of those "cocktails" she'd read about on the Internet. Hopefully one that would do the trick and make her feel like the people in those antidepressant ads she saw. Like the sad cartoon person who takes the pill and watches the storm cloud over her head suddenly float away. None of the antidepressants so far had done anything even remotely like that.

She was going to start running again, too.

And showering regularly.

And then when she felt better, she'd—

"So. Where did it come from?" her mother asked.

"What?"

Her mother's eyes skidded over her as she pulled into the parking lot of the supermarket. "The joint. On my dresser. Where did it come from?"

Crap. The joint. She'd forgotten all about that.

While Josh had still been in their mother's room the previous night, Alexa had grabbed his joint from his desk. She'd smoked it and put the spent roach on her mother's dresser, then she'd finished off the second bottle of wine. When she'd gone to sleep, she'd been inebriated. And she'd totally forgotten what she'd done . . . until now.

She'd just wanted her mother to know that Josh wasn't so perfect. That he made mistakes, too. But now that she was sober, she realized it had been a total asshole move. Josh had been a good brother to her, and he was the closest thing to a best friend she'd ever had. So why would she want to hurt him? Was she *that* horrible a person? She was beginning to think she was. "Was it yours?" her mother asked.

Alexa's cheeks grew warm. She shifted in her seat. "I don't know what you're talking about." As she waited for her mother to speak next, she bit down so hard on her bottom lip she tasted blood. She was being a coward and she knew it.

Out the corner of her eye, she saw her mother shoot her a sidelong glance, but she didn't say anything.

❖❖❖

ALMOST IMMEDIATELY AFTER walking into the too brightly lit supermarket with her mother, an overweight man in a mustard-yellow shirt hurried toward them. He smiled, revealing stained teeth that nearly matched his shirt. He had bulging pockets under his eyes . . . eyes that were superglued to her mother.

"Well, there she is!" he said, clapping his hands.

"Good morning, Wayne," her mother said.

"And who would this be?" he said. "Your little sister?"

Alexa scowled, finding the comment insulting.

"Wayne, this is my daughter, Alexa. Alexa, this is Wayne. He's the manager here."

Wayne bowed. "At your service."

What the hell is wrong with this guy? Alexa already knew she didn't like him. He was weird. And he talked too loudly.

The man's beady little eyes took her in quickly, then darted back to her mother. "So, what can I help you with today, Diane?"

Wayne talked nonstop as he escorted them around the store, his excited, high-pitched words feeling like tiny knives slicing Alexa's brain. He talked to her mother even as they checked out, then pushed their cart to the parking lot, where he proceeded to unload the groceries into the back of her minivan. When she couldn't take it anymore, Alexa snatched a shopping bag out of his hands. "I think we've got it from here," she said, sharply. "Why don't you go back inside and creep out some other customer?"

The man's smile fell off his face.

"Alexa!" her mother snapped.

Feeling a burst of anger, Alexa turned to her mother. "What, Mom? What did I do this time?" she fumed.

The man's small flinty eyes slid over Alexa. She could see his pulse throbbing in his bulbous neck. "You should never talk to your mother like that." He turned and walked away. Her mother glared at her before chasing after the guy. No doubt to apologize.

Crap, why did I even say that? Alexa wondered, the sudden burst of anger already extinguished. She bit into her lip again. The sting from the pain made her eyes water. Her brain chemicals were majorly screwed up. She was so sick of it.

She climbed in the car and waited, knowing her mother was going to be livid. And she was right—when her mother returned, her ass had barely hit the seat when she started laying into her.

"That was the rudest, most hateful thing I think I've ever heard. I am embarrassed and appalled, Alexa Anne!"

Alexa shrugged.

"Why does every single thing that comes out of your mouth have to be so full of hate? Is your life really *that* miserable?"

Yes.

Alexa's face burned hot, but she didn't say anything. Her mother never snapped at her like that. She usually had patience with her. *A lot* of patience. What was happening this morning?

Besides, she hadn't meant to say anything hateful . . . her brain was just throbbing, and she couldn't take the man's constant *babbling, babbling, babbling,* and the way he'd been so disgustingly overly helpful with her mother had made her skull feel like it was being sent through a cheese grater.

"He had creepy eyes," she muttered.

"I don't care if he had horns and a forked tongue. You do *not* talk to people that way. Ever! Do you understand me, young lady?"

As they pulled out of the parking lot, her mother clearly furious with her, Alexa felt small.

And even more alone than ever before.

CHAPTER 17

DIANE CAREFULLY APPLIED her makeup, then glanced nervously at the clock on the bathroom wall.

She still had to pick an outfit. As she brushed on more mascara she mentally walked through her wardrobe. Just a couple of hours ago, she had been sitting on the couch, checking out her new iPhone and nursing her hangover from the night before. Then Ellie had reminded her she had a date with Rick.

There was nothing like a sense of urgency to shock someone out of a hangover. She had found the slip of paper with his number that he had given her the night her tire had blown out, and she'd had every intention of canceling, but Ellie snatched it from her hand, stuck it down her pants, and refused to give it back.

What had she been thinking, accepting a date with him? Well, the answer was that she hadn't been. She'd been drunk.

When she'd woken that morning, the house had smelled of bacon and coffee—compliments of dear Ellie—and her body felt like it had been hit by a semi. She had lain in bed trying to piece together the images from the night before. But it was as if her mind was slogging through a thick sludge. Her recall was clear up until the last hour at the bar. Rick driving them home. Helping her out of his car.

Then that was pretty much it. It was scary. And irresponsible.

She didn't remember going inside the house. Getting in bed. But she did remember Alexa telling her she hated her.

Twice.

Tears welled up in her eyes now, thinking about it. But maybe it had been a dream. She wasn't sure, but she knew it hadn't felt like one. It had felt very real.

She wondered if Alexa had noticed she was drunk last night. If Josh had. When she'd discovered the joint on top of her dresser, she had asked Ellie about it, but Ellie just shrugged. Then she'd asked Alexa. After Alexa claimed she didn't know anything about it, she had asked Josh . . . and he'd come clean and told her that he smoked every now and then.

"After all you've gone through with your lungs?" she'd asked.

He'd shoved his hands in his pockets. "Sorry."

"Why? Why would you do that to yourself? You know better."

He'd shifted on his feet. "It relaxes me."

She, of anyone, knew how it felt to feel anxious. To need an escape valve. "Are you having anxiety again?" she asked.

"Yeah, sometimes."

Their therapist had prescribed something for his anxiety attacks. "Do you take the prescription Dr. Carol gave you?"

He shook his head. "Those pills make me feel like a zombie. I don't like them."

"Is your anxiety . . . is it about Dad?"

Josh looked away. "Yeah, maybe," he mumbled.

She sat on the end of her bed and wrung her hands together. "I know it was devastating for you guys. For all of us. I'm so sorry. Do you want to talk about it?"

"No, thanks. I'm fine."

"Are you sure? I can set up another session for you with Dr. Carol."

"No, I'm good."

She knew Josh had smoked pot before. She'd smelled it on him the day of his father's funeral. And at least once the week after the funeral. She hadn't been hard on him at the time because of what he was going through, but she was his mother and couldn't condone his using drugs, especially with his lungs.

"You know I'm going to have to ground you, right?"

"Kind of figured," he said.

"No friends and no games for a week. And I want your stash."

"Sure, whatever," he said and left the room.

❋❋❋

THE DOORBELL RANG at exactly seven p.m. . . . just as Diane was walking downstairs.

Right on time.

When she opened the door, her stomach felt jittery. Rick stood in the doorway in a button-down shirt and tie, holding red roses. He looked even more handsome than the previous night, if that was even possible.

Unfortunately, both kids were in the living room. She'd been so stressed thinking about Josh's pot smoking and getting herself ready in time for her date, she hadn't thought about them actually being present when Rick arrived.

She quickly made awkward introductions. Josh was his usual laid-back self and gave Rick a cool nod and a "What's up?" Alexa, on the other hand, stared at him, unblinking.

"You're going on a date?" she'd asked.

"We're going to dinner," Diane said.

"Which is a date, right?" Alexa asked, her eyes never leaving Rick.

"Alexa, let's go find a kitten you can kick." Ellie laughed, her hands on Alexa's shoulders. "That should make you all warm and fuzzy."

A few minutes later, Rick opened the passenger door for her. "Tough crowd," he said.

"I'm so sorry about my daughter. She's—"

"Just being protective of her mother," he said with a smile.

If only that were true.

In the car, she thought again that maybe it hadn't been the best move for her to go on this date. Or to let Rick see where she lived the evening before. If she could do it all over again, she wouldn't. But what was done was done. Tonight she wouldn't worry about the what-ifs. She would just try to enjoy the night. She actually longed to feel like she had last night, because it had felt so damn good.

She caught the scent of Rick's cologne again. Something about it . . . about *him* . . . stirred something inside of her. Something that had been dormant for a long time.

He flipped on the radio and the local deejay was talking about the murder again. ". . . the girl's body. At this time, New Cambridge detective James Chavez—" Rick switched the radio off and glanced at her. "Talk about a mood killer."

Wondering if the police had released news of a new development in the girl's murder investigation, Diane almost asked him to turn the radio back on, but she thought better of it. She'd have plenty of time to find out later.

A few minutes later they arrived at SeaSides, one of the many restaurants in Fog Harbor that Diane had not yet visited. It was a small, intimate restaurant. They were seated at a table with a gorgeous ocean view. When the hostess walked off, they looked at each other, and she suddenly felt awkward. It was as if the date had officially started and she wasn't sure what to do. As though sensing her discomfort, Rick offered his hand across the table.

"Hi, I'm Rick. We've actually met a few times."

Diane laughed and shook his hand. "I'm sorry. You don't look familiar."

Rick smiled. "Really? Changed your tire in the pouring rain? Drove you home when you didn't have a car? I'm typically soaking wet, if that helps."

Diane feigned confusion. "Yeah. No, sorry."

Rick snapped his fingers. "The grocery store. I rescued you from a herd of stampeding potatoes? You have to remember that."

Diane pretended to think hard about it, and then shook her head. "Hmmm. No. Doesn't ring a bell."

Throughout the night, Rick was easy to talk to, and conversation flowed naturally. She was surprised at how comfortable she continued to feel with him. He asked about her kids. Her writing. And when she answered, he seemed to listen with rapt attention.

But when it came to her questions for him, he continued to be more reserved . . . uncomfortable talking about himself. Still, she found him fascinating. Intelligent, thoughtful, funny. Their conversation shifted seamlessly back and forth between personal stories, philosophical points of view, books, and movies. During dinner she watched him closely, noting his constant assessment of everyone who came in, of everyone around them. He always seemed to be on guard. Relaxed, but not. She wondered if he'd always been that way or if it was a result of his training in the Marine Corps and experience in Iraq.

As the evening wore on, the conversation—and the wine—continued to flow. Rick would lean forward, intent on her every word. He seemed to be watching her lips when she spoke. She found something about it sensual, and waves of heat coursed through her middle.

Ellie had once again been right. Diane had definitely needed some adult attention.

The night was unseasonably mild—a welcome break from the rainy weather they'd been experiencing. So after dinner, they went for a walk along the harbor. They eventually settled on a bench and sat in silence, watching the lights from the few remaining fishing boats as they floated in with their day's haul. It was the first time they'd stopped talking since dinner began. But it didn't feel uncomfortable at all.

It felt good, exciting, peaceful . . . familiar.

❦❦❦

A LITTLE AFTER eleven o'clock, Rick walked Diane to her front door. He stopped at the bottom porch step, and she turned to face him. "I had a great time," he said.

"Me, too."

"I'd like to do it again. Soon."

She felt a smile spread across her face. "I'd like that very much."

He cupped her chin with his hand and leaned toward her. His lips were warm and his kiss was soft and gentle—and sent sparks through every inch of her body. He pulled away, never taking his eyes off hers.

Wow.

"I'll call you."

Her heart hammered against her chest so hard she could only nod in response.

He waited until she unlocked the door, then walked back to his truck. She shut the door behind her and leaned against it and closed her eyes.

Wow. Just wow. Was this really happening?

After all, just a couple of weeks ago she hadn't even been aware he existed. She'd also been against a relationship or fling of any sort.

She kept her eyes shut, as if it would prolong the evening just a little bit more, until she heard his truck drive off.

When she opened her eyes, she noticed the house was very dark, still. Then she heard Ellie rustle in her sleep on the couch and murmur something unintelligible.

Diane started for the stairs but realized she was way too wound up to go to bed. As she walked into the kitchen, she slowly drifted back into her reality and felt a pang of guilt about not hanging out with Ellie on her last night in town. But Ellie had orchestrated the whole date and had practically shoved her out of the house.

She also remembered wanting to see if any new developments in the Katie Worth case had been reported. But she decided to hold off a little longer. She wanted to occupy her mind only with thoughts of Rick right now and cling to the high from her date. The fun, exciting feeling she was experiencing.

She decided to pour a glass of wine and went to the cabinet where she kept it. But she was surprised to find nothing there. There had been two bottles there just yesterday. Her thoughts immediately traveled to Alexa. Then she remembered her sleeping friend mumbling on the couch. Of course. It was Ellie. Still . . . two bottles were a lot, even for her.

As though hearing her thoughts, Ellie muttered something else in the distance.

Diane decided on chamomile tea. She picked up Josh's laptop, which he'd left on the kitchen counter, then tiptoed upstairs. Josh's door was cracked, and she peeked inside. His room was bathed in blue light from the video game that was still on. She glanced at the TV screen. A soldier stood in limbo on some sort of spaceship, still waiting for direction from Josh's controller.

Josh was slouched in his beanbag chair, sound asleep with his game controller still in his hands and his headphones still on. She placed his laptop on his bookshelf, removed his headphones, and took the controller out of his hands. Then she laid a blanket over him so he'd be warm. She sat perched on his windowsill and watched him sleep for a few minutes. It was something she used to love doing but hadn't done for ages.

After leaving his room, she tiptoed past her office, where Alexa was sleeping on an air mattress. In her bedroom, Diane went to her window and looked out at the inky night. The half-moon was partially hidden by cloud cover, and the harbor was illuminated by blinking lights of the various boats that had docked for the evening.

She cracked the window and sat in her chair, drinking her tea while listening to the hypnotic sound of water lapping against the sides of the docks.

She replayed the night again and again, and every time her heart expanded a little more. She really hadn't expected it to go so well. For them to hit it off quite like that. She smiled at the memory of their kiss on the porch . . . and kept forcing back the needling little voice in her head that told her that things were not going to work out like she hoped. *That something was very wrong.*

CHAPTER 18

THE NEXT AFTERNOON Diane walked into the crisis center and waved to Mary Kate, who was talking with an elderly woman Diane hadn't seen before. She usually volunteered only on Wednesday evenings, but Mary Kate had asked her to fill in for a volunteer who had canceled at the last minute, and she'd wanted to help out.

Knowing that Josh would be at school all day and Alexa would be moping around the house still waiting for her car to be fixed, Diane had said yes. She didn't have the energy, or desire, to battle with her daughter. Plus, the housekeeping service was at her house—courtesy of a Happy Maids coupon Alexa had given her as a Christmas gift last year. Diane had thought it odd when her daughter had given it to her. Alexa knew that Diane liked to clean. Excelled at it, even. She remembered their conversation when she'd opened the coupon gift Christmas morning.

"Well, don't you like it?" Alexa had said with that challenging look on her face. As though she were daring Diane to tell the truth.

"What is it?" Josh asked.

Diane had smiled. "A coupon for a deep cleaning."

"Deep cleaning of what?" Josh asked.

"The house."

Josh had snorted. "The house? Why would Mom need that? That's like her favorite hobby."

"Maybe she needs a break," Alexa had spat.

Diane had butted in. "I do. It was a great gift, honey."

She had placed it in a desk drawer later that morning, where it had sat for eleven months, gathering dust.

Not that she had forgotten about it. Alexa hadn't let her. She asked frequently if she'd used it. At least now Alexa would be there to see the proof.

The older lady the cleaning company had sent had shown up while Diane was feeding the ducks and Ellie was packing to go home. The woman had come into the yard and talked about ducks for a full ten minutes before Diane was able to extricate herself to drive Ellie to the airport.

Diane beelined for the coffeepot at the back of the office, then settled into her usual cubicle, which she'd been happy to see was unoccupied. She'd had a great morning, unusually stress-free. She'd woken without the usual sense of unease, then enjoyed the fresh sea air and the warm rays of sunshine and again basked in the afterglow of her date. So far it had been a great day.

The phone rang just as she was getting settled.

"This is Sally."

There was no immediate response on the other end. She waited a few seconds, then said, "It's okay. You're safe to talk here. Is something bothering you?"

"Hello, Sally." It was the robotic voice again.

A cold slab of dread pressed down on her chest. It was him again. Her pulse racing, she stood to try and get Mary Kate's attention, but the woman was facing the opposite direction.

The voice continued. "Do you remember me?"

Diane sat back down and took a deep breath. "I do. You used that voice machine . . . or whatever that thing is called . . . the last time, too. You don't need to use it, you know. These calls are confidential."

The line was silent.

Diane wondered again if the police had tapped the lines. Surely they had, right? "What's your name?" she asked.

There was a long pause before the caller answered.

"That's not important."

"Okay . . . fair enough," she said, her adrenaline pumping. "When we spoke last time, you knew the victim's name," she continued, "but it hadn't been released yet."

Another pause, then: "Are you asking me how I already knew it?"

"Yes."

"You answer me."

"I'm afraid I'm not following."

"Well . . . how do you think I knew?"

Diane felt a jolt in her stomach.

"Remember I asked you, 'what if it doesn't stop?'"

"Yes."

"So . . . what if it doesn't?"

Diane's palms grew damp as she tried to figure out what to say.

"There's another one. Her name was Jill," the caller said.

She heard a click.

Stunned, Diane listened to the silence on the other end . . . until she got the rapid tone that alerted her that she needed to hang up.

Mary Kate walked up behind her. "Hey, I am so sorry I couldn't make it for Thanksgiving," she said. "I came down with the worst case of the flu."

Diane turned to her, her face hot.

The skin between Mary Kate's eyes creased. "Diane, are you okay? You don't look so good."

"Was another girl murdered?"

Mary Kate stared at her. "What? Not that I know of. Why?"

●●●

HER BLOOD ELECTRIC from the call, Diane pulled out of the crisis center and drove straight home. She wanted to get to her computer and check the news. She wanted to see if anyone had been reported missing recently within a fifty-mile radius.

When she pulled up to the house, she noticed Josh's Jeep wasn't there. She looked at the time. School had let out, and she knew he didn't have plans because he was grounded. She parked her minivan and texted him. He replied back immediately, saying that he was with Alexa, picking up her car. That he'd be home in twenty minutes.

Relieved to know where both of her kids were, she went inside, intent on getting to her computer. But as soon as she opened the door, she froze. Her house smelled different. Then she remembered the maid service. She also noticed three paperback copies of her latest book on the coffee table. On top was a sticky note from Mr. Davidson, asking for her to sign them.

She ran up the stairs and powered on her computer. She searched for any news she could find. Any local girl found murdered, reported missing. Fifty-mile radius. Hundred-mile radius.

Nothing came up.

Mary Kate had again assured her she would report the call to the proper channels, which Diane now understood would include the investigating detectives. But Diane wasn't comfortable waiting to learn more information if she didn't have to. She decided to text Lance. Find out if he knew anything.

> DIANE: Anything new w/ the case u can share? Or hear of any new victims?

When she didn't get an immediate response, she went downstairs and paced the living room. But after a couple of minutes she realized her anxiety wasn't going away. She grabbed several slices of bread and went out to the backyard to feed the ducks. Feeding them always helped calm her.

But the ducks weren't there.

She looked around, making little clicking sounds with her tongue to attract them. But they didn't come. Had they finally flown south for the winter? She didn't remember them doing that last year. But maybe they had.

She tore up some bread and sprinkled it on the ground, then, still full of restless energy, decided to take a quick walk. At the end of her road was a nature trail that led into some woods. It was a popular trail, so she felt safe walking it alone. Maybe it would be a good way to clear her mind until she had the chance to talk with Lance.

She walked at a steady pace, the gravel on the trail crunching beneath her feet. She made a conscious effort to try to relax and focus on the nature around her. Most of the area birds had departed for their annual sojourn south, but a few straggling wrens chattered in the trees. The ground was covered in dead leaves.

As she walked, she watched the waves in the distance as they broke against rocks, sending up small explosions of seawater and foam. She looked at the sky and noticed dark clouds were creeping in from the west. She pulled her coat tighter.

Then she heard a loud croaking sound . . . and she paused.

She'd heard it before but never paid attention. Was it one of the seals that had migrated into the harbor recently? Or was it maybe a bird?

Then she glimpsed something orange in the distance between a cluster of oaks. She saw it move. It was a person wearing an orange shirt. She froze, then heard the bird call again. The person turned toward her and froze as well.

"Diane?" she heard in the distance.

She recognized the gentle, slightly high-pitched voice. The familiar rising intonation. It was Wayne.

He walked toward her, a pair of binoculars around his neck and a beige hiking vest over his bright orange shirt. "Well, this is a surprise," he said, smiling.

She looked at the patch on his vest. It was a logo with a picture of a bird and the words *Fog Harbor Audubon Society*. "Bird-watching?" She vaguely remembered him talking about bird-watching before.

He nodded, still smiling, but seemed strangely subdued. Then Diane remembered the last time she'd seen him. How rude Alexa had been. Was he still embarrassed?

She was certainly embarrassed *for* him. For Alexa. For herself.

The breeze kicked up, blowing Diane's hair into her face. "Was that you making that sound? Was it a bird call?"

Wayne's eyes brightened at the question. "It was. Did it sound real? It's a great blue heron. Magnificent creature. I just love watching them."

Wayne talked about being grateful for the break in the rain, and the storm that seemed to be brewing. How he had taken advantage of the nice weather to squeeze in a quick bird-watching trip. "This little nature preserve is a prime spot," he said. "You can pretty much see every type of bird and fowl in the region. Right here."

Diane nodded.

His expression grew serious. "Diane, I'm sure it's none of my business, but one of my customers mentioned that you're seeing that Marine, Rick Hyland? The one that was in the store when—"

"Yes, I know who Rick is. Why?"

"It's really not my place, I know, but how much do you know about him?"

She frowned. "What do you mean?"

"It's just I heard he did a couple of tours as a sniper. And while I really respect that, I do, I need to warn you. Those guys, you know, they see stuff over there, then they come back and they're never the same. I've seen documentaries on it. There's a syndrome . . ."

Diane felt her frown deepen. She didn't like where the conversation was going. Yes, Rick had been a sniper. He'd done a couple of tours. But he should be congratulated for that, not judged. "What are you trying to say, Wayne? That you think Rick's dangerous?"

"Well, I . . ."

She was starting to lose her patience. "Is there something specific that you've heard? Something concrete that you think I should know?"

"No, I don't think there is." A smile spread on Wayne's face. "I guess I'm just protective of you, Diane. I don't want to see you hurt."

She could see Wayne meant well, but this was the last thing she wanted to hear right now. Wayne didn't know Rick. "I appreciate that, Wayne. But I better get going."

"I hope I didn't make you angry."

Diane heard the sound of brush snapping. She turned her head and saw another person in an orange shirt appear about a yard away. A round woman with frizzy red hair. Wayne turned toward the woman and smiled. "Well, there you are," he said. Then his eyes flickered back to Diane. "Diane, I want you to meet my friend Brenda. She's a fellow bird-watcher, too. My partner in crime."

Wayne has a girlfriend? Well, good for him.

Diane said hello and shook the woman's hand.

"It's so great to meet you. Wayne bought me copies of all your books. I'm on my third one now," Brenda said. "They're just fantastic!"

Diane smiled, then took a couple of steps back, wanting to get back to the house. "Thank you. I'm glad you're enjoying them. It was nice meeting you, Brenda . . . and seeing you, Wayne," she said.

"See you at Brookmart soon?" he asked.

"Sure."

As Diane walked back toward her house, she tried hard to put what Wayne had said about Rick out of her mind—and she realized she felt more ill at ease than when she'd left the house. She checked her messages again. Still nothing from Lance. If he didn't reply by the time she got home, she'd call the police and ask directly.

She needed to know if this guy was just an attention seeker . . . or if he was something more.

She hurried back up the path toward her house. She was just a few feet from her property line when she noticed a plastic bag hanging from a hook at the bottom of the deck.

She walked closer to investigate. It *was* a shopping bag. Weird. Who would have put that there? She peeked inside, then, seeing the contents, a bolt of terror shot through her.

❖❖❖

ALEXA PULLED INTO her mother's driveway and parked her car. Her thoughts were blaring so loudly in her head they seemed to be screaming at her. Agitated and dizzy, she fumbled through her purse until she found more of the prescription samples she'd discovered buried in the back of one of her mother's cabinets. Doubling up the new antidepressant hadn't helped. In fact, she felt worse.

She punctured the foil pack with her thumbnail and pushed out a pill. One of these pills had to help. Even just a little bit.

She needed relief, dammit.

She couldn't wait for a doctor's appointment.

As she tossed the pill onto the back of her tongue, she recalled how angry her mother had been when she snapped at her outside of Brookmart. It had hurt. Never in her life could she remember her mother being angry with her. Disappointed, yes. But angry? No, never.

A loud noise made her jump.

It was Josh banging on the driver's window.

She scowled at him.

"What's that?" Josh asked through the glass . . . pointing at the pack of pills on her lap.

"Dammit! You scared the crap out of me!" she hissed, throwing the pill packet back in her purse.

He glared at her through the glass. She knew he was angry at her for outing him with the pot. "Are those Mom's sleeping pills?"

"No!"

"Right," he said. He shook his head in disgust, then stalked up the driveway.

She got out of the car and followed her brother back into the house. She just needed to grab her laundry really quick, then she'd leave. But as she walked, she started feeling dizzier.

She stepped unsteadily into the tall foyer.

"You okay?" she heard Josh ask.

"I . . . I don't know," she said. But when she looked up, she realized he wasn't talking to her.

He was looking in the opposite direction. Toward the back of the house.

"Mom?" Josh said. He sounded worried.

Alexa looked past Josh and saw her mother standing at the sliding glass doors that led out to the deck. She was pale.

"What is it, Mom?"

"One of the ducks," she said. "Someone . . . killed it." She pointed to the deck. "They put it in a shopping bag and hung it up . . . like they wanted me to find it."

"What?" Josh said. He crossed the living room and stepped onto the deck.

Alexa watched silently as her mother called 911 and told them what had happened. She wanted to leave but knew it would be wrong. So she sat uncomfortably with her mother in the living room as Josh made her a cup of tea. A few minutes later, her mother got up to use the bathroom.

"Mom loved that duck," Josh said. He was staring off into space, looking perplexed. He wiped his nose with the back of his hand.

She felt bad for him. He'd always loved animals. Years ago, they'd lost three dogs, one right after the other. They'd all run away. Their mother had driven her and Josh all over the neighborhood looking for them, posting reward signs. But no one ever called. Her mother figured they'd been hit by cars and had holed up in the woods somewhere and died.

"Who would do something like that to a duck?" he said. "How screwed up would you have to be to kill a helpless animal?"

Alexa started to nod but then noticed the way he was looking at her. She didn't like it.

Wait—was he accusing her of something?

Or was she just paranoid?

Yes, she was a screwup, and yes, she'd been at the house alone all day, but she would never do anything like that.

Right now, though, she felt too awful to say any of that. She just wanted, needed, to be at her apartment, buried beneath her blankets.

Today had been too hard. She knew she needed to apologize for outing him with the pot. But she'd have to wait.

When Josh began channel surfing, she quietly slipped out of the living room, then out the front door. She got into her car and reversed out of the driveway.

The sun was sliding below the horizon as she passed the police cruiser approaching her mother's house.

CHAPTER 19

THE NEXT MORNING Alexa opened her eyes, and her brain slowly sputtered to life.

She could smell the sharp odor of vomit in the apartment and tasted its horrible tang in her mouth. Her body clearly hadn't liked her mother's prescription samples. Either that or she'd had some kind of awful drug interaction.

She glanced at Trish's side of the apartment and was relieved to see Trish wasn't there. Her stuff was stacked neatly on her bed in boxes, bins, and duffel bags. It was moving day. Trish was leaving for her new apartment. Alexa was relieved. If she'd ever needed privacy, it was now. She hated that she'd let anyone see her like this. This wasn't her, this complete mess of a person; at least it wouldn't be for long.

Memories of driving home from her mother's house yesterday rose from the fog in her mind. She remembered little snippets of the drive. Of having trouble staying in her lane. Driving over a curb.

Had she really hit a mailbox?

She'd had no business being on the road. How she made it back to her crappy apartment in one piece and without killing anyone was nothing short of a miracle. She shuddered, thinking she'd done that.

Was this what rock bottom felt like?

Everyone hating you?

Including yourself?

Feeling like total crap?

She cringed at the horrible taste in her mouth again. If this wasn't rock bottom, she didn't want to see what was. She grabbed the rest of the prescription samples and the salad bowl that held a shallow pool of puke and slowly, carefully made her way to the bathroom. Her first step was met with some lingering dizziness, but after the fourth step she started to get her equilibrium back.

When she reached the bathroom, she hurled the pills into the overstuffed trash can, dumped the contents of the bowl into the toilet, and washed it out. After brushing her teeth, she went to the kitchen and gulped down some water. Then she grabbed her backpack and took out a notebook. She went to the apartment's tiny kitchen table, flipped to a clean page, and began writing.

Enough was enough. She was tired of being critical and nasty and cynical and depressed and unhappy—and feeling so incredibly awful all the time.

She decided to make a list of things she could do to get out of this rut. No more waiting for the doctor on campus to help her. It was time for her to make things happen for herself . . . before they got even worse. She had always been told she was headstrong, so she was going to make it work in her favor this time.

She scribbled quickly at first.

1. Run every day.

2. Eat healthier.

3. Figure out what to do about school. Take time off?

4. Get a job. Fill out applications at nearby restaurants.

5. Pay back Mom for tuition, car, rent, etc.

The next action item came to mind quickly, but her hand hovered above the notebook for a moment before she was able to bring herself to actually write it.

6. Apologize to Josh (for being an ass and a terrible sister).

She gritted her teeth. That one would be hard. She couldn't remember the last time she'd apologized to anyone. But it would kill her if she wound up pushing him away, too. He was her favorite person in the world, although she was pretty sure he didn't know it. How could he, after how she'd behaved over the years, especially recently?

The next one was even harder:

7. Apologize to Mom (for being a super-awful daughter).

How the hell was she going to pull this off? Just the thought of it made the knots in her stomach twist even tighter. Maybe if she could find some of her mother's wine first, some liquid courage, she could do it.

She shook her head.

No.

It was time to put on her big-girl panties. She was going to do things right this time. Besides, she was pretty sure her mother would be hiding the wine now. Just like the pills.

Alexa's stomach rumbled. She was starving. She went to the fridge and looked inside at its meager contents: a half-eaten bowl of congealed ramen from several days ago. Two Diet Dr Peppers, both open, one nearly empty.

Both flat. A half-eaten burrito from Taco Bell. Crumbs. A dead bug on its back.

Eeew.

She shut the refrigerator door and went back to the table. She studied her list again. She was going to do this. *Everything* on her list. Even number five. And she was going to do it without pills, alcohol, anything. She was going to be strong like Josh, even if it killed her. She was committed. And her newfound drive made her feel good.

Now, time to get started! She'd start with number one.

Run every day.

She scanned her side of the apartment to see if she could spot some clean yoga pants.

She couldn't.

Suddenly her eyelids felt weighted down. Then a long yawn came out of nowhere, making her eyes water. She stared down at her list again. The ink wasn't even dry yet and it was already kicking her ass.

Okay, maybe she'd start . . . after a short nap.

She crawled back onto her mattress, told Siri to wake her in an hour, and pulled the covers over her head.

❖❖❖

ALEXA'S EYES POPPED open. There were voices outside her apartment. Trish and some guy. She tensed beneath the covers.

Jesus, no, no, no.

Not right now.

She didn't want to be seen. Either she needed to make a run for the bathroom or try to hide. A key twisted in the door. Crap! She wouldn't have time. She folded herself into the fetal position to make herself as small as possible beneath the blankets.

"Oh, man. It smells like something died in here," the guy said.

"Eew, it does," said Trish.

"You guys get hit by a tornado?" the guy asked.

"No, that's Alexa's side of the room. That's just how she lives. She's, I don't know . . . a little weird."

Weird? Alexa squeezed her eyes shut and tried to fall back to sleep. She didn't like where the conversation was headed. The last thing her raw mind could handle right now was being humiliated. She didn't want to know what Trish thought about her, especially if the first word out of her mouth was "weird."

"Weird?" the guy asked.

"Yeah. I mean, not like pushing-a-grocery-cart-down-the-street weird. Just . . . awkward. And like clumsy," Trish said.

Alexa's eyes welled up with tears.

"She sounds like a real winner. I'm glad we're getting you out of here."

"She's not *all* bad. I kind of feel sorry for her. What I don't get, though, is . . . like, her mother is a really big-time author and supercool, but it's like she didn't rub off on her at all. I don't understand how a mother and daughter can be so different."

Alexa's nose was running. The worst part about what Trish was saying was that it was all true. She honestly couldn't argue with a word she'd said. Trish was only confirming that Alexa wasn't the only one who could see it, which somehow made it so much worse than it already was.

She *was* awkward.

She *was* weird.

But she was also suffering.

She tried to hold it in, but the tears just rushed forward, like water gushing through a dam that had suddenly broken. Her shoulders started shaking and she couldn't stop them no matter how hard she tried.

"What the—?" she heard the guy say.

"Oh my Gawd. She—"

No. Just no, Alexa thought, her heart pounding so hard she was certain they could hear it. She cried harder. A big, ugly cry. Her nose was running even worse now, and her cheeks were all wet and slippery.

"Alexa?" Trish said, suddenly next to her, her Georgia accent thick. "Are you under there, hon?"

❧❧❧

ALEXA WAS MORTIFIED.

Trish had tried talking to her for a few minutes, but Alexa had ignored her. She just lay there, frozen in shame. After a while, she heard Trish walk back to the front of the apartment. She listened to the two whisper for a few seconds. Then she heard the guy laugh, and they left the apartment.

Alexa stayed under the covers for at least a full ten minutes after they'd gone, wishing she could just disappear forever. She knew she was a mess. She hadn't needed to hear anyone say it.

It's time for this to stop, she thought to herself again, now more committed than ever. She was angry. And not at Trish or the asshat guy she'd brought to the apartment, but at herself.

I don't care how crappy your head feels, how tired you are . . . this ends now.

Fueled with self-loathing rage, she threw off the blankets, dug through her pile of clothes, and got dressed. She was going to work on her list, starting now. After all, the list was her only hope. She was going to start with number one. She was going running. Then afterward, she would grab a few things and drive straight to her mother's. She'd stay there until Trish was all moved out. She didn't want to see her again.

Ever.

When she opened the apartment door, a wall of wintry air smacked her in the face. She peered out and saw that the afternoon was dark gray. It looked like it was about to storm. She had the urge to turn around. Put it off just a little longer. But she wasn't going to back down now. She'd just have to get her run in fast. It didn't have to be a long run. She just needed to get the ball rolling so she could check it off her list.

She stretched outside of the apartment building for a few minutes, then broke out into a slow jog. Almost instantly her leg muscles began to burn.

Then her lungs. But she set her jaw and ran across the parking lot, then she took a right past the building and forced herself to keep going.

She was so done with Trish *and* the awful medication. She never wanted to see either one of them again. She didn't even want to know what permanent damage she'd done to her brain over the last year, experimenting with all those chemicals that had done nothing but make her feel even crazier. The only thing that had ever truly helped when she was feeling down was running.

About ten blocks later freezing rain began to pelt her scalp and face like tiny knives. Feeling satisfied that she'd made a decent first effort, she turned around and headed back to her apartment.

I don't understand how a mother and daughter can be so different.

Those words were already haunting her. Maybe she didn't want to be so different. Maybe she *hated* that she was so different. Maybe some of her anger at her mother had in part been frustration at not being able to be more like her. But seriously, it was none of Trish's business.

An overpowering wave of emotion washed over her again and she burst out crying. She stopped on the sidewalk and bent over, her hands on her thighs. Her tears blended with the rain, falling onto the sidewalk.

The rain was coming down harder now, pelting her back. Her legs were screaming in pain, her lungs on fire.

She was cursing herself for becoming so out of shape when she heard the rumble of an engine behind her. She ignored it. The vehicle honked, and she could hear it idling beside her, but she pretended like she didn't hear it.

"Alexa? Is that you?" It was a man's voice.

Who the—?

Reluctantly, she straightened, her blonde hair plastered to her forehead. She shielded her eyes from the rain and could make out an older model white van idling next to her. "Get in. I'll take you back to your apartment," the man said. But she still couldn't place the voice. The rain was too noisy.

So she stepped closer to make out who was inside.

CHAPTER 20

THE SUN WAS descending as Diane decided to call it a night. She'd been writing straight through since seven a.m., trying to get the first two-hundred-pages of her manuscript completed before turning it in to her publisher at the end of the week.

A patrolman initially responded to the 911 call, then just a few minutes later, Detective Chavez arrived. They talked about the duck at length and about the anonymous caller's second call, with him asking many of the same questions he had during their first conversation.

He also asked if she or Josh had any enemies. She'd never known Josh to have even one. He'd always gotten along well with everyone. And Diane couldn't think of any enemies she had, even though the first person who'd come to mind when asked had been Alexa. Not that she saw her daughter as an enemy, of course, but she felt her daughter saw her that way. Still, Alexa would never hurt an animal like that. She might not know her daughter that well these days, but she knew that much.

Before leaving, Detective Chavez said he couldn't be certain the caller at the crisis center and the duck were in any way connected, but he encouraged her to keep her eyes open. She assured him she would and asked if the lines at the crisis center were bugged. He told her he was unable to share details of an open investigation. Just to call if anything else strange happened. She again assured him she would.

Josh's punishment had been lifted, and he was spending the night at Bruce's house, where he and a few friends were breaking in a new video game. Since he had been coughing earlier that afternoon, she hadn't been crazy about him staying up all hours of the night. But she'd said yes already, so there was no benefit to worrying now.

Lance had never texted her back. She really needed to clear the air with him. Clear the air and tell him the whole story about the anonymous caller and the duck. Get his thoughts on it all.

Diane's phone chimed. A new text.

RICK: May I make you dinner tonight? Seven o'clock?

Diane sat back in her chair and smiled. Her first inclination was to say no. But . . . what the hell? She had a great time with him on their date. And like Ellie said, she should live more.

Worry less.

With everything she'd been through with Josh, Frank, and now Alexa, she'd worried enough for several lifetimes. Besides, being with Rick felt therapeutic—and she could use a little therapy right now.

DIANE: I'll be there. Address?

❖❖❖

TWO HOURS LATER Diane was in her car, following her GPS's instructions to Rick's address. Her stomach flip-flopped with butterflies—but she also couldn't help but feel a little foolish that she had agreed to go to a man's house in the middle of nowhere.

In fiction writing, they called heroines who did foolish things like this TSTL, which stood for "too stupid to live." But she trusted Rick for some reason. She didn't find herself frightened in the least.

Was she just being irresponsible?

She knew that if she'd learned Alexa had done the same thing, she'd be horrified.

The navigation system told her he lived only six miles away, but as her car crawled deeper into the woods, she began to wonder if the GPS had gotten the coordinates wrong.

A few minutes later she arrived at an old, run-down cabin with peeling gray paint. The windows were high and small. Three vehicles were parked on one side of the cabin. She recognized one of them as Rick's truck.

She second-guessed herself again as she eased her minivan next to his truck, but then Rick stepped out onto the porch and grinned at her. He looked handsome in a black T-shirt and jeans. She returned his smile and climbed out of her car, into the chilly evening.

"It's not much to look at on the outside, but it does the job."

Diane pretended not to notice. She walked up the porch steps and handed him a bottle of wine. "Thanks for the invitation. It came at the perfect time." As he hugged her, his five o'clock shadow gently brushed her cheek, and she felt her heart skip a beat.

While the house left much to be desired on the outside, the inside was a different story. It looked as if it had been recently renovated and had a warm, manly, rustic charm. Classical music played softly from stereo speakers as Rick walked her into a large, immaculately clean room that opened into the kitchen, separated by a large counter. In the living room, hardwood floors and exposed wooden beams made the perfect frame for a deep brown leather couch and recliner. The couch sat in front of a large fireplace, a fire already burning.

A few pieces of big, sturdy, wooden furniture filled out the room. Next to a large window was a bookshelf full of hardback and paper-back books.

"Great place," Diane said. "And cozy. Any chance I can have a tour?"

She took in the sweet and spicy smell of firewood, and the scent of leather as Rick showed her around the cabin.

The bathroom had a large cast-iron claw-foot bathtub and white pedestal sink; the floor and walls were covered in black-and-white tile. Diane couldn't believe how clean it all was. Did he ever even use it? It certainly didn't look like the bathroom of any man she'd ever known. She was impressed.

The bedroom was small but cozy. The full-size bed took up most of the room. It was draped in a burgundy-and-brown comforter and topped by a large wooden headboard. The only other furniture in the room was a large oak dresser. Again, everything was immaculate and in its place.

He led her back out into the living room. He pointed to a closed door and explained it was a utility room with the washer and dryer.

Diane gestured to the doors on the opposite side of the front foyer. "And over there?"

Rick smiled. "Oh, you don't want to see that. Let's just say it's the working part of this cabin."

"*Working* part?"

"Well, to be frank, it's sometimes referred to as a *kill room*. It's where hunters clean and prep their spoils. Not glamorous in the least."

"Gotcha. Yeah, we can skip it."

He placed his hands on her shoulders and planted a kiss on her forehead. "I need to check the grill. Just make yourself at home."

Her forehead still tingling from the kiss, Diane set her purse on the table and looked around the room again. Something about the masculine yet tidy and well-organized space made her even more attracted to Rick.

She went to the bookshelf and studied his books. Some hunting books, history books, biographies, medical titles, books on fishing, a large collection of survivalist books, how-tos for living off the grid.

On a lower shelf she was surprised to find an appreciable selection of mystery and suspense paperbacks. Names of her colleagues: Michael Connelly, Patricia Cornwell. Even some true crime: Anne Rule, Gregg Olsen.

She turned and noticed a gun cabinet on the wall behind the couch. It was stocked with at least a dozen rifles, pistols, and what looked like an automatic military weapon. She hadn't seen so many weapons in one place outside an armory she'd toured while researching one of her books. Was he a collector? He was a former Marine sniper, so it would make sense.

Next to the gun cabinet, against the sliding glass back door, was a large stack of neatly labeled bins. Medical supplies, antibiotics, water, MREs, seeds. Either he was planning a long camping trip or he was taking this survivalist hobby of his very seriously.

A side door snapped shut and Rick walked back into the kitchen. He smiled at her, then without missing a beat, he grabbed a bottle of wine from a wine rack built into the wall. She watched as he uncorked it quickly, easily . . . confidently.

He poured her a glass. "Merlot. That's what you were drinking the other night, right?"

She nodded.

Dinner was steak and grilled vegetables. Served at his sturdy farm table, it was all simple but elegant. And frankly, she was having such a good time she would have been happy with a peanut butter and jelly sandwich. Again, they talked and laughed easily. As on their first date, the conversation moved effortlessly among many subjects. Diane pointed to the supply bins along the wall.

"So, I have to ask. Are you preparing for an invasion?" Diane asked.

He laughed politely at her question and shook his head, almost as if he was reading her mind. "Don't worry. I'm not a wacko hermit preparing for the end of days. I just like to be prepared. For anything.

At the very least, if I get snowed in this winter, I'll be self-sufficient for months."

"And the books? Are those to keep you occupied during your shut-in?"

Rick laughed. "Unfortunately, those are books I've already read."

"You like mysteries, huh?"

Rick nodded. "There's nothing like a good mystery. I don't know if you noticed, but I have one of your books on my bedside table."

Diane blushed. "You do, do you? Well, I hope you like it."

His green eyes caught the light from the fireplace. "Love everything I've read so far."

After dinner, they moved the conversation to the couch. She turned so she could face him, and he put his arm behind her, lightly stroking her shoulder as she worked on her second glass of merlot and talked. When he got up to stoke the fire, she admired the steady confidence in his movements. The way he walked, talked . . . even listened.

She also realized, again, she was doing the majority of the talking. But when she tried to turn the tables and ask him questions, he would deflect them back with questions for her. It was obvious he wasn't used to talking about himself. Knowing he'd done two tours in Iraq, she had a feeling why.

At one point, she found herself telling him about the female duck she'd discovered on her porch.

His face darkened. "What did the police say?"

"To keep my eyes open."

He seemed to think about that.

She wanted to tell him about the caller at the crisis center, and that she'd spoken with not just a patrolman, but also a homicide detective, but she decided to keep that information to herself for now.

She surprised herself by talking about her concerns about Alexa instead. How she wanted desperately to be close with her daughter. For

Alexa to no longer be angry. How she seemed so unhappy—and how she felt her hands were tied because as much she wanted to help her, Alexa wouldn't let her.

She also shared how badly she wanted her family to just come together and feel whole for once. How it was something she'd wanted since she was just a child, but had never had. Also that she'd never give up trying.

After she'd talked for what seemed like forever, she noticed he seemed troubled. "What's wrong?" she asked.

"Do you want my opinion?"

It was respectful for him to ask. But she had a feeling that she knew what he'd say. She could see it all over his face. He would agree with her therapist. And Ellie. And Josh. He'd probably say she should back off. Hold Alexa accountable for the way she treated her. Also for stealing.

Having listened to herself talk aloud so openly and honestly about it, she realized how right they all probably were. Or . . . maybe in a way she had realized it all along but just wasn't ready to accept it. "No, thanks," she said and changed the subject to his passion for survivalism.

As she listened to him talk, she couldn't help but think he guarded his words. Usually people did that when they had something to hide, she thought, but of course there could be many other reasons.

"When I was overseas, I saw such . . . decimation," he explained. "In cities. These people had been living comfortably—just like us. And then *bam*." He clapped his hands softly for effect. "It was just all gone."

"You think that could happen here?"

"Maybe. We've grown so complacent and reliant on conveniences around us. It makes us vulnerable. I prefer to be prepared for pretty much anything."

They talked for a long while. As they did, Diane was vaguely aware of the sky outside growing blacker and a beam of moonlight appearing, streaming in the window behind him. She took long turns talking and short turns listening, all the while staring into his green eyes.

She couldn't get over how attracted she was to this man. And every time she saw him the attraction just got stronger. She didn't remember chemistry with Frank . . . or anyone else . . . being even close to as intense.

"What?" he asked.

She smiled. "Nothing. Just listening."

Silent now, he watched her for a moment. The way he stared made every nerve in her body tingle. Then he grinned, the dimple in his left cheek becoming more pronounced. "This is really nice."

"This?"

"Tonight. You being here. Us . . . together."

He reached out and brushed her jawline with his fingers. It made her shiver. His gaze was so serious, so intense, she was dying to know what he was thinking. She was about to ask when he suddenly pulled her close. When he kissed her, she tasted the malt of his beer. Then he pulled her effortlessly onto his lap and the kiss grew stronger, more passionate, sending shivers up and down her spine.

She felt a physical hunger that she hadn't felt for a long time. It had been building in her since the night at the bar. Maybe even at Brookmart that first night, the night of the potato avalanche—in a much less intense way.

Sitting on his lap, she could feel he was aroused. And that made her even more excited. The harder he kissed her, the more she wanted to be kissed, and to—

He groaned, then gently pulled back. He looked deeply into her eyes, then he shifted on the couch and turned her so that they were both facing the fireplace. She nestled deep into his chest and felt a rare sense of peace, security.

"I think you're incredible, Diane," he said quietly.

"Likewise," she said, smiling inside.

They both sat in silence, the fire in the fireplace crackling in front of them, and soon Diane felt her eyelids get heavy. All the wine had caught up to her. Or was it the sense of calm and contentment she was feeling—sensations she hadn't truly experienced in years? She didn't care which it was. She felt amazing. There wasn't one worry on her radar. She was taking a vacation from worry for a little while. She was just going to enjoy this.

A few minutes later, she drifted off in his arms. Into a deep, peaceful sleep.

❖❖❖

DIANE'S EYES POPPED open at three in the morning. She lifted her head from Rick's chest. They were both sleeping on the couch, Rick still holding her tight.

She untangled herself and leaned in to kiss him good-bye. "I need to go," she whispered.

He reached for her hands. "Are you sure?"

"Yes."

He yawned. "Okay, then. Let me at least warm up your car for you." He grabbed her keys from the kitchen counter and went outside to start her car for her—and she used the time to go to the restroom.

Then he walked her to her car and even offered to follow her home. But she assured him she was okay. She had slept off the effects of the wine. She'd be fine.

Before she left, he kissed her. Desire again threatened to overtake her, and she found herself pulling away before she changed her mind about leaving.

As she wound her way through the dark woods, she felt as if she was driving on a cloud. She could tell she was falling for this guy. Hard.

And she hoped that wouldn't turn out to be something bad.

❦❦❦

AT FOUR A.M., after much tossing and turning, Diane still couldn't sleep. She sat up in bed, grabbed her iPad from the bedside table, and decided to check again for news of any local disappearances or murders. Just as she pulled up her browser, she heard a noise downstairs.

She grew still and listened.

There it was again.

A surge of fear traveling through her, she crawled out of bed and reached for the large can of pepper spray she kept in the bottom drawer of her nightstand. She grabbed her iPhone with her other hand, then crept into the hallway.

A small night-light in the hallway cast a bit of illumination that helped her see where she was going. She was at the top of the staircase when she heard the sound again. It sounded like a baby crying.

Well . . . maybe.

Then she heard another sound.

Like someone was scratching at the sliding glass doors that led to the deck. The same door where she'd found the dead duck.

Was someone trying to break into the house?

She dialed 911 on her phone. She would press Send if she needed to. But when she heard the sound next, it sounded less like a baby, or a person at all, and more like an animal. She stood by the back door, her finger on the trigger of the pepper spray.

"Who's there?" she called as bravely as she could.

There was no answer. Then a moment later, the crying sound again.

She reluctantly set her phone down on the floor and flipped on the porch light. She peered outside. It was a dog, just skin and bones. It was staring at the door as though waiting for someone.

She opened the door and was startled by the loud batting of wings. A bird disappeared into the dark sky. The dog stepped backward and stared at her woefully with big, brown eyes—his shaggy hair unkempt and knotted with burrs.

He took another step back and shivered.

Diane's heart melted, and she dropped to her knees. She set the pepper spray aside.

"Hey there, fella. Where did you come from?" she asked, reaching out her hand. But the dog backed away in fear. He was distrusting. Someone in his past had probably given him good reason to be. She realized that he might have smelled the duck carcass on the deck. Either that or he was drawn to the bread Diane was still putting out for the ducks.

Somewhere nearby an owl hooted.

"It's okay. I'm not going to hurt you."

The dog shifted side to side, his tail wagging softly to her voice.

"You must be so cold."

He stared at her.

"One second. I'll be back." She gently closed the door and locked it, then hurried into the kitchen. When she returned, she had two biscuits in her hand. She opened the door and found the dog standing in the same spot. She broke off a piece and placed it on the deck in front of him.

He sniffed curiously at the food, then stepped forward and gulped it up in one bite. Then he looked up at Diane for more. Diane set another piece just inside the door. This time the dog approached much more warily, but the lure of the baked treat was stronger than his fears. He gobbled it up, too, licking the floor, intent not to leave behind even one morsel.

Diane knelt down and held out the remainder of the biscuit in the palm of her hand so that she could get him inside the house. The dog stepped toward her and pulled the biscuit out of her hand and devoured it.

Now that he was inside the house, she sidestepped him, closed and locked the door, then went to the kitchen and grabbed another biscuit. She also grabbed a jar of peanut butter and swathed a thick amount inside the bread. She placed it on the ground and the dog went right for it.

"I'll get you some water, too."

As the dog ate, Diane snapped pictures of him with her phone. She wondered where it had come from. He had obviously been outside for a while, because he was thin enough she could count his ribs. After he finished eating, he still wouldn't let her touch him, but he did inch closer to her.

After a while, Diane grew tired and knew she needed to try to go to sleep again. She made a bed out of some old towels and placed it by the warmth of the wall heater in the laundry room, then with the help of some more peanut butter, the dog followed her into the laundry room. As it sniffed the towels, Diane quietly walked out and shut the door.

Back in bed, Diane posted the dog's pictures on Fog Harbor's Facebook page and asked if anyone had any information.

Then, satisfied she had done all she could do for the night, she lay back down in bed.

But her eyes soon popped open to the sound of the dog whining downstairs. Diane closed her eyes and waited for him to stop. Ten minutes later he was still whining, so she sighed, got back out of bed, and went downstairs.

A couple of minutes later she crawled back in bed, smiling contentedly. She looked down at her new furry friend, who was curled up on his makeshift bed, which she had moved next to her bed.

"Good night, Biscuit," she whispered before turning out the light.

CHAPTER 21

ALEXA JOLTED AWAKE and looked around, struggling to get her bearings. Something was very wrong.

Why was she in a car? Had she sleepwalked again? She remembered running, then seeing a van . . . then someone calling out to her. Then it came back to her. She was in her car, in her mother's neighborhood. She wiped the fog off the driver's-side window and squinted into the darkness outside. It was still nighttime.

And she was freaking freezing.

She started her car and stared at her fuel gauge. There wasn't much gas left, but she needed to run the heater for a little while—just until the interior warmed up.

After Lance had pulled up in his van and driven her back to her apartment, she had packed quickly in an attempt to leave before Trish returned to retrieve her things. She couldn't bear to see her after what she'd overheard, so she had planned on sleeping at her mother's.

But when she got to her mother's house, the driveway had been empty. In her haste to get out of her apartment so quickly, she had forgotten to grab the spare key to her mother's place, so she couldn't get in. So now she had no key, no phone charger, and no cash to get gas.

Ugh.

Where could her mother and Josh be? Neither of them ever stayed out all night, especially her mother.

Could she be with that guy she went on the date with? she wondered. The thought turned her stomach.

She'd texted Josh three times throughout the night, and he hadn't answered any of them. Was he still angry with her? She had thought about texting her mother but just couldn't bring herself to ask her for help.

She was parked just a couple of streets from her mother's house. All night, she'd been alternating between running the engine so the car would heat up, then shutting it off to conserve gas until it got too cold to take it anymore. She rubbed her eyes and peered into the rearview mirror. God, she looked like crap. She had barely slept at all.

She replayed Lance stopping beside her in his van. "Nice van," she'd said, feeling self-conscious and wiping at her nose. As she'd talked, the freezing rain had started coming down even harder.

"Thanks. It was my brother's."

She'd held her hand in front of her face so the freezing rain didn't blind her. "And you stole it?" she asked, fishing for something, anything, to say so they wouldn't have awkward silence. She hadn't realized what would come out would be so dumb.

"I inherited it when he killed himself."

She flashed back to her father.

"Need a ride?" he asked.

"I'm good."

"C'mon. Seriously. You can't run in this. Let me take you home."

"Okay," she said as she opened the passenger door and climbed inside.

As she fastened her seat belt, he shifted into drive and they started rolling forward. "Your discipline is admirable," he said.

"Discipline?" she asked.

"Yeah. You know. To go running in this weather."

Obviously he didn't know her. She was the least disciplined person on the planet. But she tried on the word anyway. *Disciplined.* It had a nice ring to it. She liked being thought of in that way.

This is my daughter, Alexa. I'm incredibly proud of her. She's very disciplined.

Two minutes later, they pulled up to her apartment building and he asked for her number. But of course she wasn't going to get her hopes up. He was probably just going to text her to ask for Trish's number. That seemed more likely.

She thought back to what he had said about her. That he admired her discipline.

Discipline.

It sounded so much better than the words Trish had used. She absentmindedly touched her hair and immediately realized how dirty and oily it was. She needed desperately to shower. And yes, apologize. The sooner she did it, the better. The little fire inside of her was burning hot again. She was so determined to do everything on her list, to make some serious changes in her life, even if her head was pounding—a sure sign of pill withdrawal. She sighed. It was going to be a long day.

She watched the sky lighten a little, and a quiet grayness spread over the street. The sun was coming up. She looked at the clock on the dashboard: 5:12 a.m. The last time she'd driven by her mother's house was three a.m. and neither her mother nor Josh had yet returned home.

She'd check back in a few minutes. But first, there was something she had to do online. Something she'd been meaning to do for a little while, because she'd never felt right about it. She picked up her phone, pulled up a browser and the website she wanted, then scrolled through some content she'd posted. She searched around for a way to delete everything. But just as she had it figured out, her phone went black.

Crap! And no phone charger.

Groaning, she shifted her car into drive and decided to drive back to her mother's house to see if anyone had returned.

❖❖❖

DIANE WAS POURING her first cup of coffee when she heard a knock on the door. Biscuit rushed to the front door, barking his head off.

Diane's chest constricted. It wasn't even six in the morning. Who would be at the door this early in the morning?

Could Josh have gotten sick? Hurt?

The thought sending spikes of fear shooting down her arms, she hurried to the front door, hoping beyond hope that it wasn't a police officer coming to tell her there'd been some sort of an accident.

But when she swung the door open, she saw Alexa.

She exhaled loudly, relieved. Then she took a good look at Alexa and noticed she looked more disheveled than usual. She also realized that it was odd for her to be there at such an early hour. "My God. Are you all right?"

Instead of the usual scowl, Alexa gave her a tight smile.

Diane blinked. *Did Alexa actually smile?* Granted, it looked like it had been painful, but she'd still attempted it. She couldn't remember the last time Alexa had smiled at her. It had been years.

Hold on. Am I still asleep?

She decided to tread lightly—and not say anything about her being a mess, because she didn't want to upset her. "You're up early."

"I just wanted to get my day started. I didn't finish my laundry last time I was here. Is it okay if I do it now?"

"Of course. It's in front of the washer." Diane had found Alexa's duffel full of laundry in her office the evening she'd found the dead duck, and she had moved it to the laundry room. She would've washed and folded it for her, but she wasn't sure how Alexa would have felt about her handling her things.

Another awkward smile crept across her daughter's face, then she turned and headed to the laundry room.

What the hell's going on? Diane wondered, pulling a carton of eggs out of the fridge. A few minutes later, Alexa emerged from the laundry room.

"Eggs and coffee?" Diane asked.

"Yes, thanks."

"Thanks"? The smiles? Who is *this young woman?*

Diane handed Alexa a cup, then began frying the eggs. She watched Alexa as she sat at the bar, silently stirring her coffee with her finger, as though lost in a thought. She looked up a couple of times like she wanted to say something, but Diane pretended not to notice.

"You guys get a dog?" she asked.

"He's a stray. I'm trying to find a home for him."

"Josh doesn't want him?"

"Josh hasn't seen him yet. He showed up this morning."

"Showed up?"

"Yeah. On the deck."

"Oh. Where's Josh?"

"Spending the night at a friend's house."

Alexa nodded and stared at the dog for a minute. Then she made a face and shifted in her seat. "I'll be right back," she said, and headed toward the foyer. Diane heard the door to the half bath close loudly and the faucet squeak on, then she thought she heard Alexa vomiting.

She wouldn't ask. The last thing she wanted to do was to get on Alexa's bad side. This morning had been surprisingly pleasant.

Diane left the plate of food on the counter for Alexa, then reached for her phone to see if Josh had texted her. But she was surprised to find her phone was dead. That was weird. She was sure she just had a full charge.

She went upstairs to her office and plugged the phone in, then sat talking to Biscuit, who had followed her up, while she waited for it to charge.

When her phone beeped to let her know it had powered back up, she grabbed it and swiped the lock screen. It opened to an Amazon page. But she never shopped Amazon on her phone.

She took a closer look at the Amazon page and noticed who was signed in:

writewellorquit777

Diane's brain stalled. writewellorquit777. That was the username of the reviewer who wrote those hateful reviews about all of her books.

She turned the phone over in her hand. It looked like her new phone. Then she pressed the home button to close the Amazon page and look at the apps: Pandora, Candy Crush, Hulu, Netflix. She felt a catch in her throat. She'd mistakenly picked up Alexa's phone.

And Alexa was writewellorquit777.

❋❋❋

FEELING AS THOUGH someone had punched her in the stomach, Diane set Alexa's phone down on the table next to the staircase, then quietly walked into the bathroom and closed the door behind her.

She gazed at the woman who stared back at her in the mirror. She looked tired.

She *was* tired.

Tired of struggling with her daughter.

Tired of trying and failing.

Tired of being on the receiving end of her daughter's disdain. Her daughter hated her. Truly hated her . . . she had to; how else could she do something so malicious? She felt herself start to crumble.

As she always did when the stress became too overwhelming, she reached under the sink and grabbed some cleaning supplies. She sprayed the cleaner in the bathtub and unwrapped a new sponge, then started scrubbing.

She was angry, but she knew good mothers didn't get angry with their children.

Or, did they?

Tears stung her eyes and she began to cry. Alexa's attitude toward her was like a stain that she couldn't wipe clean. It tarnished everything.

She scrubbed harder. So hard the skin on her knuckles split. Ellie had been right. What was she teaching Alexa with her never-ending patience? That it was okay to treat people like doormats?

Because it wasn't.

She wanted more than anything to protect Alexa. But she could only protect Alexa so much . . . because she had no idea how to protect her from herself.

"Mom?" Alexa called from outside the bathroom door.

Diane stopped scrubbing. She cleared the tears from her throat. "Yes?"

"Have you seen my phone?"

"On the table next to the stairs."

A long pause. "Uh, thanks."

Diane stood up and tossed the cleaning supplies into the sink.

She closed her eyes and took a deep breath. When she opened her eyes, she looked at her reflection with a new sense of resolve.

Okay. She'd taken the wrong approach with Alexa. She was fully on board with that now.

But now she was going to take the right one.

CHAPTER 22

ALEXA STARED DOWN at her phone.

Her Amazon app was open, just as she had left it, and she was signed in as writewellorquit777.

Crap, crap, crap, crap, double crap!

Had her mother seen it?

And why did her mother have her phone anyway? Was she spying on her? Or had it been an accident?

Hearing footsteps coming down the staircase, she quickly tossed her phone on the couch and pretended to look out into the yard.

"Alexa?"

A cold flush spread through her. She squeezed her eyes shut. She didn't like her mother's tone. She *had* seen, hadn't she?

"Alexa?" her mother repeated.

Reluctantly, Alexa turned around.

Her mother stood in front of her, her eyes red and glassy.

Oh, no. She did.

"What awful thing did I do to you to make you hate me so much?" she asked.

"I . . . I don't."

Her mother shook her head. Alexa noticed she was clenching her jaw. She was angry.

"It's pretty obvious you do."

"I don't know what you're talking about."

"I'm not stupid, Alexa. I saw your phone."

"What?" Alexa pretended not to understand.

"Why would you put all that energy into writing those nasty, *hateful* reviews for my books? And, my God, for, what? Almost five years now! Why go to all that trouble?"

Alexa's eyes filled with tears. It was time to come clean. To apologize to her mom. She just wished she'd done it before something like this had happened. She swallowed hard. "No. Look, I actually came to—"

But her mother wasn't listening. "I love you more than anything, Alexa. And I always will, no matter what you do. You're my daughter, and that bond is very special to me. But . . . you go out of your way to hurt me. All the time. And it ends now."

The air left the room.

Huh?

What ends?

"I am tired of being your punching bag. I'm not going to do it anymore."

Alexa felt like someone big was pressing down on her chest. Instead of apologizing, she heard herself say, "Why were you looking at my phone anyway?" The words had just come out—and she regretted them as soon as they were out of her mouth.

Her mother stared at her with clear disappointment. They stood in the middle of the living room, silence growing between them.

Alexa felt like she was in a corner. Her ears burned hot. "You have no business looking at my phone!" she shouted.

Her mother's face reddened. "I *pay* for your goddamn phone! And I pay for it with royalties from those so-called lame-ass books I write!"

Alexa's breath caught in her throat. She took a step backward, stunned to hear her mother speak to her with such anger.

"So just because you pay for my stupid phone, you think you own me?" she yelled. "You think because you give me money that you can just do what you want? I'm not a kid!"

"Do you ever listen to yourself?" her mother asked. "Because you sure as hell act like one."

"Oh, I'm the one acting like one? Who's checking someone else's phone? Who's getting passed-out drunk? Who's picking up guys at bars and sleeping at their house overnight?" she asked, her words taking on a noticeable bite.

Her mother's face reddened. "You want to talk about getting drunk? About stealing alcohol? What about sleeping pills? You want to talk about that? God knows what else you do to yourself, Alexa. You have the world at your feet, but all you seem to want to do is make a mess of everything . . . and step on those who care about you!"

They stared at each other for a long moment, then her mother's voice softened but sounded more controlled, which was somehow even scarier. "All I've ever wanted is for you to be happy. All I've ever tried to do is be a good mother to you. But it doesn't matter. You clearly have decided to hate me. You think that it's fine to disrespect me . . . and even steal from me. And I'm tired of waiting for you to grow out of it. I'm done."

Done? What?

The room felt as if it were closing in on her. "It's because of that guy, isn't it?" Alexa heard herself say. "Is that it? Now that you're screwing him, I'm just in the way? Do you really care more about getting laid than about your own daughter?"

"I want you to leave," her mother said calmly. "You owe me an apology for that and everything else . . . and until I get one, and until you start treating me with respect, I don't want you here."

Her mother turned and started up the stairs. "Finish your laundry and leave."

Alexa could barely breathe. *What just happened? I came here to apologize. To start making things right. This was supposed to be a new start.*

She stomped into the laundry room and pulled her wet clothes out of the washer, stuffing it into her duffel bag. There was no way she was going to wait around for it to finish.

Tears in her eyes, she grabbed her keys and left.

CHAPTER 23

FOUR NIGHTS LATER the roaring in his head had morphed into something even more mind piercing: the sound of someone shrieking.

The loud, ear-piercing wails shredded his mind, sending him pacing. He was sweating, trying his best to keep it together, but it was getting difficult.

He couldn't, wouldn't, go out tonight. It was way too soon. He had to stay put. But it was taking everything he had to stay in. He'd always prided himself on his self-control. Where had it gone?

Stop. Things are going so well.

You don't need to do this anymore.

You don't even want *to do this anymore, do you?*

No. He didn't. Not anymore.

But it was fighting him. His skull felt like it was in a vise. He held his head between his palms, trying to keep it in one piece. He clenched his teeth, willing the shrieks, the screams to go away.

Who was screaming?

Was it Jill?

Katie?

Or someone . . . or some*thing* . . . from before?

Or, a thought even more frightening . . . maybe it was him?

Oh God.

He tried to concentrate on the goldfish. He scooped it up with the side of his hand and let it squirm its soft little body against his palm and plop down into the larger fishbowl, its new, bigger home.

He watched it swim in circles for several seconds before it finally calmed down and began to explore the little pirate cove he bought for it to hide in. After all, everyone needed a place to hide.

He set aside the old bowl and tried to keep his mind on the fish, but he was shaking. His high after being with Jill had been a letdown. It had lasted all of an hour, much less than Katie. And much, much less than his other victims.

Within two short hours he began feeling worse than before he visited her, and the itch had already started all over again.

And it bothered him that they hadn't found Jill yet. It had been five days. Had no one missed her? Had no one but him noticed she'd suddenly stopped updating her social media accounts?

He turned a thought over in his mind. A surefire way to alert them to what had happened to Jill . . . and within minutes, if not seconds.

But it was risky.

It could change everything for him. But wasn't that what he wanted? At least on some level?

He turned the thought over in his mind a few times, then went to retrieve her phone and the battery. He shoved the battery in and slid the backing of the phone back on. Then he opened her camera app and sifted through the six photos he'd taken of her, paying careful attention to the details of each one.

In each of the photos her neck was turned at a slightly odd angle, and for once she wasn't making the awful duck face. Her mouth was relaxed, actually, her lips parted. Her eyes were half-open, staring at the bedroom door.

Had she been thinking about the door?

Hopeful somehow she would be able to slip out of his grasp and escape?

Or had she already given up?

He selected the best photo of the six and, holding his breath, uploaded it to Facebook.

If they didn't know she was gone, they would know now.

This was going to be her most popular post ever.

He removed the battery from the phone again and put it away, then his eyes flickered back to his laptop, and he watched.

Not a minute later, the first of the comments rolled in . . .

> Jackie Taylor: Dude, what are you doing?
> Charlene Hickey: Dude, that is NOT funny!
> Tim Egan: WTH? Wasn't Halloween almost
> two months ago?
> Steven Dennison: Best pic ever! Sharing!
> Kristy Lipton: Is this some kind of a joke?

He was much calmer ten minutes, 203 comments, ninety-four likes, and sixty-six shares later as he continued to watch everything unfold on Facebook:

> Jeff Voorhees: What are those marks on your
> throat? Seriously. This pic is disturbing the
> shit out of me.
> Terry Clark: Call me!
> Eddie Raymond: Why aren't you answering
> your phone?
> Sarah Brighton: Dude, seriously . . . I just
> called the cops. Are you okay?
> Amy Davis: This isn't funny, Jill!

Todd Jackson: I just reported this to
Facebook.
Crystal McGee: Answer your door, hon!
Beth MacDonald: Jill, honey, this isn't funny.
Please answer your phone.

He watched, his blood electric, until Facebook took down the photo.

The screaming had stopped for now . . . and his world, at least for a little while, was almost okay again.

CHAPTER 24

DIANE OPENED HER eyes. It had been five days since she'd stood her ground with Alexa. She hadn't reached out to her since . . . or to anyone else, for that matter.

She'd also come down with an awful sinus infection, one she'd been battling for most of the week.

The only places she'd gone were the veterinary clinic to get Biscuit checked out and then the pet store for dog food and supplies. She'd placed two additional ads on social media, and so far no one had claimed him. It looked like she might be keeping him after all.

Rick had shown up midweek, surprising her with chicken noodle soup he had picked up from Brookmart's deli. He said Wayne had helped him select it. He had stayed and played video games with Josh and visited every afternoon since. It made her happy seeing Josh with a male figure again. A solid one.

He was solid, wasn't he?

Her thoughts circled back to Alexa, like they always did. Her eyes welled up with tears and she sniffed into her pillow. She'd Skyped with Dr. Carol back in New Jersey twice since having the discussion with Alexa—and she said Diane had done the right thing. She advised her to give it time. She hadn't banished her daughter. She'd just erected healthy boundaries by telling her she didn't want to see her until she was ready to apologize and be more respectful. Dr. Carol said that odds were, she'd come around.

But what if she didn't?

It had been a tough decision, even tougher to enforce it and not reach out to her in the days afterward, but she knew that she'd done the right thing. Still, it was painful to rip off a Band-Aid.

Diane forced herself to get up and dress. Then she deep cleaned her house most of the day, listening to music she hadn't heard since her college days: Evanescence, Radiohead, Green Day. The music brought back old memories of her time spent with Ellie, of the days when things had been great with Frank. It was almost unfathomable how different her life was back then.

At six o'clock, Rick showed up with Thai takeout he'd picked up in New Cambridge. Josh was with his friends again and Diane didn't want to be alone.

When she answered the door, she smiled, again taken by how attracted she was to him. But a second later Biscuit sidled up next to her and growled at him, baring his teeth.

"No sir," Diane said. "That's not nice. Rick's my friend." She knelt down and scooped the dog into her arms. She petted him, trying to calm him down, but the dog kept growling. "Sorry. I don't think he likes men much. He growled at Josh, too. I'll just put him in the kitchen."

"And I will make sure to stay *out* of the kitchen," Rick assured her with a grin.

Diane left Biscuit in the kitchen with a bone and led Rick to the dining room. She'd already lit candles and dimmed the overhead lighting. She took the takeout from Rick and brought it to the table. Halfway there, Rick walked up behind her and circled his arms around her waist. "You didn't tell me you had a dog."

She leaned back into him. "I didn't. Well, I don't. He just showed up last week. I have ads out to find his owner . . . or even just a good home for him, but so far, no one's bitten."

"That explains why he's so skinny," Rick said. "Poor little guy."

Rick plated the food while Diane went back to the kitchen for drinks. A few minutes later, they were ready to eat.

"So," she said. "Tonight, let's talk about you."

He stirred his tom kha gai with his spoon, then peered at her with those intense, green eyes of his.

God, he was handsome.

"What would you like to know?"

"A lot of things."

"Like?"

"What makes you happy?"

His mouth curved into a smile. He picked up his beer and took a long pull. Set it down. "Being in nature makes me happy."

"Yeah?"

Rick nodded. "Without question. It wasn't always important to me, but as I got older and experienced more, I realized I need it. In fact, I'd like to completely live off the grid one day."

"Why?"

"Like I told you the other night, I think it's important to be self-reliant. It can come in handy."

Diane nodded.

"And there's something else. Something else that makes me happy."

"What is that?"

His eyes became intense. "Being in the company of such a beautiful woman. And not just physical beauty. Inside and out. Someone with substance. I'm not sure how I got so lucky to cross paths with you."

Diane's cheeks heated up. "Thank you. But it's a small town."

He stared silently at her for a long moment. "So, how are things going with Alexa?" he asked, picking up his beer again.

As usual, he was shifting the topic of conversation back to her.

"No. Tonight let's talk about you."

"But I'm not half as interesting."

Diane raised an eyebrow. "I wouldn't be so sure about that."

He shrugged. "I'm just not used to talking about myself. Besides"—he smiled playfully—"I've read the articles. Women hate guys who go on and on about themselves."

"I think there's a difference between sharing a little bit and going on and on incessantly. And I feel I've gone on and on incessantly. I'd like to know more about you. So, please. Tell me more."

Rick sat back in his chair and studied her with a thoughtful expression. "Okay. Well, you know I grew up in Texas, right?"

She nodded. "Go on."

"Played football in high school, like pretty much everyone else. I lived in this really small town that practically closed down on Friday nights so everyone could go to the games. Worked on my dad's dairy farm for a while. But I wanted to get out, serve my country, see the world. So I joined the Marines. Did a couple of tours overseas, came back. Now I spend my time doing odd jobs; I research survivalism and sustainable living. I run every day, with little exception. Lift some weights. I eat right. Lots of the same meals: chicken and vegetables. I hunt when I can. Make it to the supermarket maybe twice a week. I hang out at The Bar maybe once a week. Play video games. Like I said, boring."

"Your lifestyle shows an exceptional amount of control. The eating, exercising."

"Maybe. But I'm not perfect, of course."

"You said you served in Iraq twice, right?"

His eyes dimmed a little. "I did."

"If you aren't comfortable—"

"No, it's fine." He cleared his throat. "I was a scout sniper. And even though I don't like to talk about it a lot, I'm glad I was. I was doing my duty. But I saw things. Things that, as hard as I try, I can't get out of my head. Things I don't want to remember or continue trying to make sense of. When I came back, I tried to go back to work for my dad. Just slip back into my old life. But I couldn't. I don't look at the world like I did before. Our government. Life. I realized a lot of what I believed . . . that I'd been wrong."

She reached across the table for his hand. It was warm, strong. She squeezed it, and he squeezed back. "I can't imagine."

His eyes were serious. "It stays with you. Messes with your head. Sometimes I get migraines. A little anxiety. But nothing I can't deal with."

He squeezed her hand again, and his now-familiar grin returned. "So to end my story, I decided to get a fresh start. Moved here to be close to the water, and . . ." He lifted her hand up to kiss it. "Things have been looking up ever since."

❦❦❦

AFTER DINNER, DIANE and Rick moved to the living room. She didn't expect Josh home from Bruce's for at least a few hours, so she knew she could relax.

Rick tended to the fireplace while she refreshed their drinks in the kitchen. When she returned to the living room, the fire was already roaring.

She dimmed the lights and let the fire cast its warm glow over the room. Rick sat on the couch and watched her, smiling. She loved the attentive way he looked at her, his quiet confidence, his exceptional sense of control. In fact, she loved everything about him—everything she knew of, at least.

164

He patted the couch cushion beside him, and when she sat, he set his beer on the coffee table, then took her wineglass and did the same with it. He turned his attention back to her and stared into her eyes. And that was all it took for her to get aroused. Not wanting to wait any longer, she leaned into him and kissed him. He kissed her back, cupped the back of her neck, and pulled her closer. Then his lips moved from her mouth to her chin, to the base of her neck. Every nerve ending in her body tingled. As he continued to move south, the kisses grew harder.

She knew at that moment she wanted more of him.

All of him.

Tonight.

She couldn't remember ever feeling such urgency to be with a man. But what if Josh came home early?

It took all of her energy to push Rick away. "Not here," she whispered. She grabbed his hand and led him upstairs. A minute later, they were in her bedroom with the door locked. He pulled her close and kissed her again. Then, effortlessly, he picked her up and laid her on the bed. Pressing his hot mouth against hers again, he slid a hand under her blouse and pushed the cup of her bra to the side. He massaged her breast, and her body trembled. Then he did the same with the other one. He sat her up, slipped her blouse off, and tossed it to the floor. Then he unclasped her bra, and she felt her breasts spill out.

She fumbled with his shirt buttons and he helped her pull it off. Then they worked on his pants. When those were off, he slid his hands around her back and pulled her close, so that they were skin to skin. He kissed her, then his warm breath was next to her ear. "Are you sure you want to do this?" he whispered, his voice hoarse. "Because if we don't stop now—"

"Don't you dare stop," she whispered.

He pulled back from her so he could see her eyes. He looked into them and smiled, then he laid her on her back again and slid his hand down her side until it reached the hem of her skirt. She arched her back so he could unzip it and pull it off. Then he pulled a breast into his mouth and groaned, sending every inch of her skin prickling with need.

After a moment his lips traveled to her rib cage and down to her stomach. Then she felt his hot breath as he kissed her through her panties. Just when she didn't think she could take it anymore, he hooked the elastic over his thumbs and yanked them down. His hand traveled back up her thighs to where her panties had been, and he stroked her gently, then hard, making her cry out.

A moment later he lay on top of her, the heat of his erection pressed against her. She guided him between her legs and moaned as he entered her. She held her breath and didn't let it go until he was deep inside her, filling her up.

Afterward, she lay in his arms, her head pressed to him, listening to his heart thudding in his chest. She had never experienced that kind of passion before. Never felt this kind of chemistry with anyone . . . ever. It had by far been the most incredible sex of her life.

Ellie had been right.

She *had* needed this.

Maybe her worries about Alexa had become unhealthy. An obsession.

Right now she felt content. Safe. At home. And she didn't want to forget one second of it.

Half an hour later, she kissed one of his broad shoulders and sat up. She wanted so badly for him to stay, to be able to fall asleep in his arms, but Josh would be coming home, and she didn't want him to know Rick had been there. At least not like this.

"I'd love for you to stay, but Josh . . ."

"I understand." He kissed her forehead, then got up and dressed, and she led him to the front door. His eyes were half-closed, tired . . . his short, dark hair was standing in all directions.

Before opening the door, he pulled her to him again and kissed her. He started to say something but stopped himself.

"What?"

"It was just a really great night. Unbelievably amazing."

"It was."

He kissed her again and walked out the door. Diane watched him leave, sorry to see him go. She had butterflies in her stomach—and already felt a sweet but painful longing to be with him again. Despite everything she'd told herself since Frank's death, she knew she'd fallen in love.

❂❂❂

LATER THAT NIGHT, Diane jerked awake. The house felt like a meat locker. The room was pitch-black, although she knew she'd left the bathroom light on.

But the bathroom light wasn't on now.

And the house seemed uncharacteristically quiet.

All she could hear was the rain outside pummeling the house and the wind pressing against the windowpanes.

What time was it?

She fumbled in the darkness for her phone. It was 10:07 p.m.

A bolt of lightning pierced the sky and was followed by a deafening clap of thunder. She heard whining downstairs. Biscuit. She'd forgotten him in the kitchen.

Dammit.

She sat up and shivered.

Biscuit whined again. Probably frightened by the loud storm outside. She tried to turn on her bedside lamp, but it wouldn't work. Her chest constricted, and all the tension that sex had alleviated came flooding back. "What the—?"

Then it hit her.

No lights. No heat. The power had gone out.

Using the flashlight on her iPhone, she walked slowly into the hallway. She peered into Josh's room, but he wasn't home yet.

Biscuit whined louder.

The sleeping pills she'd taken to get some rest after the excitement with Rick had her feeling woozy. As she made her way downstairs, she heard a loud bump and a tapping sound.

The hair on her neck stood up.

Had the sound come from the attic? The roof?

As she continued downstairs, thunder rumbled, rattling the dishes in the cabinets.

The dog's whimpering stopped. She peered into the living room, the last embers from the fireplace casting an eerie red glow in the large room. She made her way to the kitchen. "Biscuit?"

She opened the door off the kitchen, and Biscuit bounded out and ran to the sliding glass door. He sat by it, panting in anticipation.

"Poor boy. You just needed to go out, didn't you?"

When Diane opened the door, he shot across the deck and down into the yard, ignoring the storm.

She heard the noise again. Now, with the back door open, she could hear it more clearly. It was coming from outside.

She stepped out into the darkness. Looking up, she saw the source. A tree branch had broken in half and was swinging in the storm, knocking into the side of the house, near the roof.

Relieved to have discovered the culprit, she stepped back inside just as Biscuit came bounding back in. As she closed the door, the porch light flickered back on, then the heater kicked on, too, breaking the silence.

The power was back.

She grabbed a blanket, got comfortable on the couch, and turned on the television. She was lying there when Josh got home, then long after he went up for bed, and was still trying to muster the energy to peel herself off the couch when a local news anchor appeared on the screen and announced they had a breaking story.

The newscast cut to a reporter standing in front of an apartment complex. A caption was splashed across the bottom of the screen: SECOND COLLEGE STUDENT FOUND SLAIN. DEAD GIRL'S PICTURE POSTED ON SOCIAL MEDIA.

CHAPTER 25

ALEXA SNIFFED BACK tears. She was still withdrawing from her antidepressants, and she couldn't stop crying.

She was also getting "brain zaps." She'd learned on the Internet that they, too, were typical withdrawal symptoms. Typical, but not easy to get through. She was determined to get the drugs out of her system and try something else. What, she didn't know yet. She just knew the drugs weren't working. Sighing, she lay down and picked up her iPhone. Her mother hadn't texted her for over a week now. Not one word. She went through her texts to make sure she hadn't missed any.

Nothing.

She felt gutted.

Her mother had never gone longer than a few days without texting her. She winced, thinking back on the last conversation they'd had. At first she was in utter disbelief that her mother would actually kick her out. She fully expected a call or text by the time she drove back to her apartment. That her mother would apologize after she'd had the chance to cool down and think more clearly.

But she hadn't.

Since their argument, she had been replaying her mother's words over and over. The disappointment on her face. The anger. She never in a million years would've thought she'd see her mother that angry with her. That her mother would ever turn her away.

But she had.

It had to be that new boyfriend of hers. Alexa was angry just thinking about the guy. She flung the blanket off and stared at the popcorn finish of the ceiling, waiting for her eyes to adjust to the murky light in the room.

She missed her mother.

She actually missed her.

There, she'd admitted it.

She felt a longing that she hadn't felt since she was a little girl, waiting at the window for her mother to return home from the hospital. Most of her childhood had been spent alone and waiting. She'd always had a difficult time fitting in with her peers, so school had been lonely. Then she'd get home, it was lonely, too. The lonesomeness back then had made her sad at first, but then it had grown into anger, and after a while she began to wake up every morning with the overwhelming urge to scream, smash things, lash out.

But she didn't feel anger now.

Just longing, regret . . . and intense loneliness. She'd thought a lot about it over the last few days and realized that aside from her mother and maybe Josh, no one else in the world loved . . . or even cared . . . about her.

Not really.

And maybe now she'd screwed things up so badly, even they didn't anymore. The thought terrified her.

She wanted to text her mom. To say she was sorry. But she couldn't. At least not yet.

A text came through. Lance. He had been checking in on her. And she was starting to believe that maybe he really was interested. She opened his text. It was just a smiley face. He probably just wanted her to know he was thinking about her. He was nice like that.

She sent him a smiley face back and smiled for real. She liked that his texts had started getting a little flirty.

Well, *a lot* flirty.

But she wasn't completely sure about how she felt about him. On one hand, she felt giddy and hopeful when he texted. It was the only thing she had to look forward to every day. On the other, she read his texts with a sense of disbelief. After all, how could he possibly be interested in her when there were women like her mother and Trish in the world?

She was a complete and utter wreck. A loser. Like Trish had said: *weird*. It made no sense. But when she was able to suspend her disbelief, it did help slice through some of the loneliness and bring some excitement into her screwed-up life.

The good news was that she was making some progress with her list. She'd gotten a job at a restaurant near campus and had been running every day since her fight with her mother. Just a short distance, but it was something.

She'd even cleaned up her apartment and was washing her hair every day. Everything she did still seemed like a battle and took forever to do, but she was doing it. And each accomplishment made the next thing she did a little easier.

Another text came in. *Probably Lance again*, she thought.

But it wasn't. It was from Trish. She read the words and her stomach roiled.

Anger swelled inside her chest.

What the hell? Why would she . . . say that?

If she'd had any doubts about hating Trish before, she didn't now.

CHAPTER 26

DIANE STOOD BUNDLED up outside on her deck, a light dusting of snow falling around her and in her hair. Listening to the rowboats knock into the piers, she watched the water shimmer beneath the moonlight.

Inside, the house was wrapped in holiday spirit. The fire in the fireplace was burning. Josh and Rick were playing Call of Duty, a military special ops video game that Rick had brought over. A Frank Sinatra Christmas album was playing softly from the speakers in the living room. But she felt far from festive. When she looked at the large tree in the corner, decorated in white lights and an ornament collection that had grown throughout the years, she could conjure up only two things: the scene of her daughter sitting alone in that tiny apartment and the fact that a serial killer was on the loose.

At ten that morning Detectives Chavez and Johnson had been at her front door, wanting to speak to her again. She'd brought them into the dining room, where they proceeded to tell her the name of the second murdered college student: Jill MacDonald.

The fine hairs on the back of her neck immediately rose. The caller had said the girl's name would be Jill.

There was little doubt in her mind now that the caller was the killer . . . or was at least involved with the killer somehow. But why the hell reach out to *her*?

The detectives spent over two hours with her, going over both of the phone calls again. Asking about her family, the other volunteers at the call center, about her past. They told her that she was the only volunteer who had been called. And they must have asked her five times, in five different ways, why she thought the caller would specifically seek her out. And in five different ways, she had told them she had no idea.

Before leaving, they'd wanted to talk to Josh. And they'd asked for both Alexa's and Rick's phone numbers and addresses.

After they left, she decided to scrap her plan of leaving the ball in her daughter's court, at least for now, and called her. She didn't want her by herself now. Not with a predator on the loose. When Alexa didn't answer, she left a voice mail telling her that she would probably hear from the detectives and asking for her to come stay with her and Josh until the police caught the person behind the murders. But Alexa didn't return her calls or her texts.

It was the end of deadline week, and Rick had come by every day to help her with nonwriting tasks, like preparing dinner. He also entertained Josh. Not only did they play video games together, he'd also taken Josh hiking. Ten- and fifteen-mile hikes in the eastern Massachusetts wilderness, something Josh otherwise would never have thought to do but seemed to really enjoy. With Rick's help, she'd been able to shoot the manuscript off to her editor on time.

In other circumstances, she'd be relieved right now that the manuscript was out of her hands and happy that what she had going on with Rick was working out so well, *so perfectly*, but the darkness pushing in on her was eclipsing everything.

As she stood in the kitchen, trying to clear her mind enough to start prepping for Christmas dinner, she felt Rick's arms encircle her waist. He pulled her in tight and said softly in her ear, "Change tactics. Call her again and *specifically* invite her to Christmas. But just Christmas. Maybe she'll say yes, then come around about staying here."

Diane wrapped her hands around his and nodded.

"I'll call her," Josh said, messing with a GPS locator that Rick had let him borrow in case they got separated during their hikes. Diane hadn't even noticed he was within earshot of the conversation. He pocketed the device and pulled out his phone. "I'll do it now."

❖❖❖

ALEXA HAD TRIED not to think about Trish's text, but it was next to impossible. It had been a warning about Lance.

> TRISH: Need 2 warn you about ur mom's friend, Lance. I saw ur phone number n his contacts and don't know if u r seeing him, but I was w/him and afterward . . . OMG. He was SO weird. Such a DICK. He didn't txt me or anything. I don't want him 2 do that to you.

Alexa had reread the text over and over again—and still didn't know what to think about it. Trish said she'd been with Lance.

What did "with him" mean?

Had they hooked up?

The mere thought of it made her feel sick. But Alexa decided not to reply and ask questions. She didn't want to give Trish the satisfaction of seeming concerned.

She got up and went to her apartment window and looked out. The world outside looked cold, gray. Two homicide detectives had visited her that morning. She'd been reluctant to open the door but felt she had to when they announced who they were. They said that they were working the college girls' murder cases. They'd stayed for thirty minutes, asking her questions about her mother and about the guy her mother was dating.

She flinched, thinking about the Jill MacDonald girl who had just been murdered . . . how the murderer posted a picture of her, dead, on social media. Facebook had pulled the post, but not before people had copied it and uploaded it to several sites. She wished now she hadn't seen it for herself, because she couldn't get the visual out of her head.

She was aware that the killer could be, probably was, somewhere nearby right now. Close by when she went on her runs. But she knew she wasn't half as gorgeous as Katie or Jill had been, so she wasn't really that frightened.

She closed the curtains tightly, then walked to the bathroom and tried to focus on getting ready for Christmas dinner. She'd been surprised when her mother had called to ask her to stay with her and Josh until the killer was caught. She'd been almost certain that her mother didn't care about her anymore. But she didn't want to stay at her mother's house. She wanted to stay in New Cambridge, where her new job as a waitress was located . . . and continue to work on herself. Now that she had the ball rolling, she was inspired.

But Christmas dinner was a different story. When Josh had called to invite her, he'd said that their mother really wanted her there. She was surprised by that, too. What surprised her the most, though, was that she was actually looking forward to it.

She had grown so lonely she had a need—almost a hunger—to be around people. Plus she wanted her mother to see her now.

Although she was still struggling with random crying jags, they were much better, only coming in waves, and the other symptoms had, thankfully, disappeared. She'd been increasing her distance with her runs. Half a mile had turned to one mile, and now she was running two miles twice a day. Her muscles ached right now, but in a good way. She'd also lost five pounds in the last week . . . much of it from water weight, leaving her face looking thinner and her ankles looking normal again. She needed her mother to see her hard work, that she was changing.

She'd decided not to enroll in any new courses until her mind was working right. No need wasting the money if she was just going to continue to flunk out. She'd just work as many shifts as she could at the restaurant and save up enough money to pay her mother back, and she'd keep working on herself. She wasn't sure how she was going to tell her mother she'd flunked out this past semester, but she was trying not to worry about it just yet.

She stepped into the shower and let the hot spray thunder down on her skin. She was going to look nice at Christmas dinner. She was going to show her mother and Josh that she wasn't a loser after all. That she really was trying this time.

❖❖❖

WHEN ALEXA PULLED up to her mother's house, Josh was standing in the driveway. He opened her passenger door and jumped in.

"Change of plans," he said.

Alexa frowned. "What do you mean?"

"Power's out."

"What?"

Josh nodded. "Something about an old transformer or something. Landlord's gonna look at it later."

"So where are we going?"

"We're relocating to Rick's house."

Alexa sank down into her seat. She shook her head, her stomach churning. "No. I'm not going."

"What? Why?"

"I don't—" She decided to be careful what she said.

"Rick's really cool. You'll see. Go to Main Street and I'll steer you from there."

Alexa couldn't afford to piss her brother off again, so she bit her lip and followed his directions. But the deeper they drove into the woods, the worse her stomach felt. "It's creepy out here."

"Look, why don't you keep your mouth closed unless you have something nice to say," Josh warned. "Don't ruin this for Mom."

"Seriously, though. Look around."

"At what? A bunch of old oak trees? It's nature. Hardly creepy."

Alexa knew Josh was right. She would need to just suck it up. Be nice to Rick. Try to be pleasant. Perform like everyone else did, whether they were happy or not.

Not cause any scenes.

Just because she'd rarely done it before didn't mean she didn't know how to. They drove the rest of the way in silence; the only words spoken were Josh's directions. Finally they pulled up in front of Rick's cabin.

"Is this place for real? It looks abandoned."

Josh opened the passenger door and swung his legs out. "It's really cool inside."

Alexa's heart pounded as she got out of the car. Brittle leaves snapped beneath her shoes as she walked toward the cabin. She could hear a dog barking inside. Her eyes started to water.

No, don't cry. Do. Not. Cry, she told herself.

That was the last thing she wanted to do.

Well, at least one of the last things. The *last* thing she wanted was to spend Christmas at some strange guy's house. A strange guy who she knew she didn't like.

She scraped the rubber soles of her shoes on the welcome mat and stepped in. The interior was warm and smelled of oregano, and she could smell a fire in the fireplace. It was the way her childhood home had smelled in the wintertime when her mother was cooking spaghetti sauce.

"Merry Christmas." She looked up to see her mother was smiling at her, but the smile looked different. Polite, and like she wasn't sure if she should mean it. Alexa noticed her mother also looked too thin. And she didn't try to hug her like she usually did.

Rick appeared in the hallway in a black T-shirt and jeans. "Merry Christmas, Alexa," he said. "Make yourself at home."

Alexa stiffly muttered her hellos, then followed them into a large living room. Josh was sitting in a recliner, already queuing up a video game. It irritated her that he seemed to feel so at home. She found a place on the couch and sat down.

"Want some soda?" Rick offered. "Coffee?" His voice was friendly. She looked deep into his eyes and wondered if it made him happy to see that she'd been cast aside. Seriously, it was like she'd been pushed away, and he'd just slipped in and taken her place. "Coffee . . . please," she said. Rick told her to relax and he'd bring it over.

Alexa sat on the couch, looking around. Josh was right. It was a pretty cool place. But she still wasn't comfortable.

A few minutes later, Rick handed her a cup of coffee and sat down across from her.

Oh God, he's going to try and talk to me. She bit down on her lip and stared at him.

When he spoke, he kept his voice low. "Hey, thanks for coming. Your mom really misses you."

That surprised her. She had assumed her mother liked it better without her around. Alexa felt tears surge forward again, but she fought them.

Her face felt like concrete as she tried to smile. The smile wasn't real, and she was sure it showed. It was hard being nice to Rick, no matter how kind he was to her. She would pretend to play nice with him, but she would make it clear that she was only there for her mother and Josh.

●●●

"WHAT IF . . ." JOSH was saying at the dinner table, introducing another one of his lifeboat scenarios. Alexa managed not to roll her eyes. She concentrated on her manners instead.

Since she'd been there, it was more than obvious everyone was trying their best to keep things light. She knew all eyes were on her, and she knew she was being graded for her behavior.

She ate the spaghetti, the whole time in complete surprise that her notoriously cautious mother would date this guy. Yes, he seemed nice . . . but what did her mother know about him? She'd always preached about not trusting strangers, and this guy, wasn't that what he was? And not only that, he had a collection of guns in a glass cabinet by the back door—and her mother didn't like guns. Josh had also mentioned the guy used to be a Marine sniper.

A Marine sniper!

That meant he had actually killed people.

Then there was the teeny, glaring fact that he lived in this creepy little cabin in the woods. What the hell? It all left her bewildered. But she didn't say a word. She said just enough to be polite.

"Have you gotten your grades from last semester yet?" her mother asked.

"Not yet."

Her mother nodded. "What have you been doing with your time?"

"I started running."

Her mother's face seemed to brighten. "You did?"

Alexa nodded. "I'm up to two miles, twice a day."

"That's wonderful!"

"Got a new job, too," she muttered. "At a restaurant by campus."

Her mother seemed genuinely pleased. She asked more questions, and Alexa answered them all as carefully as she could.

"Oh, I almost forgot," her mother said. "Your friend Trish stopped by the house yesterday."

Alexa's pulse sped up. Trish was *not* her friend—and why in God's name would she stop by her mother's house?

"She dropped off a story she'd been writing," her mother said.

Alexa pushed at her spaghetti with her fork. "Was it any good?"

"I haven't had a chance to read it yet. I was writing when she stopped by, so she gave it to Rick."

Alexa didn't like that Trish had stopped by, but she wasn't about to say anything negative. "Cool."

When dinner was over, Rick brought a board game to the table.

"Okay. Now it's time for my family tradition," he said. "A rousing after-dinner game of Risk."

"Bring it on!" said Josh.

Alexa barely succeeded at not rolling her eyes again.

Diane cleared the table as Rick set up the game.

"I'm going to pass," Alexa said. She noticed her mother looked a little disappointed. But they didn't hound her about it.

"Where's the bathroom?" she asked.

Rick pointed to a door on the other side of the living room.

Once safely behind the privacy of the bathroom door, Alexa let out a deep breath. She had made it this far. How much longer did she have to stay before she could *leave*?

She looked at herself in the mirror and turned on the faucet, splashing cold water on her face. After patting dry, she looked at herself again. Then, with just a slight hesitation, she opened the medicine cabinet. Some prescriptions. One she recognized as an antidepressant that she'd tried. It was prescribed to Rick.

He takes antidepressants?

After a couple of minutes, she left the bathroom. But when she realized that the other three were already engrossed in the game, she seized the opportunity to investigate a little more.

The next room was a bedroom. Probably Rick's. She slipped in and looked around. The room was immaculate. Everything was in its place. The bed was so tightly made you could bounce a quarter on it. The dresser was bare except for a few neatly placed items: a small plant, a comb, a bottle of cologne, and an article titled "Living Off the Grid," held together by two paper clips. She carefully opened the drawers of his dresser, sifting through his clothes for anything hidden underneath.

But everything was folded neatly . . . and she found nothing strange. She pulled on a middle drawer. But it wouldn't move. She pulled again, then realized it was locked.

Why would he lock a drawer . . . unless there was something in it he wanted to hide?

It had a keyhole lock on it, just like her mother's jewelry box. She glanced at the bedroom door, then grabbed a pin from her hair, straightened it, and jiggled it in the lock. Not two seconds later, she heard a click.

Presto!

She quietly opened the drawer. It was stuffed with bills and official-looking papers.

Alexa heard the three laughing in the other room. She glanced over her shoulder at the door, then pulled out some of the paperwork to see what else was in the drawer, sifting the crisp papers between her fingers. Then something glossy fell out. She picked up the object and gasped. It was a photo of a woman dressed in skimpy red lingerie. She was posing on a bed.

Eww. Who the hell is she?

And . . . did her mother know about her?

Her pulse sprinting, she pushed the picture aside and sifted through more paperwork. A contract of some sort, passport, old driver's license. Some old letters, foreign money. Then she got to a large envelope underneath. The US Marines logo appeared at the top of the return address. She pulled out the letter inside and read the first two lines.

She felt her eyes go wide.

She stuffed the letter back in the envelope, tossed in the photo, and folded the envelope into threes before stuffing it in the waistband of her jeans.

She felt the air move behind her.

Someone was standing in the doorway.

●●●

TWO HOURS, ANOTHER cup of coffee, and half a slice of cherry pie later, Alexa was able to politely leave.

Once outside, she tossed her keys to Josh. "Drive."

"What? Why?"

"Just drive now."

They both jumped into the car and pulled away.

"So are you gonna tell me what the hell you were doing going through Rick's stuff?" Josh demanded. "Damn, why do you always do weird crap like that? It's one thing to go through Mom's stuff, but Rick's? What were you thinking?"

Alexa waited for him to calm down before saying anything.

"So, what'd you take?" he asked.

"I went through his stuff because I don't trust him."

"You don't trust *him*? Hey, *you're* the one stealing crap."

Alexa pulled the envelope from her purse and scanned the whole letter. "It's a form DD214. A *dishonorable* discharge from the Marine Corps."

Josh hesitated, then said, "Yeah. So?"

"Josh, it's a discharge for assault and battery. That means he, like, pummeled somebody."

Josh was silent.

"And he had pictures of some woman half-naked in his drawer. Look."

She pulled everything out to show him. He slowed the car a little and glanced at the photo and the document in her lap.

After a moment he sped up again. "I'm sure there's an explanation."

"For which one? The assault and battery or him having a half-naked picture of some chick while he's dating our mother?"

"Both." But he sounded unsure.

"He was kicked out of the Marines for assault and battery, probably for beating some poor woman to a bloody stump. And let's not forget, he was a Marine sniper. He's killed people."

Josh snorted. "Yeah, he killed the enemy. And he did it to protect *you*. All of us."

"He has antidepressants in his bathroom. He's got issues."

Josh glanced at her, his eyes flashing. "You of all people should not be judging people for that. And I took antidepressants before. Almost everyone has. The whole *human race* has issues."

She could see he was getting angry with her. But why? Shouldn't he be *thanking* her for discovering this stuff so that they could warn their mother? "He's a creeper. And we need to tell her," Alexa said.

"So now all of a sudden you pretend to *care* about her? You're really a piece of work, you know that?"

Alexa bristled.

"Stop doing this, Alexa. Just stop already."

"But I'm just trying to protect her."

"No. You're not."

"I am, too!"

"You never think of anyone but yourself and you know it," Josh said, his voice raised. "And all that crap you said at dinner about running now and getting a job. You made all that up, too, didn't you?" His words stung. "No. It was true."

"Whatever," Josh said. They rode in silence for a couple of minutes. When Josh spoke again, his voice was calmer. "He's a nice guy. Mom likes him. I like him. And Mom really needs someone. She's lonely, and he makes her happy. Please, leave them alone." He turned onto the paved road, then glanced at her. "There's an explanation for everything."

CHAPTER 27

ON NEW YEAR'S Eve, Diane stood on the deck, staring out over the harbor. Soft, delicate flakes of snow fell as she gazed out at the docks and boats decorated with Christmas lights.

She was still haunted by the caller. Every time she thought about him, her stomach knotted up.

When she'd woken that morning, the pit in her stomach had grown into a sinkhole of worry. She was going to have to talk with Dr. Carol about it. She couldn't go on like this much longer.

An old Motown tune played inside. Ellie, who had flown in the previous night, had clearly taken charge of the music. Diane thought back on how differently Alexa had handled herself at Christmas dinner. For once she hadn't seemed angry. Uncomfortable, yes. Stiff and awkward, yes. But her attitude had definitely improved. She'd also said she'd taken up running again and had gotten a job. Diane hoped that was true.

Maybe Diane's tough love, although short-lived in many ways, had worked. Maybe Alexa was turning her life around. Maybe . . . she would be okay after all. Of course, she still hadn't apologized, but maybe that would come with a little more time. Right now that hardly seemed important. Her daughter's safety trumped everything. She would ask her again tonight to come stay at the house. Maybe this time she would say yes.

Diane scanned the yard for the ducks. She hadn't seen them for a long while.

She glanced back inside at the festive partygoers in her living room. She was having a small, intimate New Year's Eve gathering. Half a dozen friends Diane had made at the crisis center over the past year, including Mary Kate. She'd even invited Wayne, who was no doubt sharing all the latest hot gossip with everyone. Ellie was laughing with Diane's landlord, Mr. Davidson, and probably already knew him better than Diane did after a whole year of living here. That was how Ellie operated. Lance had been invited, but so far he hadn't shown up.

No matter how hard she tried to fake it, Diane just couldn't get into the party mood. In fact, she never would have thrown a New Year's Eve party, but Ellie had planned to be in town and had insisted.

She looked back at the dark harbor. Josh had driven to New Cambridge to pick up Alexa, because her car was acting up again, and should be back any minute. There was a good chance of another snowstorm, though, and she worried about them being on the road.

Diane suddenly heard oohs and aahs from the women behind her. She turned to see Rick walking in the front door, carrying a vase of red roses. She felt a smile forming on her face, and suddenly everything seemed a little better.

She walked over to Rick and took the flowers.

"Thank you."

"Happy new year, beautiful."

She noticed he was carrying something else in his other hand. "What's that?"

He held it out. It was a beef bone. "For Prince Biscuit," he said. "Where is he?"

Diane smiled, loving the fact that he'd also thought about Biscuit, who she'd grown attached to and was now pretty sure she'd be keeping. "Upstairs. My bedroom."

He looked around at the room. "And your kids?"

"I sent Josh to go pick up Alexa. She's having car trouble again." She heard a car pull into the driveway. "I bet that's them now."

❖❖❖

ALEXA WALKED INTO the foyer with her brother. She didn't want to come. She would have much preferred to stay buried under her covers watching a movie on her iPhone rather than be forced to hang around with people she didn't know. People she was certain she wouldn't like. But she didn't want to disappoint her mother.

Besides, she had big plans for tonight. She was going to apologize to her mother once and for all. She'd apologize to Josh, too . . . and tick the two most difficult (and important) things off her list.

She scanned the room and saw Ellie already staring at her. She knew Ellie thought she was going to behave like a brat, but she wasn't. She'd changed. Ellie would see.

She watched her mother make a beeline toward her and Josh. "Thanks for coming."

Again, a polite, hesitant smile.

Her mother was quickly whisked away by her landlord, who wanted to talk to her about something dull like furnaces or something.

After a few minutes Alexa withdrew from the crowd and hurried upstairs. She needed to take care of something before she did anything else. Her mother's bedroom door was shut. No doubt because the dog was in there. Alexa walked in and found Biscuit standing at the door, his tail wagging in anticipation. She knelt down and petted him, and he picked up a bone and offered it to her. Then he glanced past her into the hallway and whined.

"Trust me. You're much better off up here."

Biscuit looked unconvinced and kept staring past Alexa into the hallway.

Alexa wiped her palms on her jeans, and as she headed downstairs, she heard her mother and Josh in Josh's bedroom. Her mother was insisting he do a breathing treatment. He'd been coughing up a storm in his Jeep on the way here and really did need one. Knowing she'd have a few minutes unobserved, she headed straight for the kitchen, trying not to make eye contact with anyone.

The kitchen was empty. Thank God.

Privacy.

She had one more thing she needed to do before she could face the night.

On the island, she found something that would work. A bottle of vodka. She had planned to allow herself this little slip.

Just this one.

After all, tonight would be difficult . . . and she was certain even the strongest people in the world let themselves slip sometimes.

She wouldn't get drunk. She'd just have a little bit. Enough to take the edge off. Besides, who *didn't* drink or do pills on New Year's Eve, right?

She grabbed a red plastic cup and poured it half full with the vodka, then topped it off with Coke, then she went to the half bath. When she emerged from the bathroom several minutes later, half of her drink gone and the other half tucked inside the cabinet beneath the bathroom sink, she noticed a bunch of ladies and the creepy manager from the supermarket gathered around Rick. He was saying something, and they seemed to be hanging on his every word.

She watched him with the others and wondered why everyone seemed so taken with him. Even Josh. And even after what she had told him. It made her angry. Rick had gotten a dishonorable discharge and had that half-naked photo, but for some reason, *she* was the bad guy.

Fine. She would pretend to like him tonight.

But sometime after tonight, when the time was right, she was going to talk to her mother about what she'd found. Her mother needed to know. She would appreciate knowing.

She found a seat on the arm of the couch and listened to the conversation. Rick was saying something about living off the grid. He talked about gardening, preserving food, natural antibiotics. Everyone seemed so fascinated, but she found it boring. She noticed the supermarket manager looking at her. When their eyes met, he quickly looked away. She could tell he didn't like her, and she couldn't blame him. She *had* been rude that afternoon.

She refocused her attention on Rick and listened quietly, relaxing as the alcohol hit her bloodstream. When it did she felt a burst of joy and began to feel lighter, more confident. She let her eyes travel the room again and noticed her mother was watching her. Alexa smiled at her, and for once it was easy.

The buzz felt so good that after a few minutes she went back to the bathroom and drank down the rest of the drink so she could keep it going.

When she emerged this time, she felt *really* good. She walked back into the living room and leaned against a wall. Minutes later, voices sounded like they were under water, distant. She watched Josh coughing and her mother leading him upstairs. She heard the words "pneumonia" and "hospital" and "breathing treatment."

The room started to spin a little. Alexa blinked. She tried to focus on something close to her. Her eyes found a bouquet of roses on the counter. Needing to do something to keep her hands busy, she reached for the card and read it. It was from Rick to her mother.

To new beginnings, it read. *Love, Rick.*

Gross.

Feeling nauseous, she fumbled to put the card back and lurched forward. As she did, she bumped the vase and watched as it teetered off the edge of the counter. Everything seemed to happen in slow motion. She grabbed for the falling vase but couldn't catch it in time, and it crashed to the floor near her feet, the glass shattering loudly.

The party stopped.

Alexa stared down at the mess in front of her. She was too frightened to look up. When she finally did, her mother's face was pale.

"It was an accident," she said, feeling bile rise in her throat.

She saw something she didn't like in her mother's eyes.

Disbelief.

Her mother didn't believe her. Alexa felt herself bristle. Suddenly she didn't want to be there anymore. She turned to head up the stairs to get Josh and ask him to bring her home.

"Alexa?" she heard behind her. It was her mother. "You've been drinking, haven't you?"

She kept walking.

"Alexa," her mother said, her tone firm. "Where are you going?"

Alexa turned and looked at the floor. "To get Josh. I want to go home."

"Please. I'd like for you to stay here."

"I don't *want* to stay here," she said defiantly, "and *you* can't make me."

She wanted her mother to apologize for not believing her. But she didn't.

"Josh shouldn't be on the road in this weather," Rick said. "If she wants to go back to New Cambridge, I'll drive her."

Alexa glared at Rick, but when he walked into the foyer, she followed him. When she got to the front door, her mother appeared with her purse.

"I lost my balance!" Alexa shouted. She couldn't believe her mother didn't believe her. And she didn't want to control herself. Not now.

Her mother stood silently, her arms folded across her chest. There was disbelief in her eyes. Alexa's eyes traveled to Rick, and anger rose to the surface. "He's not as great as you think, Mom. Did you know he has a half-naked picture of some lady in his bedroom that he keeps locked up?" she said, slurring. "Did he tell you he got a dishonorable discharge from the military for assault and battery?"

Her mother's forehead creased. "Why, Alexa?" She shook her head. "Stop. Just stop."

"But I'm serious! I have no clue why you even trust him! He's a creeper, Mom. It's so obvious!"

Alexa looked past her mother and saw Ellie standing in the hallway, watching. She had a feeling she was going to regret saying these things tomorrow. But right now she didn't care.

Rick opened the door and freezing air came rushing in.

"Go home and sober up, Alexa," her mother said. "We'll discuss this later."

Alexa's heart sank. She wanted to reach out to her mother. To grab her arms and say, "But he is! Believe me, not him!" and "I need help! I don't know why I do these things. Why I am screwing up so badly tonight? I was trying so, *so* hard!"

But instead she found herself just glaring at her mother. Then she turned and followed Rick out into the dark, snowy night.

❖❖❖

A FEW MINUTES later Alexa sat in Rick's truck, her mind racing.

The truck was freezing. The cold leather seat pressed against her back, sucking heat from her body.

Rick flipped on the heater, but the loud fan only spit more cold air at her. He backed out of the driveway and began the trek to New Cambridge. She glanced sidelong at him and could see his jaw was set. Maybe from the cold but more likely from trying to hold in his anger.

But he had no right. He had inserted himself into her spot in her family. And as far as she was concerned, this whole mess was his fault.

Well, some of it, anyway.

She tried to piece together the moments that had just happened back at her mother's house, but it was all already a blur.

Tears pricked at her eyes. *Oh, God, please don't cry. Not in front of him.* But she couldn't control it. She burst into tears.

Rick didn't say a word. As far as she could tell, he never even looked at her. She wiped the tears from her eyes, then opened the glove compartment to grab some tissues.

But when the little light in the glove compartment blinked on, she didn't see any tissues. She just saw a pair of thick gloves and some rolled-up cord. Brushing those to the side, she saw something else. Something that glinted beneath the light.

A gun.

Her eyes widened. She'd never been so close to a gun before. Why did he have it in his truck?

"What do you need, Alexa?" Rick asked. His voice was deep, gravelly.

She didn't know how to answer him. She had completely forgotten what she was looking for.

He reached over and shut the glove compartment door. She stared straight ahead into the night. Fat snowflakes lit up in the headlights, rushing at the truck before being cast away by the windshield wipers. The motions were hypnotic, and Alexa could feel her eyes droop.

And a few miles from her apartment, against her wishes, she felt them close.

CHAPTER 28

HE WAS PULSING with need. Just one more, then he would stop. Things were going so well for him. Better than they ever had. Definitely better than he had expected them to. And he didn't want to risk everything.

But he needed this tonight.

And he would make it good.

Facebook had taken down Jill's photo one hour and thirteen minutes after he'd posted it. It took the media four more hours to report her murder . . . and an additional three hours after that to release her name. And it had only taken half that time for his high to dull and for him to feel completely on edge again.

He knew what this was called: escalation.

Snow had come down in a dense flurry earlier in the night and was now blanketing the ground. It glittered on the small patches of grass that bordered every apartment door.

Tonight he was visiting another girl . . . one he'd just started watching recently . . . Trish Underwood . . . and she would be his last.

She and a neighbor had just parked in front of their apartment complex. They'd gone to a New Year's Eve party and were now getting out of a vehicle. They lingered at the open trunk, pulling out color-ful gift bags. Then they laughed as they tried not to slip on the icy pavement.

The neighbor shouted bye and tottered into her apartment, and a few seconds later Trish went into her own.

Trish was another one of those girls who made those horrible kissy duck faces on social media. She was lucky—or maybe terribly unlucky—that she was just so damn beautiful and he was able to over-look it.

He waited a few minutes, then trudged across the pavement and knocked on her door. Almost instantly he heard her unlock the dead bolt. She opened the door. "You forget something?" she asked.

He lunged inside and clamped a gloved hand over her mouth and watched her eyes go wide. He twirled her so that her back was facing him, and as she squirmed, trying to free herself, he closed and locked the door. Then he headed to her bedroom.

"You know you shouldn't open the door for just anyone. Are you really that stupid?" he seethed.

The palm of his hand tickled as her breath crashed against his skin. She was saying something, and her head was moving side to side.

He saw flashes of red.

He whipped her around again, and now they were facing one another. In the dim light of her room, her big, beautiful blue eyes were pleading.

And she was trying to say something.

"Scream and you're dead," he whispered, loosening his grip on her mouth. He pinned her down on the bed and crawled on top of her.

She stared up at him in horror. "Please, no. Please . . . don't," she cried, tears glistening in her eyes. "I . . . I don't understand. What . . . why?"

Why?

"Because," he whispered, his teeth clenched, "it's all I can think about."

She shook her head, and more tears slipped down her face.

He continued, "And because if I don't do it, I'll lose my mind."

Her head went from side to side. "No, please. Don't. I'll do anything you want." She tried to smile, bat her eyes, to convince him. To use her young feminine wiles. The kind that led to creating horrible and unnecessary pain for others. She was trying to exploit his weakness. But sex *wasn't* his weakness. *"Anything—"*

The roaring was back. The screaming . . . slicing his mind.

The mind-bending commotion had come back so quickly he nearly screamed himself. Adrenaline flooding his body, he clamped his hand over her mouth again and reached for the cord. "But I don't want anything from you . . . but this."

CHAPTER 29

AS SOON AS she saw the van pull into the parking lot the next night, Alexa began to wonder if she had made a big mistake.

After all, she was pretty certain what Lance would want. She hadn't needed to read between the lines very much in his texts, and she'd played along.

But she'd said yes when he'd asked to hang out, because she had been incredibly lonely since the scene she'd made at her mother's New Year's Eve party the previous night. And she was scared that if she said no, he would stop texting her. Plus maybe, just maybe, it was a small way of getting her mother back . . . *for not believing her.*

Her mother had blown up her phone that morning with calls and texts, again wanting her to come stay at the house. She said she would turn her office into a bedroom for her to stay in until the guy was caught. When Alexa hadn't answered her messages, she'd shown up, knocking at the door again. Alexa had pretended not to be there. She wasn't ready to talk to her yet.

But she was also lonelier than she could remember ever being.

An hour after her mother left, Alexa had finally texted her.

ALEXA: Why does Rick have a gun and a roll of cord in his glove compartment?

Her mother had taken exactly four minutes to respond.

DIANE: Personal protection and to tie things down. He hauls a lot of stuff. Why, Alexa?

Alexa wasn't sure if her mother was burying her head in the sand or not . . . but the fact that Rick had those things did seem pretty creepy, especially in light of everything else. But right now she had to put all of that out of her mind, because Lance was there.

She hurriedly gave herself one final inspection in the full-length mirror. Her new jeans actually fit her well, and she liked the way her shirt hung. She'd even managed to whip her blonde hair into submission.

He knocked on the door and Alexa took a deep breath.

Here goes nothing.

She opened the door and was greeted by a big smile—and she was knocked off balance again by just how hot he was.

He stepped in and looked around. "Nice place."

He was just being polite, of course.

She closed the door behind him, in disbelief that a guy as good-looking as him was in her apartment . . . there to see *her*. She couldn't help but stare at him as he scanned the room. Then he turned to her and smiled, holding up the brown paper bag.

"I brought refreshments."

She smiled, hoping he meant alcohol.

"Come see." He walked to the kitchen table and started pulling out its contents: a two-liter bottle of Coca-Cola and a pint of Jack Daniel's. He looked at her, and a grin inched across her smooth face. "You won't tell your mom, right? I could get into *a lot* of trouble for this."

"Of course not." She grabbed two cups from a cabinet.

As he poured their drinks, Alexa caught the smell of whiskey on his breath. He'd already started drinking. She was a little surprised, considering he was a cop and he'd been drinking and driving.

She could hear his phone vibrating in his pocket, but he made no effort to check it. She thought again about what Trish had texted about him . . . about how weird he'd acted with her . . . but quickly pushed it aside when he handed her a drink, then held his own up high.

"To a great night with a good friend," he said.

A good friend?

She smiled and clinked cups with him. Then gulped down as much as she could swallow.

The whiskey made her feel warm; better and more relaxed.

"So . . . I think we should have some tunes. What do you think?" he asked.

"Yeah." She went back to her mattress and found her phone. She pulled up her Pandora app and started looking for a station. "What do you like?"

"Something mellow," he said softly, and she watched his eyes slide over her. It made her knees weak.

"Here. You find something," she said, feeling self-conscious.

He took the phone from her, and she took more sips of her drink. She still needed more to completely relax.

"How's mellow/acoustic/indie sound?" he asked.

"Great," she said, although she was pretty sure she would have said that no matter what he'd suggested.

A Ryan Adams song started playing.

Lance got up and refreshed her drink, filling it to the rim again, then he sank back into his seat. "So thank God the holidays are over, huh?"

She nodded.

He finished half his cup, then wiped his mouth with the back of his hand. "I don't care much for this time of year."

"Yeah, me either." Actually, she didn't care much for any time of year. It was all hard to stomach. He squirmed in his chair and made a face. "Sorry, but these chairs are uncomfortable. How about we go over there?" he said, pointing to her mattress.

She bit down hard on her lip. "Yeah . . . um, sure."

He walked over to the mattress, kicked off his shoes, and grabbed two pillows, using them to make a backrest. Then he scooted back on the mattress until he was sitting up against them. Alexa followed him and sat at the foot of the mattress, putting as much space between them as possible.

"My brother . . ." His voice trailed off as he took a sip of his drink. "He killed himself this time of year. Two years ago."

She remembered him mentioning something about that. She watched him fashion his hand into a makeshift gun, put it up to his head, and pretend to fire it—and the horrible memory of her father flashed into her mind.

"Sorry," she said. "I know that sucks."

"Understatement."

They talked for a little while. About his brother. All the reasons why the holidays sucked. When she got up to make another drink he placed his hand on her stomach to stop her, and his touch sent an electric jolt through her body so strong she could hardly breathe.

"Let me get it for you, beautiful."

Beautiful? Her breath quickened.

He made himself another drink and topped off hers again.

This time her drink was even stronger, which was fine with her. She drank it, and they both listened to the music without saying a word.

It was nice, not having to try to be clever. Or even normal. But even though she wasn't talking, the wheels in her head were still churning at breakneck speed. What was going to happen? Was he going to try anything? After all, he was sitting on her bed, so—

As if to answer her questions, Lance suddenly reached out and cupped the back of her head. Then he pulled her face close to his and kissed her.

Hard.

She'd never been kissed that way before. It felt good. Exciting. A flush of heat rushed through her body. He stared into her eyes as he caressed her hair. It felt good to have someone touching her. She couldn't remember the last time someone had, unless she counted the awkward hugs from her mother.

He slipped his hand across the small of her back and pulled her forward. Her breath hitched and another wave of electricity passed through her, this one even more intense. He kissed her harder, then he slid his hands beneath her shirt and yanked it over her head.

Cool air hit her stomach and back as his fingers fumbled with the clasp of her bra.

"I, uh . . ."

"It's okay. I just want to see you," he said, unhooking her bra and pulling it away from her body, exposing her breasts. She trembled, partly with excitement, partly out of fear. She felt self-conscious and exposed and unsure as he stared at her breasts. But when he smiled hungrily at what he saw, she felt something she'd never felt before . . . desired.

In one sudden movement, he laid her back on the bed, then crawled on top of her. He kissed her hard again.

And again.

And she kissed back.

This time just as hard. Her face stung from his rough kisses but she didn't care.

He began unbuckling her jeans.

❋❋❋

IT WAS OVER before it really even started. When Lance was done, he rolled off her and lay quietly. She noticed that they were no longer touching.

And she sensed he was *avoiding* touching her.

She pulled the covers up over her exposed skin and tried not to think about the burning between her legs. Her raw cheeks from where his face had scraped hers.

The silence was broken by the sound of his phone vibrating. He groaned and got up. He pulled his pants back on and slipped on his shirt without even looking at her.

"I've gotta run," he mumbled.

He pulled on his coat, grabbed his keys and his phone.

And before she could figure out what to say, or if she should even say anything at all, he was gone.

CHAPTER 30

DIANE LEFT FOR the crisis center ten minutes early. She was going to put in for a leave of absence before her shift. Josh had developed a respiratory infection and she needed to take care of him. Plus the thought of the creepy caller phoning in again was too much for her to handle. She wanted nothing more to do with him.

Again she wished Alexa had taken her up on the offer of staying at the house. Yes, she was upset with her for her behavior during the New Year's Eve party . . . and for going through Rick's things and making those claims, especially aloud, where some of her guests could hear. But Alexa's safety was far more of a priority for her . . . and she really wanted her home.

She'd spoken to Rick at length about Alexa's allegations. The dishonorable discharge. Photos of a scantily clad woman. And he'd explained everything to her satisfaction. He'd been given a dishonorable discharge due to an assault and battery charge filed by a superior. They'd both been drinking one night, and his commanding officer had become belligerent with him and a small group of buddies. After several minutes of being on the receiving end of some choice words, Rick said he lost his temper and hauled off and punched the guy. He said it would have been just another fight except the guy was his commanding officer. He said he was unceremoniously court-martialed and discharged for it. And that he wasn't proud of it. That it had been a mistake. Albeit a rather big one.

The photo was of an ex-girlfriend. He said it must have been tossed in with all of his other keepsake letters and documents when he moved in. The drawer stayed locked because it contained important documents. She'd also asked him about the gun and the cord that Alexa had seen in his glove box. Those were easily explained away, too. As far as Diane was concerned, all of his answers sounded honest. And she believed him.

Arriving at the crisis center, she parked and hurried to the door. When she was just a couple of feet away, it swung open and Lance walked out. "Hi, Diane," he said, his face spreading into a smile. He held the door open for her.

It had been weeks since she'd seen him. Her pulse quickened. "Lance. Can we talk?"

His smile dimmed. He glanced at his watch. "Sure. But we need to make it quick. What's up?" He stepped outside with her.

"Look. I know things have been a little strange between us. But I just wanted to apologize for the weirdness on Thanksgiving," she said, hugging herself against the brisk wind.

Lance looked confused. "Weirdness? I don't understand."

"You know, Thanksgiving night. Right before you left."

Lance laughed. "I don't know what you're talking about."

He wasn't making this easy.

And she didn't believe him.

"Sorry." His smile reappeared on his lips, but his eyes didn't seem to be smiling. "Look, I've got to go or else I'll be late for my shift at the station. I'll see you around, okay?"

He was blowing her off again, just as he had with the text messages. She was disappointed.

She watched him head across the parking lot. When she walked in, Mary Kate was on the phone. She gave Diane a wave, then started talking with whomever was on the other end of her line.

Diane decided to talk with her after her shift about the leave of absence, so she grabbed a cup of coffee. On her way to her cubicle, she noticed two police officers sitting at a table in the back.

What are they here for? she wondered. She glanced back at Mary Kate, wanting to ask, but she was still on the phone.

Not two minutes later, she took her first call. "This is Sally. How can I help you?"

There was no response.

"This is Sally. How can I help you?" she repeated.

Still nothing.

"It's okay. You're safe to talk."

She waited. Staring up at the clock on the wall, she prayed for a normal voice to respond. A desperate soul needing to reach out. A college student crying. An elderly woman at the end of her rope. Someone human. A normal call. *Anything* but that mechanized voice.

It was the mechanized voice. "I hurt people. I don't want to, but I can't stop. I did . . . for a while. But I don't think I can anymore. My brain isn't working right anymore. I'm. Having. A. Crisis."

The hairs rose on the back of Diane's neck. Then something caught her attention. Distorted but somewhat familiar music coming from the other end of the line.

But what was it?

She strained to hear but couldn't make out the words. But she knew she'd heard it before. She felt a stab of pain in her head. The onset of a rare headache.

"Hello?" she said, holding her head. "Are you still there?"

The line went dead.

CHAPTER 31

THE NEXT AFTERNOON Diane snapped her laptop closed and thought back to what the anonymous caller had said. As soon as he'd hung up, the two police officers she'd seen earlier brought her into the back office, and not five minutes later, Detective Chavez arrived and there were more questions. He also told her they'd gotten a recording of the call.

Diane went to the living room and stoked the wood in the fireplace. It cast a warm, orange light over the cabin. If it weren't for a low-grade sense of disquiet buzzing in her head, being at Rick's would feel cozy and safe. But something new was bothering her, had been since her shift at the crisis center. She had the sense that her mind was rejecting something. But what?

Rick was in the shower and Josh was sprawled out on the couch, wearing headphones, taking a catnap. His respiratory infection had flared for a couple of days, but fortunately had gotten much better. She watched him sleep, happy that he felt completely at home at Rick's. It was a good thing, considering they were seeking shelter because of another power outage at her place.

She was also pleased to see that he was wearing his wrist brace. In fact, he'd been taking extra-good care of himself this past week, slowing down when his body asked him to . . . and also taking a little break from his gaming, which had always been such a difficult thing for him to do.

Biscuit seemed at home, too, lying on the kitchen floor, gnawing a new beef bone, again compliments of Rick. Over the weeks, Rick had managed to gain Biscuit's trust, and next to Diane, Rick had become the dog's favorite human. She'd noticed that Rick seemed to have that kind of effect on almost everyone he met. It was easy for others to warm up to him.

Diane picked up her Kindle. She'd just downloaded a thriller she'd been wanting to read. It had been a long while since she'd been able to simply sit and enjoy a book. But then she remembered she needed to change over the laundry.

She went to the laundry room and pulled a load of Rick's laundry from the dryer. He'd been nice enough to let them stay at his house and use his washing machine, so when she'd finished her own laundry, she'd decided to help him with his.

After she loaded the machine, she noticed something had fallen on the floor between the washer and dryer. A folded piece of paper. She picked it up and unfolded it. It was an address.

512 Oakton Ave

She went into the kitchen and tossed the paper on the kitchen counter in case it was important. As she was walking back into the laundry room, her phone rang. She didn't recognize the number but answered anyway, thinking it might be the power company.

"Hello, Ms. Christie? This is Happy Maids."

The housekeeping service she'd used.

"You used our services one time in early December."

"Yes. I remember."

"I'm Stan Vinditti, the manager. Our receptionist just found an incident report from that visit that had been misplaced."

Diane was confused. "Incident report?"

"Yes ma'am. And, um, this one is a little different than the usual ones." Stan cleared his throat and spoke in a professional tone, as if he was reading the report verbatim. "'Happy Maids representative Maggie Lucent reported finding a dead duck in the backyard of the property while taking out the trash. Unsure what to do and thinking it might be a family pet because she'd seen you feeding it, she placed it in a plastic bag and hung it on a hook by the back door with a note. She didn't want an animal to find it first and . . . well, you know."

A wave of relief rushed over Diane as Stan continued.

Good news for once.

So the duck's death hadn't been anything malicious. She remembered again how the female duck had been moving slower than usual on Thanksgiving morning. Maybe she'd simply been sick and died of natural causes.

"We make a point of following up on incident reports. I apologize it's taken me so long," Stan continued. "I hope Miss Lucent's actions were acceptable to you."

Diane was only half listening. "Huh? Oh. Yes. I'm glad you called. I wasn't sure what happened. I found the duck but there was no note. But it had been windy, so it probably just blew away. Please tell Miss Lucent thank you for me."

She hung up, feeling lighter. Amid the murders, the anonymous phone calls, and everything with Alexa, at least she could rest a little easier knowing what had happened to the duck.

Rick emerged from the bathroom in a clean T-shirt and shorts, toweling his damp hair.

"Who was that?" he asked.

Diane shook her head and told him what she'd just heard.

"Well, I'm happy to hear the good news," he said.

"Me, too."

He gave her a big hug and kissed her. As always, a shiver of pleasure passed through her.

Josh sat up and thumbed something into his phone. Without looking up, he said, "I hate to break up the lovefest, but can I go to Bruce's house?"

Diane frowned. "Are you sure you don't need more rest?"

"Mom. I've been resting all week."

She examined him, noting that the dark circles beneath his eyes hadn't gone away. But that would probably still take a day or two.

"I feel fine, Mom. I promise. And if I start feeling bad again, I'll come back. Scout's honor."

"Sure. Go ahead." Diane had barely gotten the words out before he was headed for the door.

"I think we cramp his style," Rick joked. But he didn't look well, either. His face was tight, and he looked tired.

"Are you okay?"

"Another migraine's coming on," Rick said, grimacing. "If you don't mind, I need to lie down for a little while."

Rick had been having a lot of migraines lately, and resting in the dark was about the only thing that soothed them.

"Sure. Can I get you anything?"

"Thanks, but I'm pretty sure I've got everything I need," he said and kissed her on the forehead.

❋❋❋

DIANE WAS POWERING up her Kindle when she heard Rick's bedroom door click shut softly. She started reading chapter one of her new thriller, then felt herself drifting off. The next thing she knew, she opened her eyes, relaxed but disoriented.

Had she really fallen asleep? She looked at her watch. Yes—at least thirty minutes had gone by. She yawned and stretched and with bleary eyes glanced at the images moving on the television screen. When she processed what she was seeing, she felt the color drain from her face.

It was a photo of Alexa's friend Trish. Below the picture was the caption: THIRD STUDENT FOUND SLAIN.

"Oh my God!" She fumbled with the remote, looking for the volume. She turned it up as the footage cut to a reporter in front of an apartment building.

"The latest victim, Trish Underwood, was found in her apartment last night, just a few blocks from the University of New Cambridge . . ." As the reporter continued, Diane flashed back to Trish showing up at the house just a few days earlier and giving Rick the story she'd written.

The news report cut to the reporter again, who was on the scene—and something behind her caught Diane's eye.

It was a street sign that read Oakton Avenue.

Oakton Avenue? Where had she seen—

She felt her body stiffen.

Her adrenaline pumping, she went to the kitchen and unfolded the slip of paper on the kitchen counter.

512 Oakton Ave

It was the same street.

Could 512 Oakton Avenue be Trish's address? Certainly not, right? She stared at the handwriting. It didn't look like Rick's. It didn't look like any handwriting that she knew.

And she always noticed handwriting.

Could Trish have given it to Rick when she stopped by? If so, why? But then she remembered how Trish had flirted with Lance. Obviously she was open to dating older guys. Had Trish made a pass at Rick? If so, why hadn't he hadn't told her? Could he have planned to see the girl behind her back?

Her thoughts were a tangle—and she wasn't sure which was greater: her shock at finding out Trish was murdered or discovering that Rick might have her address.

Holy crap, what's going on?

She stared at the address and realized her hand was shaking. Her imagination was getting the best of her. She should just ask him. Besides, Oakton was a big street. But not much of it was residential. Just a piece of it near the college. So it was probably just a coincidence.

Something is very wrong.

Suddenly Rick slipped his arms around her waist. She pulled away from him and turned around. "Did Trish give you her address?" she asked, trying to keep her voice even, casual.

Rick frowned, his eyes bleary from sleep. "I'm sorry?"

"Trish. Alexa's friend. Did she give you her address?" she asked, her words coming out way too fast.

He seemed to be processing the question. "Back up. The young lady who came to your door the other day?"

"Yes."

"Her address? No, why?"

Diane showed him the slip of paper with the address on it and watched his face. His expression remained neutral. "Where did you get that?"

CHAPTER 32

A FEW MINUTES later, Diane was flying down the dirt road, heading away from Rick's cabin. She had left suddenly, stopping only to scoop up Biscuit on her way out.

It had started snowing again, and she struggled to see the road, which was already disappearing under a blanket of white powder. As she sped around a corner, she hit a patch of ice, and her minivan slid sideways, narrowly missing a tree.

Biscuit whined in the backseat.

She stopped to catch her breath and pulled the address out of her pocket. Determined to prove to herself that it was just a coincidence, and that the address written down did *not* belong to Trish's new apartment, she threw the minivan in gear again and sped toward New Cambridge.

Thankfully, the main road was much less treacherous, the snowplows having already made one pass to clear it.

Her mind was racing as fast as her car.

She was breathless. And thoroughly confused.

Rick suddenly seemed like a stranger, and she realized again how little she knew about him. She thought about how he hated talking about his past. And she now wondered if his story about the dishonorable discharge had been true. The photo of some half-naked lady. The gun and cord that Alexa had seen. The fact that the murders coincided with his move into town.

Maybe Alexa had been right after all.

Maybe he couldn't be trusted.

Or had Alexa's claims tainted her perspective, which was leading her on a wild goose chase?

Stop jumping to conclusions. There's an explanation for this, she told herself. *He's given you no reason to assume the worst.*

He's been so kind to you. He's very attentive and considerate. Absolutely, completely normal. But she, more than anyone, knew that didn't mean anything. She remembered Lance's words at Thanksgiving. Words that she knew were true:

"They're masters at blending in. Hell, most of the time they seem more normal than you or me."

Her phone rang. It was Rick. It was the third time he'd called since she'd left so abruptly. She ignored his call. As she entered New Cambridge, she double-checked the address again.

She saw the sign for Oakton Avenue and turned left. She scanned the houses for their street numbers: 1025. She needed 512. Five blocks away. As she turned onto the road, she slowed down. Up ahead there was a cluster of police cars and news vans.

Her hair stood on end.

They were on the 500 block.

She parked on the side of the road and walked as close as she could until a police officer stopped her from getting closer.

An apartment building was cordoned off with police tape. Various uniformed police officers, detectives, and medical examiners walked in and out of it. She craned her neck, trying to see the address above the door.

Then she saw it: 512.

She looked down in disbelief at the address written on the paper.

It was the same. She'd been right. It was Trish's address.

CHAPTER 33

PARALYSIS WAS SETTING in. The ability to think of nothing but his addiction. Things were not going as planned, and his self-control, at least what was left of it, had vanished into thin air.

He was a mess as he stood in the supermarket, watching Sarah Turner shop the frozen aisle. A bead of sweat dripped off his brow and onto his cheek.

He wiped it away and pulled his hoodie even tighter around his face. He'd been out driving when she'd Facebooked a photo of two cereals a few minutes ago, asking her friends which one she should choose: Froot Loops or Cap'n Crunch. She'd even tagged the photo so everyone could see exactly where she was shopping: Brookmart.

She was beautiful but insipid.

He watched her, for the first time fully aware that he would never be able to stop. This was his lot in life, no matter if he liked it or not—and it frightened the hell out of him.

When their eyes met, she grinned at him and stood a little straighter. Her boobs suddenly looked bigger, her behind stuck out a little more. He knew she wouldn't smile—wouldn't go through the trouble of trying to look good for him—if she had any idea of the horror festering inside his head.

Any idea of what he wanted to do to her.

She'd posted a makeup tutorial on YouTube just three days ago, and he'd watched it at least fifty times so far. He'd memorized her full, pink lips. Long, dark, gorgeous hair. Light, wide-set eyes that looked vacant when she spoke.

She grabbed a frozen meal, then walked the opposite way. A few minutes later, she glanced at him again. This time when they gazed at one another, he glimpsed something untrusting in her eyes. Like he was starting to worry her a little, freak her out.

Good girl. Self-preservation.

Give me a reason to let you live. You can do it.

She glanced back in his direction as she paid the cashier, then hurried into the parking lot.

He started to follow her but froze when he heard a voice behind him. "Hey! I thought that was you!"

It was Wayne. The store manager.

He cursed Wayne from beneath his breath. And in the distance he watched her slip into her car.

He turned around and smiled. "Hey, Wayne. How's it going?"

●●●

TEN MINUTES LATER he pounded on the door to Sarah Turner's apartment. "Fog Harbor Police! There's been a bomb threat! We're evacuating this building."

He heard footsteps, then the sound of a chain lock sliding. Sarah opened the door, her eyes wide, a fork in her hand. "Oh my God! What's—?"

They stared into one another's eyes for a quick moment, then he rushed her, sending the fork flying into the air.

215

There was a dull rumble in his head as they struggled. Then the rumble turned into a roar. In one smooth movement, he slammed the door behind them and clamped a hand against her mouth. He lifted her off her feet and carried her toward her bedroom. She bit at the palm of his hands, kicked wildly at his shins. But he couldn't feel anything but adrenaline, heat. When an elbow rammed into his solar plexus, he dropped her to the kitchen floor. She yelped as her body crumpled to the green linoleum.

Straddling her, he covered her mouth again and watched her struggle for air. As her chest jerkily rose and fell, he anticipated the high to come, to envelop him, to wipe away the anger, the hatred. Quiet the horrible noises.

As he waited, he observed the panic in her eyes, the tears spilling down her face.

He waited some more.

But the high didn't come. Instead the screaming returned, and now it was a deafening roar. Every muscle in his stomach clenched so tightly he could barely breathe.

Nauseous, he gagged twice—then shook his head. He didn't want to do this. No, not anymore.

He released the girl's arms and climbed off her.

They stared at one another, both surprised by what he'd just done. He could hardly believe it. It was almost like someone else was driving . . . had made the decision for him.

Like *finally* something else had intervened.

But he didn't have the desire to grab her again. He just wanted her to go. Her eyes, wide as saucers, darted to the apartment door.

His breathing grew heavy, agitated. "Get out of here," he barked.

"Wha-at?"

"Go! I'm serious. Fucking run before I change my mind!"

She scrambled to her feet, then she froze at the edge of the kitchen and the living room and stared at him like a deer in headlights.

"I won't tell you again. *Go!*"

He watched as she bolted out the front door of her apartment. His thoughts traveled to Diane, and his heart raced. In all the time he'd been watching the girls, and making plans for them, he'd been watching her, too.

He'd contemplated telling her, *tried* telling her, but hadn't been able to.

He wasn't sure how the rest of it would unravel, but he knew this was the end for him—at least how he knew it.

He wondered how much Diane would hurt when she found out.

How much she would grow to hate him.

And he was sure he didn't want to know.

***

HER MIND SPINNING with confusion, Diane made her way back to her minivan. At best, Rick had accepted Trish's address and had kept it secret from her. At worst, he could be responsible for the girls' deaths. What she knew for sure, though, was that he wasn't the honest, upstanding guy she'd thought he was.

She needed to sort this out. And she wanted her kids close by until she did.

Running on adrenaline and instinct, she drove to Alexa's apartment, but her car wasn't there. She dialed Alexa's number, but there was no answer. She texted her. She was out somewhere. Maybe at that job of hers. *Where did she say she worked?*

She called Josh. He answered on the third ring.

"Hello?"

"Josh. Where are you?"

"Um, at Bruce's. Remember?"

"I need you to drive home."

"But Mom, we just started a new game," Josh protested. "Bruce got it today and—"

Diane interrupted him. "I don't care. I need you home. *Not* the cabin. Our house. Do you understand?"

"Do we have power?"

"Yes," Diane lied, having no idea. Anything to get him home.

"Can I at least eat here first?"

"No. I'll make you something. Just come home."

Josh didn't reply for a second. When he did, his voice was different. Concerned. "Mom? Is everything okay? You're acting weird. What's going on?"

"Just come home!" she said firmly. She tossed her phone on the passenger seat and raced toward her house.

❖❖❖

TEN MINUTES LATER Diane burst through her front door and slammed it behind her. She flicked the switch on the wall and the lights came on.

Thank God. Mr. Davidson must have fixed the fuse box.

Functioning on autopilot, she went into the kitchen and started making a sandwich for Josh. Her thoughts went back to the address that was stuffed in her pocket.

Where did she go from here?

She had no clue.

Obviously Rick wasn't going to tell her the truth. But was it really possible he could have killed Trish? Any of the three girls?

She needed to talk to someone, but who?

Maybe Lance could give her a better perspective. Help her think it through. She needed a voice of reason. But the question was . . . would he talk to her? She called him, but there was no answer. She texted him that she might know something about Trish's murder. There—that would surely get him to call back, whether he was upset with her or not.

Josh walked in just as she'd plated the sandwich. He still looked tired. But he also looked worried now. "What's going on?" he asked again. "You're kind of scaring—"

Before he could finish his sentence, he broke into a coughing fit. He covered his mouth and turned away until it was over.

"When did you start coughing again?"

"I don't know. I guess an hour or so ago. But, Mom, tell me what's going—"

More rapid-fire coughs. "You need a breathing treatment," she said.

When he was done coughing, he grunted, "Fine, but you're still not answering my question."

She didn't know *how* to answer his question.

"Mom?"

She filled the teakettle with water before placing it on the burner. She needed to stay busy. Stay preoccupied. Get his treatment ready for him. Unravel her knotted thoughts slowly, one by one. That was the only way she'd be able to think more clearly.

"Seriously. Are you going to tell me what this is about?"

"I just needed you home."

"No, you didn't. Something happened." He was becoming more frightened.

She sat down across from him. "Okay. You remember Alexa's friend from Thanksgiving? Trish?"

Josh nodded. "Yeah."

"She was murdered."

Josh's eyes widened. "What? You're kidding me."

"No."

He sat down next to her. "Whoa. No freaking way. Same guy?"

"I'd imagine so."

"Trish . . . man, that sucks." He shook his head. "Does Alexa know?"

Diane's phone chimed and they both looked at it, seeing Rick's name show up on the screen. Diane silenced the call, then turned back to Josh.

"I don't know if she knows. I drove by her apartment but she wasn't home. And she hasn't returned my calls. Do you remember where she said she works?"

"Some restaurant, but I don't know which one."

"Can you text her for me? You might have better luck."

"Yeah, sure." Josh pulled out his phone and texted Alexa. They both waited for a response, but there was none.

"She'll get back to me. She always does," Josh said.

A few minutes later, Diane grabbed Josh's nebulizer. There was only one packet of saline left. She always used two. Dammit, she would have to go to Brookmart. But later. Not now. As she prepared a treatment for Josh, she realized her teeth had begun chattering. She poured a glass of wine, then she brought the nebulizer to her son. For once he took it without protest.

Watching him inhale the first few breaths of medicine, she realized her heart was racing. If she didn't calm down soon, her mind was going to snap.

CHAPTER 34

THE STEAM FROM Diane's hot bath filled the air and fogged up the mirrors. She lit a lavender-scented candle to help relax her mind. The arteries in her neck pulsed. Tears of frustration rolled down her cheeks. This entire time she hadn't wanted to think negatively about Rick. She had wanted to think he was a good guy. But that had been irresponsible. Even more irresponsible was giving him access to her kids.

But what exactly had Rick done? Had plans to cheat on her? Had he *already* cheated on her?

Or, much more frightening, was he a murderer?

No way. No way, because she would've known—*sensed*—something wasn't right with him, right? And she hadn't had that sense at all.

Of course she knew people only saw what they wanted to see. That they created the stories to justify what they wanted and what they didn't want. But she hadn't done that with Rick, had she?

Had she?

She thought back on everything she knew about him: Former Marine sniper with two tours in Iraq, a dishonorable discharge, possible PTSD, a cabinet full of weapons. He studied survivalism. Dreamed of living *off the grid*. He carried a gun in his glove compartment . . . and a roll of paracord. He'd shown up in town fairly recently and was renting the cabin—so like Wayne had said, he was basically a drifter. For some reason he'd had Trish's address written down—and now Trish was dead.

It didn't paint a good picture.

Biscuit sat at the foot of the tub, watching her. When their eyes met, he let out a little whine as though he knew something was wrong. Diane reached out and patted his head. He closed his eyes, enjoying the affection.

If Lance texted back, should she ask him to check Rick out? Just in case? Or should she just call Detective Chavez?

Her mind screamed at her to just get it over with and contact *some-one*. But her heart was arguing that it couldn't possibly be true. That there was a logical explanation. For it all.

With her free hand, she texted Alexa again.

DIANE: Call me. It's an emergency.

After all, if Rick had anything to do with Trish's murder . . . *any* of the murders, she didn't want her daughter alone.

As she waited for a response, Biscuit's tail suddenly stood at attention. He walked to the bathroom door and began to whine.

Is someone at the front door?

Diane turned off the stream of water. She listened carefully and heard voices downstairs.

She jumped out of the bath, quickly toweled off, and pulled on her robe. At the top of the steps, she could hear the voices more clearly.

Her heart sped up and she hurried down the stairs. Josh sat on the couch, playing his video game. Sitting next to him was Rick.

"Total decimation!" Josh said to the screen. "Sorry to have to do it to you, dude. I had no other choice."

Rick's eyes flickered to hers. He smiled.

Blood pounded in Diane's ears.

Standing next to her on the staircase, Biscuit growled again, this time baring his teeth. He was picking up on her stress and trying to protect her.

Rick stood up. "Diane . . . I needed to talk to you."

"Josh. Upstairs." Diane was firm, her voice clipped and controlled.

"But why?"

"Now, Josh."

Josh tossed his game controller on the couch. He walked past Diane and went up the stairs.

When he was out of sight, Diane turned back to Rick.

"I need you to leave."

He looked confused. "What's going on?"

"Please. Just leave. I'll . . . explain later." She led him to the front door.

But he didn't budge. "What did I do? Did I say something? Whatever it was, I'm sorry. And I can explain."

Her heart was hammering so hard she could barely think. "Just go," she said more loudly.

Rick dragged his hand through his hair. He walked to the front door. *Don't let him fool you*, Diane told herself. *Get him out of the house. Now.*

She opened the front door.

"If it's something I've done," he said, "I'll make it right. Just talk to me."

She searched his face, but she couldn't read him. If she was making a mistake . . . *Shit.* "Please. Just go."

Rick reached out and placed his hand on the back of Diane's neck, something she usually loved. But this time his hand felt heavy and dangerous—and she shrank away.

He dragged his hand down his face, and she noticed a vein throbbing in his neck.

"Is it something Alexa said?" he asked. "Because if it is, I can probably—"

"It wasn't Alexa," Diane said. "Please, though. Go."

Rick suddenly turned as though he'd heard a sound. Then a voice called out from behind them. "Everything okay?"

It was Mr. Davidson. Her landlord was standing on the sidewalk, his inspection binder in his hands.

"Yes. Everything's fine, thanks," she said, hoping to God that what she was saying was true.

"I rewired the circuit box," Mr. Davidson said. "Hopefully that will take care of the problem with all the outages. Everything's working okay now, right?"

"Yes, it is. Thank you."

"Okay. Sorry again about all these outages. Hopefully the problem is fixed now."

"Thanks, Mr. Davidson."

"You two have a good night."

"You, too."

Rick watched the man for a long moment as he walked off, then turned back to her. "Diane . . ."

"Go."

Rick's eyes darkened. He was getting frustrated. Or maybe angry. "Okay, if you insist. But if you feel like letting me in on what's going on, you know where to find me."

Diane massaged her temples as she watched him get into his truck and slowly back out of the drive. She wasn't sure how to feel. She was numb but far from calm.

She stepped back inside and dead bolted the door shut.

Against whom . . . she wasn't yet certain.

❖❖❖

AS THE AFTERNOON wore on, Diane watched Josh's coughing spells intensify. His respiratory infection was flaring up again. He needed more breathing treatments, but she was out of saline.

Instructing him to stay in bed with the doors locked and to not open the door for anyone—*any*one—she hurried to Brookmart.

She rushed in through the double doors of the store, blinking against the bright fluorescent lights, and hoped Wayne wasn't working. She needed to just get in and out and was in no mood for conversation.

She scanned the supermarket as she headed to the section that carried saline. So far, so good. Wayne was nowhere in sight.

She quickly picked up a box of saline and hurried toward the register. But when she was halfway down the frozen aisle, she saw a familiar face.

Josh's friend Bruce. He was with his mother. Diane had met her almost a year ago, the first time Josh had asked to hang out at their house.

When she was just a few feet away from them, Bruce looked up, and their eyes locked.

"Hi, Bruce," she said, deciding to be polite and stop for a few seconds.

"Hi, Mrs. Christie."

She smiled at his mother. "Remember me? Diane Christie. Josh's mom?"

"Yes, of course. How are you?"

"I'm good." She looked at Bruce. "Did you guys have fun today?" she asked. "Playing a new game?"

Bruce looked confused. "New game? Today?"

"Yes, this afternoon. Didn't Josh come over?"

Bruce didn't answer.

His mother spoke for him. "No, Josh wasn't at the house. We've been out all day."

Diane's heart dropped like an anvil in her chest. If Josh hadn't been at Bruce's, where had he been? And why had he lied? She fought to keep the semblance of a smile on her face.

Bruce's mother said, "I haven't seen Josh in a while. Since before Christmas. In fact, I just asked Bruce the other day where he's been."

Diane peered at Bruce. He shrugged his shoulders. It was apparent he didn't want to say anything to get his friend into trouble.

Diane spoke gently to Bruce, not wanting to spook the boy. "You haven't seen him at all? You guys haven't met at another friend's house, maybe?"

Bruce glanced at his mom, then back at Diane, and shook his head. "I haven't seen him at all during winter break."

CHAPTER 35

DIANE'S MIND FLICKERED with confusion as she drove home from the supermarket. She drove slowly—fifteen miles below the speed limit—to give herself time to think. As she got closer to home, she slowed to a crawl.

Why had Josh been lying?

Drugs? Was he was smoking pot again? Or . . . using something stronger? Or . . . maybe he was running with a crowd she wouldn't approve of.

It might also be a girl. Again, one she wouldn't approve of.

But then an idea loomed. One that sliced through her heart. She tried to push it away, but the more she fought it, the bigger a shadow it cast across her mind.

No.

As she shifted into park, her phone rang. She checked it. It was Lance, finally returning her call. She ignored it.

She opened her car door and stepped out into the bitter air. At any other time her entire body would have tensed against the severe cold. But right now she could barely feel it.

Dead leaves scuttled past her tennis shoes as she crunched her way up the gravel drive to the front door.

"Diane?"

It was Mr. Davidson. "I didn't want to say anything while your gentleman friend was here, but it's about that ladder," he said.

She blinked at him. "Ladder?"

"Yes, on the side of the house," he said, pointing to the side where Josh's bedroom was. I noticed it while we were working on the fuses . . . and I'm afraid that's a safety issue that we—"

"Can we discuss this another time?" Diane said as she made her way to her front door.

"Diane? Are you all right? Is there something I can—"

She walked into the house and closed the door.

❖❖❖

JOSH WAS IN the living room, curled up on the couch, sleeping soundly.

She watched him for a moment, then, Biscuit at her feet, she headed up the stairs. When she got there, his bedroom door was wide open.

Moonlight shone through the window, illuminating the room's contents in a cool blue hue. She could see his license plate collection hanging on the wall above his bed.

From his doorway, her eyes swept the room. She took in the gaming and movie posters on the walls. The oversized beanbag chair sat in front of his flat-screen television. An incredibly lifelike military man was floating on a spaceship on the television screen. He was moving his mouth, but the sound was muted.

She took a couple of steps into the room. Biscuit whined from the doorway as she scanned his bookshelf and noticed two books she had written. She had no idea he'd read her work. Why hadn't she known or even asked?

She'd always been so sensitive about giving him his space; a sense of privacy. When she brought clean clothes into his room, she always just hung them up or set them on his bureau and walked out of the room—always making a point to get in and out quickly.

She'd been like that with both of her kids.

Why? Why had she found that so important to do?

Next to his bed was a small metal desk. And on the desk were his goldfish bowl, iMac, and iPhone. She noticed that he'd rehomed his goldfish into a much larger bowl. She stared at the fish, and it faced her, seeming to stare right back. She reached for Josh's iPhone. She needed to know what was going on. She swiped it and saw that there was no passcode to unlock its contents.

A good sign. Her shoulders relaxed a little. If he hadn't bothered to passcode-protect it, there must be nothing to hide. She would just see who he had been texting. See if there were any clues there that would help explain why he'd been lying to her.

But before she could open his texting app, another app on his home screen caught her eye. It was called Voice Changer Deluxe. A cold flush spread through her body.

Her hands shaking, she sat on his bed and launched the app. She whispered into the microphone, and the voice that came out of the phone's speaker sounded similar to the voice that had spoken to her at the crisis center.

No. No, no, no.

She struggled for another explanation.

Her hands trembled as she opened up the main drawer to his desk. She found a baggie of marijuana, rolling papers, two joints, and a bottle of Febreze. She rummaged in the back of the drawer and pulled out three dog tags, each with the name of one of their past family dogs—Miffer, Angelica, and Toddy—engraved on it. But the dogs had all run away, so how did he have their tags?

Her mind hit a wall.

Her pulse sprinting, she opened his iMac. She powered it on, and an image quickly filled the screen.

She recoiled in horror. It was an image of a young woman with long, dark hair holding an infant. She'd seen the photo many times before. It had been left with Josh when his biological mother had abandoned him at the hospital. It was a photo of him with his mother, a young, attractive brunette. For a few years he'd kept it next to his bedside table but then had suddenly put it away.

But that's not what shocked Diane. It was what had been done to the picture. A big red X had been drawn across the woman's face. The word WHORE was written below it.

It was vile. How could Josh have done that? He never seemed angry about anything. It was so out of character. Then it hit her: the victims had been young and pretty with long brunette hair and light eyes . . . dead ringers for his biological mother.

Had he killed the girls out of anger? A sense of retribution? No, impossible. Not Josh.

Her thoughts tumbled and spun inside her head as she clicked on the computer's web browser and checked his search history. It was filled with mostly Facebook pages and Twitter accounts he had visited. She clicked one of the Facebook pages and gasped out loud.

It was a memorial page created for Jill MacDonald. She clicked on another page of his history. It was Trish's Facebook page. She clicked on another page of his history. And another. And another. They all linked to Facebook profiles, pictures of the different murder victims or Facebook pages set up in memory of them. He'd also visited their personal pages and Instagram accounts. His last visit online was timestamped just thirty minutes ago.

Her eyes floated back to the television screen: the military man floating silently on a spaceship. He was staring straight at her, his mouth moving. She found Josh's remote and turned up the volume.

"Recruit . . . we're having a crisis. We are relying on you to pick up the slack . . . when your training is complete . . . you will have become a machine . . . a work of complete perfection . . . the killing kind."

The words, the music behind it. It's what she'd heard in the background at the crisis center.

She rushed to Josh's bedroom window and threw it open. A blast of icy air blew in. She leaned out the window and vomited on the side of the house and the steel ladder that led from his bedroom window to the yard below. The world shimmered in front of her eyes.

Biscuit growled from somewhere behind her.

Then she heard Josh's voice. "Mom?"

She turned around. Josh was standing in the doorway, his dark hair disheveled. He stared at her, then his eyes flickered to his desk, his iMac. She saw his breath catch. "I . . . I . . ." He floundered and fell silent. The blood drained from his face. "I'm so sorry."

Before she was able to form any words, he whipped around and tore down the stairs.

She ran after him. "Josh!"

He was bounding down the stairs two at a time. Biscuit barked frantically from the landing above.

"Josh, don't! Stop!"

She watched helplessly as her son threw open the front door and vanished into the night.

CHAPTER 36

ALEXA FELT STUPID and used. She should have known better. Why would she think Lance, of all people, would actually care about her? What he'd done—practically shunning her after they'd had sex—it hurt . . . really badly.

She wished she could talk to someone about it—so someone could help her make sense of it all. She found herself wishing again that things between her and her mother were back to normal.

But who was she kidding?

She couldn't talk to her mother about this kind of thing. They didn't have that kind of relationship. She wished they were closer. And she now realized why they weren't. It was *her* fault.

She lay in her bed, wishing she could do so much over. She was falling backward when she needed to be moving forward. She was also starving, and there was no food in the apartment, so she was going to have to go out.

She prayed her car would start. But it was unlikely. The piece of crap hadn't started since the day before New Year's Eve.

But maybe it just needed to sit for a few days. Maybe the vehicle had just been tired, too. Maybe a miracle had happened and something good would finally happen for her. God knew she was due. Wasn't she?

Yeah, probably not.

She bundled up and stepped outside. As she trudged along the two blocks to where her car was parked, she kept reliving Lance's visit. She felt sick about it. Did he just screw her because she was available? Or was it the alcohol? Did he even like her at all? Or had screwing her and leaving been his game plan all along?

She realized a part of her was hoping that Lance would text her again. That he'd say he was sorry for just leaving like that. Say he wanted to come back and hang out with her again.

She rolled her eyes at her own thoughts.

Stop being such a loser. He used *you. He's* not *coming back.*

When she was just two yards from her car, she heard snow crunch from somewhere behind her.

Panic rose in her throat.

Was someone following her? She didn't have the pepper spray she'd promised her mother she'd always carry. She hadn't carried it in months.

Her pulse drumming in her throat, she walked faster. She could still hear the footsteps. And whoever it was, they were getting closer.

She spun around, her keys held out in front of her like a knife. And then she took a step back in disbelief.

It was Rick. And he looked really serious. Maybe even pissed.

Oh my God. What's he doing here?

"I'd like to talk to you," he said sternly.

Alexa walked backward, still moving in the direction of her car. She glanced around, in case she needed help. But no one else was in sight.

She thought of the things she'd seen in the glove box. His dishonorable discharge. Could he really be dangerous? Or was he only just a prick? She couldn't be sure.

"Alexa, stop."

"No. Why would I want to talk to you about anything?" she said defiantly, still walking backward.

"I don't care if you want to or not. This is about your mother, and it's important."

"My mother?"

"Yes."

Was he trying to trick her?

He took a step closer, and Alexa took a bigger step back.

"I want to know what you—?" Before he could finish, his phone rang. He yanked it out of his coat pocket and looked at the screen. Then he motioned for her to hold on, and he took the call.

"Hi," he said into the phone. He listened to the person on the other end, and his face tightened. "What? No, I'm not there. Where? What? Slow down."

She decided to run while she had the chance. She whirled around and bolted to her car. But just before reaching it, her feet flew out from beneath her and she smacked hard to the icy ground.

Her head pounding, she quickly scrambled to get back up. When she reached the car, she jerked the door handle up, opened the door, and jumped in. Then she locked the doors and tried to start it.

But the engine didn't even turn over.

Crap!

She looked up to see if he was chasing her. But he was exactly where she'd left him, pacing and on the phone. He wasn't chasing her at all.

She'd definitely overreacted.

She opened her car door.

"Diane, slow down," she heard him saying. "I can't understand you. Are you saying you think Josh is at the cabin?"

It was her mother on the phone? What . . . was going on?

She climbed out of the car and listened to his conversation.

"Okay. I'll be right there."

Rick started jogging away from her.

Alexa frowned, then found herself chasing after him. "What's going on? Is my mom okay?" she asked.

Rick didn't answer. He opened the door to his truck, fired it up, and threw it into gear. But before he could back out of his parking spot, Alexa reached his driver's-side window and pounded on the glass.

"What's going on?" she yelled.

He lowered the window. "Your mother is looking for Josh. She's worried."

"Why?"

"Either get in or step away from the truck," he shouted.

Alexa was surprised to hear the next words coming out of her mouth. "Okay, wait. I'm coming with you."

❖❖❖

ALEXA HELD ON to the dash with one hand and the passenger grip bar with the other. Rick was driving like a bat out of hell, weaving in and out of traffic on the highway toward Fog Harbor.

Was this all a trick to lure her out to the middle of nowhere? Had the phone call been fake? Had she just gotten in the truck of someone dangerous?

She wanted to call her mother. To call Josh. But her phone had been dead for two days now and her charger had crapped out.

She stared at Rick and realized he looked legitimately concerned. "What's going on?" she asked, out of breath.

"I'm not sure," he said, his eyes on the road ahead of him.

CHAPTER 37

DIANE SHOT UP the dirt road leading to Rick's hunting cabin, her palms damp against the steering wheel, her mind in a state of utter shock and disbelief.

She tried to conjure up Josh's behavior over the last several months. He'd been sleeping a lot, he'd often been late for school, had been having anxiety attacks and smoking dope, had become almost obsessed with his video games.

Escapism . . . anxiety . . . depression.

All classical signs of a mental downward spiral.

Or simply being a teenager.

"Goddammit!" she shouted, watching the wipers in front of her flail across her windshield.

There has to be some kind of explanation.

But . . . what if there isn't? she asked herself, panic tearing at her insides.

When the hunting camp came into view, she was relieved to see Josh's Jeep parked outside. She jumped out and ran to the door as quickly as she could without sliding across the icy ground.

Inside, the cabin was pitch-black and very still. She could smell the skunky-sweet odor of marijuana and the remnants of grilled meat. But there was no sign of her son.

"Josh?"

She crept into the living room and flipped on a light. The room was empty. Then she saw the gun cabinet. The glass panel had been smashed. Shards of glass littered the floor. Her veins turned icy. "No . . ." she murmured.

"Josh?" she called out again. "It's Mom. Answer me, please. Josh?"

She heard footfalls from behind the door to Rick's kill room. Instinct told her to approach slowly.

"Josh? Hon? I just want to talk to you, okay?"

She pushed the door open gently and was met with a cloud of pot smoke. A faint glow from two naked lightbulbs hanging from the ceiling afforded her just enough light to see.

There was no furniture other than a large piece of plywood centered over two sawhorses, creating a makeshift table. Along one wall was a large utility sink. Wall-to-wall wood shelves held tools and cleaning supplies. Two meat hooks hung from the ceiling.

Her attention went back to the makeshift table . . . and she saw a 9 mm lying on top of it. She felt a crawl of horror in her stomach.

"Josh?" she whispered.

She saw movement in the flickering shadows along the back wall. She stepped in the room to get a closer look. Josh was cowering in a corner, curled into himself, holding his knees close to his body. He was rocking back and forth, a joint burning on the concrete floor beside him.

Her heart was in her throat as she walked toward him. "Oh, Josh," she said.

"You shouldn't have come here," he said, his face slick with tears. "Please. Go."

The chill deepened in her bones. Seeing him like this made it all seem all the more real. "No. I'm not leaving you," she said softly.

He stared at her, his eyes sunken deeper in their sockets—and there was a darkness behind them that she'd never noticed before.

"I'm so sorry, Mom," he said between sobs. "I'm so, so sorry. I didn't want to do those things. I didn't. But I couldn't stop."

What? Is he confessing? No. Oh my God. NO.

Gooseflesh dimpled her arms, and she shook her head.

Feeling the dull throb of a headache coming on, she studied him and realized he looked younger to her. Smaller. More vulnerable. She remembered back to when he was little, his bare feet slapping the floor as he used to gleefully fly from room to room. At least on the days he was feeling well. She remembered the crisp rustle his diaper made when he walked. The light, clean scent of his baby shampoo.

He started having a coughing fit, and her instinct was to comfort him. "It's going to be okay," she heard herself say.

He stared at her, his face red. "No. Mom. It's not going to be okay. It's never going to be okay. Don't you understand?"

He's right. It isn't.

It was a stupid thing to say.

She opened her mouth, then closed it. She needed to ask, although she wasn't sure she could handle the answer. "Josh, did you . . . kill those girls? Trish?"

Josh glanced away. He closed his eyes and nodded. "You know I did."

His words ripped the air out of her. A part of her had still hoped she had it wrong. That he was covering for someone. That he was just role-playing. That he—

Her world narrowed. Thinking about him hurting those girls made her flesh crawl. The air in the room seemed to turn colder, and she blocked out the visuals that tried to flash in her head.

She just couldn't go there.

Not now.

Maybe never.

She'd been so terribly concerned about Alexa for seeming so lost, angry, troubled, and closed off. For being disrespectful, stealing. Only for Josh to be—

She realized the horrible irony of it all and almost wanted to laugh. Almost.

"Why? Why would you want to do those things?"

"I don't know," he said quietly. "I'm just really screwed up, Mom. I've always been."

She remembered once how she'd seen him rip a praying mantis in two when he was about eight, and just stare at it. She'd felt so sick at the time, but Frank had told her that it was just something little boys did. Another time she thought she'd caught him trying to drown a lizard, but he'd explained that he was only trying to give it a bath. She felt the hairs at the nape of her neck stand at attention. Had he been having urges to hurt innocent life all these years?

His ears were red. "I didn't want to do it anymore. I tried to tell you a few times . . . because I wanted help . . . but I ended up not having the balls."

They sat in silence. Diane thought of the robotic voice. What he had said. She closed her eyes tight and could hear both of their hearts hammering.

"Doing those things. Mom, it's the only way to stop it."

"Stop what?"

Josh gritted his teeth. "The noises . . . all the screaming in my head."

"Whose screaming?"

Josh stared into her eyes, his tears glistening. "Mine, Mom. Mine."

Bile crept up her throat again and she barely managed to push it down.

The room began to spin and she felt her knees weaken. Then she was on the concrete floor and Josh was sitting next to her, gripping her hand.

She reached out to hold him and felt his moist T-shirt clinging to his body, his ribs shaking beneath her touch.

His breaths were raspy. He needed a breathing treatment.

"Why am I like this? Am I crazy? Evil, even?" Josh asked, his words muffled.

She didn't have an answer.

"I'm so sorry, Mom. Christ, I'm so sorry I let you down. After all you've done for me." His voice broke. "I'm so sorry I hurt them. I wish I hadn't hurt them."

She wasn't sure what to say.

"Do you hate me?" he asked.

She wasn't sure. She didn't think so.

He broke away from her grasp and stared into her eyes. Again, she flashed back to memories of him as a baby. As a little boy. How sweet and funny and considerate and helpful he'd always been.

How kind he'd seemed.

Never in a million years would she have thought . . . *this*.

"Mom?"

He wanted an answer.

"No," she finally said, tears spilling from her eyes. "I love you. Even if I hate some of the things you've . . . *done*, you will always be my son—and I will always love you."

He leaned toward her and kissed her cheek.

"We'll get through this," she whispered.

He shook his head. "Don't say that." But she could see his countenance had shifted. He even smiled. But the smile looked strange; tired. Different than normal.

Bile shot up her throat again, and this time she couldn't stop it. Covering her mouth, she scrambled to her feet and rushed to the sink, barely getting there in time. She vomited long and hard into the cool steel bowl, until there was nothing left, questions still tumbling around in her mind.

Could I have stopped this somehow? Could it be genetic? Could his brain possibly have been affected by his autoimmune condition and no one was aware of it?

The questions just kept coming—and they made her feel sicker.

When she knew nothing else was going to come up, she wiped her mouth and tried to catch her breath. She turned on the faucet and splashed cold water in her mouth, on her face. Then she looked up and scanned the room.

"Josh?" She turned in a circle, searching for him.

But he wasn't there. "Josh!"

Panicked, she headed for the door that led to the living room, but something on the table stopped her in her tracks.

An envelope.

She froze and picked it up. The word "Mom" was scrawled messily on the front. But it wasn't Josh's handwriting. It was the same handwriting she'd seen at Rick's. Trish's address.

The brace, she realized.

He'd written the address while wearing the brace that he wore for his carpal tunnel and repetitive thumb injuries. That's why she hadn't recognized his handwriting. Rick hadn't written down the address at all. Trish, either.

Josh had.

The slip of paper that had fallen between the washer and dryer units must have come from her own laundry, not Rick's. Then she noticed something else . . . and her breath hitched. The 9 mm was missing.

POP! The loud noise came from somewhere outside. The sound of a—

"Josh!"

CHAPTER 38

ALEXA AND RICK blasted up the dirt road toward the cabin, scattering dirty snow, rocks, and other debris in their wake. The way Rick was driving, completely unafraid to draw attention to himself, convinced her this wasn't a trick at all.

Something was going on.

Something serious that involved her brother.

She could see Rick's cabin ahead. Josh's Jeep and her mother's minivan were out front. As they drew closer, she could see someone standing in the driveway.

It was Josh.

He disappeared into darkness just as Rick slammed the truck to a stop. But before Alexa could get the truck door open, she saw a flash and heard a loud *BANG!*

A gunshot.

What the hell?

"Josh!" she screamed and jumped out the truck. She began to sprint toward the driveway, but Rick grabbed her and held her back.

"Let me go!" she shouted and struggled to get out of his grasp. "It's Josh! Let me go!"

"Stop," Rick said. "That was a gunshot."

"But he's my brother!"

Rick wrestled her down to the snowy ground. "Wait. Here," he ordered. Then he jogged over to where she'd last seen Josh.

But there was no way she was going to wait. She sprang to her feet and ran after him. A moment later she was right behind Rick.

"Jesus Christ," he said, running his hand through his hair. She stepped beside him and saw Josh lying on the concrete driveway next to a gun, his head in a pool of blood.

She screamed.

Rick pulled her back and turned her head into his shoulder, shielding her eyes. Alexa sobbed so hard she couldn't catch her breath. *What the hell? Why? Why would Josh——?*

It made no sense.

Her heart pounded so hard against her rib cage she thought it might stop.

❖❖❖

DIANE HEARD A bloodcurdling scream outside the cabin.

Alexa!

Her pulse racing, she ran for the door but tripped on an uneven piece of flooring and landed with a thud. Wincing, she scrambled back to her feet.

Finally she got to the door that led to the living room and swung it open. When she reached the front yard, she saw Rick kneeling in the driveway. Alexa was sitting next to him, wailing.

She saw Josh's feet. His new tennis shoes he'd gotten for Christmas. As she drew closer, she noticed blood splatter on them. Vines of ice wound up her neck.

"No!"

She started toward him, but Rick caught her in his arms and held her back. "Josh!" she screamed. "Oh my God, Josh! My baby!" Her stomach roiling, she bucked and kicked, trying to break free from Rick's grasp.

Rick released her. Diane stumbled forward, toward her son. She fell to her knees beside him and stared at the blood pooled around his head.

A chill started at her head and spread all the way to her toes. She grabbed his hand and squeezed. "Please. Oh my God!"

This can't be happening! She reached to touch his head, then drew her hand back. "No! My baby," she moaned. "No. No. Noooo!"

CHAPTER 39

THE SILENCE WAS thick in Rick's truck. Alexa was riding with him as they followed the ambulance to the hospital. Her whole body felt numb, and she couldn't shake the image of Josh from her mind. Or of her mother curled up in anguish next to him. The way she'd screamed—like a wild animal. The horror on her face. Her weeping.

She could hardly believe everything that had just happened.

But it had. Hadn't it?

It seemed to have come out of nowhere. *Why would Josh try to kill himself? He always seemed to have it so together. What could have been so bad?*

She remembered him smoking the pot.

He'd been stressed.

She remembered their argument. How difficult he'd said it had been to be him growing up. How terrifying it had been for him, being so sick as a child. How his biological mother had just thrown him away like a piece of trash. How angry he'd been at their father for committing suicide . . . abandoning their family. Abandoning *him*.

She recalled the letter she'd seen her mother drop on the driveway when she'd run toward Josh. She pulled it out of her pocket and unfolded it.

Mom,

I wanted to tell you so many times. I just couldn't. I didn't want to disappoint you or cause you more pain. I love you more than I ever loved anything. But I couldn't stop. I really needed to do those things. To hurt them. Like really hurt them . . . even though part of me really didn't want to. It started back in New Jersey. Hell, it started way before then, because as long as I can remember I've always had the urge to do bad things. Terrible things. I've always been different than everyone else. Way different.

I know that's not what you want to hear, but I have to tell you the truth. I always wanted to tell you because I thought maybe then you could stop me. But I was a coward, so I hoped you would figure it out on your own. But you didn't. You couldn't.

Please don't hate me. Please don't let Alexa hate me either. And please, don't take any more crap off her. Hopefully she'll come around so you can at least have one child you can be proud of.

I'm so sorry I couldn't be better for you.

Love,
Josh

Alexa's hands trembled. What did he mean, he needed to hurt them?

Hurt who?

And what could he not stop doing?

She remembered her mother's screams again. It had ripped at her heart. She'd never seen her mother in pain like that. Suddenly she was a million times more sorry than ever for being so selfish. For being such a bad daughter. For not being a better sister. Maybe if she hadn't been such an asshole, Josh wouldn't have done this to himself. Maybe if she hadn't been such an asshole, her family would actually be happy.

More than anything right now, she wanted to be with her mom and her brother. She wanted things to just go back to normal. To go back to *better* than normal. If she could take back all the horribly selfish things she'd done, she would. She would do anything to make things right.

I really needed to do those things. To hurt them. Like really hurt them . . .

What the hell does——? Then a thought flashed into her mind and her mouth went dry.

No.

It didn't make sense. Not Josh. He'd been the golden child. The perfect one.

Josh? No. No way. No freaking way.

She reread the letter, barely able to breathe.

CHAPTER 40

DIANE SAT IN a straight-back chair next to her son's hospital bed and held his cool, limp hand as he slept. The room was cold, sterile, quiet, except for the steady beeping of the machines that were connected to Josh's body.

They'd been at the hospital now for thirty-six hours; the first twelve she'd spent in a waiting room while her son was in surgery and then recovery.

Alexa was also there. She lay curled into a ball on a blue vinyl couch against the far wall. When a nurse peeked in the room, Diane didn't even bother looking up.

"Mrs. Christie?" she said, her voice sounding far away. "The neurologist, Dr. Renshaw, will be in here in a few minutes to check on your son."

But Diane didn't have the energy to respond. She stared at her son, his face partially covered in bandages. Was her love for him so strong that she had refused to see what was happening right in front of her face? Had she somehow known something was going on but looked the other way?

She thought of the timing. Had Frank's suicide been a catalyst? Or had Josh murdered before?

She stared at Josh . . . her sweet little boy. But he wasn't so little anymore, was he? And he obviously wasn't as sweet as she'd always thought him to be. Her stomach roiled.

Oh, God. People are going to think he's a monster.

Is he?

She flinched.

Yes. She imagined he was.

Her throat was on fire from all the screaming. The crying. She'd cried for the victims. For the families that had lost their children. She cried for Josh. And for losing him.

Even if he survived this, they would take him away.

She didn't think there was a death penalty in Massachusetts, but they'd lock him away for life for sure. And who would care for him when his health was on the decline? When he needed his breathing treatments?

In hindsight, all the puzzle pieces snapped together in her mind. The dogs that had gone missing over the years. How much Josh had grieved afterward. Hurting them had been traumatic for him, hadn't it?

But he still did it . . . and had continued to.

She thought again to his lifeboat questions. Now she realized every question he asked had been a test. He was wrestling with his guilt. Wanting assurance that she'd love him—even though he'd done such heinous, *abominable* things. Wanting to know if she would be there to rescue him.

She still felt a burning need to protect him. But from what?

Justice?

But that was insane. She knew that wasn't right—and that it wasn't something she could do. This time she couldn't protect him. He was in too much trouble.

Her phone chimed, snapping her tired mind back to the present. Lance.

He had texted and called her at least four times over the past several hours because she'd left that text message saying she thought she might know something about Trish's murder.

That seemed a lifetime ago . . . when she thought that Rick could be behind the killings. Right now she was wishing he had been. It was incredible how much had changed in the span of a few hours.

"Who keeps calling you?" Alexa asked from the back of the room.

Diane glanced at her daughter. "Lance."

Her daughter seemed to recoil at the name.

Diane poised her thumbs on the phone's keyboard. She wasn't sure what to say. She was going to have to turn Josh in before they came looking for him. It was the right thing to do, and she knew the consequences for harboring a murderer, and she couldn't afford to go to jail. Alexa needed a parent.

But she hadn't been able to do it yet—because once she did, she knew there was no going back. She also worried his medical care might suffer once they knew he was a killer. She would tell the detectives, but not until she was ready. She wanted to spend a little more time with her son while people *didn't* know, because once they did, the place would become a circus.

She finally decided what to type.

DIANE: *No need to worry. Everything's fine. Just a silly idea that makes no sense anymore.*

She set the phone in her lap.

Please. Just let it go and don't respond.

But a thought bubble immediately popped up, indicating he was already responding. Then the text came through:

LANCE: Are you sure?

Before she could type a response, the phone rang. He was call-ing her.

"Shit."

She took a deep breath, mustering all her energy to sound nor-mal. "Hi."

"So what is the information you have?" Lance asked.

"Like I said, it was silly."

"I'd still like to hear it."

Her voice was thick. "No."

A nurse's voice crackled over the hospital PA, and Diane quickly covered her phone.

"Where are you?" Lance asked.

"At home."

Then she remembered gunshot injuries were reported to the police. Had Lance seen the report? If he hadn't, he would soon.

"Now's not a good time to talk," she said.

"Okay," Lance replied. "I guess I'll see you at the crisis center?"

"Yeah," she lied.

"Oh, and Diane. Since I know you're so interested in the case, I thought you'd like to know that they have a witness now." Lance continued, "He attacked a girl yesterday in Fog Harbor. He did it in broad daylight, and apparently he let her go. We're having a sketch composite made right now. We also pulled surveillance video from Brookmart, and we're working on an IP address. We're getting really close."

Diane hung up.

Josh had attacked someone else? Then let her go?

"Mrs. Christie."

Diane turned toward the voice. It was a blond doctor she'd seen earlier that morning. "I'm Doctor Renshaw, chief neurologist," he said. His face was soft, his eyes kind. "I'm here to check on your son again."

Diane nodded.

She stood and stepped back to give the doctor room. He walked past her and checked the readouts on the machines, then examined Josh.

Diane stared at the floor, feeling completely powerless. "Mrs. Christie? Are you okay?"

Okay? What an ignorant question. No. She wasn't okay.

She felt a hand on the small of her back. Rick had returned with a cup of coffee for her. His face was drawn, concerned.

He tried to guide her back to the chair, but she didn't want to sit. She looked at the doctor, preparing for the worst. Would her son survive? Earlier this morning they said that there was more than a 50 percent chance.

Dr. Renshaw took a seat in a chair and rolled it closer to her. "Your son's a lucky boy," Dr. Renshaw said.

Lucky? The word sounded ludicrous.

"Only about ten percent of gunshots to the head are nonfatal. And out of that percentage, most never fully recover."

She stared at him, waiting for him to go on.

"The trajectory of the shot shattered his jaw, which deflected the bullet. It did do some damage to the frontal lobe, but from what we can see so far, it seems to be localized. His jaw can be rebuilt.

"The frontal lobe damage could result in some changes in personality, but hopefully nothing too radical. Time will tell." He paused to let what he'd said sink in. "But like I said, he's lucky. If the angle had differed by just one degree in either direction, he would have likely suffered enough brain damage to leave him completely unresponsive."

Diane nodded, knowing she'd need time to process the full meaning of what the neurologist was telling her.

"He's not out of the woods quite yet, of course. But barring any complications, things are looking pretty good for him. Please pardon the pun, but your son literally dodged a bullet."

Rick laid a hand on her shoulder. She heard Alexa sobbing behind her.

The neurologist went on. "When he recovers, it's very likely he may suffer from ongoing seizures, the severity of which we can't know at this point. But if that happens, there are always antiepilepsy drugs. The best thing you can do for him right now is to take good care of yourself. He's going to need you, and when he does, you need to be ready."

Diane's mind raced as the neurologist left the room. The prognosis hadn't looked nearly as good just a few hours ago. Josh had shot himself in the head. How could it be possible that he might be okay?

Rick unpacked a sandwich from a paper bag he had brought back from the hospital cafeteria. "You need to eat," he insisted. "You can't just keep getting by on coffee. Like the doctor said, you need to take care of yourself."

Diane looked at the sandwich and shook her head.

"Maybe something else? I can get you whatever you like," Rick offered. He slid a chair next to hers. The metal legs screeched as they dragged across the linoleum floor. Rick took one of her hands and held it. His touch felt good, warm. She had been pouring out all of her energy; it was nice to have a little poured back in.

She considered telling Rick what Josh had done, but then decided to wait . . . just a few more minutes. She needed just a few more to muster the energy. To wrap her head around the fact that Josh had done these terrible things, if that was even possible.

"Mom, we need to talk," Alexa said, appearing in front of her. Alexa knelt down, her gray-blue eyes urgent. She looked and sounded softer than usual. Even loving, maybe. Definitely frightened. "It's important." Her eyes slid over to Rick. "And it's private. Sorry."

Rick nodded and squeezed Diane's hand. He stood. "I'll be right outside," he said and left the room.

Alexa took a seat in his chair and leaned forward. "I know, Mom," she whispered.

Diane stared at her. "Know what?"

"I know," she said. "About Josh. I found his note." She pulled the folded piece of paper from her pocket. Diane stared at it in disbelief. She took it from her daughter.

"Does anyone know yet? Besides you and me?" Alexa asked. "The police? Rick?"

Diane shook her head. "I don't think so. Why?"

Alexa lowered her voice even more until her words were barely a whisper . . . and she said something that raised the hairs on Diane's neck.

❈❈❈

A FEW MINUTES later Alexa followed her mother to a bathroom in the corridor. Her mother stared at her in surprise . . . or horror . . . or maybe both.

"Why would you even suggest such a thing, Alexa? You have your whole life ahead of you."

Alexa was crying so hard everything looked blurry. She could hardly see her mother's beautiful but pained face—or the bathroom stalls behind her. "No. You don't understand. I . . . have nothing but you and Josh. I realize that now. You're my world and I just could never see it. I'm flunking school. I'm depressed and scared and I can't figure it all out myself. I've been trying, and I just can't. Not alone. I need you. And I think maybe you need me, too."

She looked deep into her mother's eyes. "Let me help. Please. I want to. For me as much as for you and Josh."

She watched her mother stare at her. The shock that had been on her face had transformed into something different. Was she considering it?

"We can't let them take him," Alexa continued. "They'll try to kill him if we don't get him out of here. Give him the death penalty—or lock him up forever. We can help him. You used to be an emergency room nurse. And you've been taking care of his medical needs for years, so you'll know what to do. It's *Josh*. We can't let that happen," Alexa pleaded. "That would kill you. You know that. That would kill you, and I'd . . ." She paused and sniffed. "I'd never get you back. I'd lose you both."

Her mother peered down at the scuffed tiles and seemed to think about it all. Alexa grabbed her slight hands and squeezed them. They were cool beneath her touch.

Please say yes, she thought. *Please.* Because she knew that if Josh was taken away, there'd be no family any longer. No second chance to be who she wanted to be. Selfless, a good person. A good daughter. A good sister. This was her opportunity to finally be there for her mother and brother—and in a meaningful way.

A big way.

She was more than willing to trade in her miserable life for one that could be better. To get a clean slate somewhere where no one knew them. But her mother needed to be on board. To say yes.

When her mother looked up again, her eyes looked different, maybe a little wild. "It's been years since I've been a nurse," she whispered. "I . . . This is insane."

She's thinking about it.

Her mother stared at her. "And Josh . . . you know he killed those girls. You know that, right? He's a killer, Alexa," she said, her eyes glistening with tears. "I still haven't completely—"

"But he's still Josh," Alexa said. "We can help him stop. We can. I *know* we can."

Her mother gazed at her.

"But we can't wait long," Alexa said. She wiped at her cheeks with the back of her hand. "Lance . . . he's been blowing up my phone. I think he knows something, Mom. This isn't going to stay secret much longer. We have to make a decision, and fast."

●●●

AT NOON, DIANE had been nodding off at Josh's bedside when she felt someone nudge her.

"Diane," Rick said. He smiled and pointed to Josh. "He's awake. I'll go get the nurse."

Diane stood up and grasped Josh's hand a little tighter. "Josh, honey. I'm right here."

He blinked at her as though confused. "You're in the hospital, and you're okay." She squeezed his hand again. "You're going to be okay."

His eyes welled up with tears. They streamed toward his ears and were soaked up by his bandages. He shook his head.

"Are you in pain?" she asked.

He didn't say anything. He just stared at her.

Tears filled her own eyes to the point she could no longer see.

A nurse walked into the room. Then Dr. Langley, the intensivist on duty. Diane backed away from the bed so that the doctor could get close. He leaned over Josh and smiled. "Well, hello there, Josh," he said gently. "I'm Dr. Langley. You probably don't remember me, do you?" He smiled again. "I just need to check a few things, okay?"

He held his index finger up to Josh's face. "I want you to follow my finger. Can you do that for me?"

He moved his finger back and forth in front of Josh's eyes. Diane watched as one eye tracked perfectly. But the other only moved in spurts.

"That's good. They're both moving. One eye's a bit lazy, but that can be expected. Can you say something for me, Josh?"

Josh's mouth opened a little, but only a wheezing sound came out. The doctor patted his shoulder. "It's all right. Don't force it."

The doctor spent another few minutes with him, checked the machines for reports on other vitals, then asked Diane to join him in the hallway. Diane hesitated, not wanting to leave her son. But Alexa appeared next to her and took hold of his hand. "I'll stay with him."

Out in the hallway, Dr. Langley set Josh's medical file in a hanging basket on the door. "I understand Dr. Renshaw's been by and spoken to you?"

Diane nodded.

"He's doing so much better than expected, Mrs. Christie. You have quite the fighter there. That boy really wants another chance at life," Dr. Langley said. "I've ordered another CT scan for the morning, as well as a consult with plastic surgery. If all looks like it does today and Dr. Renshaw or Dr. Pendi don't have different recommendations, your son will be moved to a general ward as soon as tomorrow night." He smiled and patted her on the shoulder. "But as of now I feel fairly comfortable telling you that I think your son's going to be okay."

After the doctor left, Diane held Josh's hand until he fell back to sleep. Then she gestured for Alexa and led her back to the lobby bathroom.

Her blood was electric. "Are you sure about this?" she asked her daughter.

"I've never been more sure about anything," Alexa answered.

"Because what you're talking about is very wrong."

"It doesn't feel wrong."

Diane had to agree—and she found it shocking that she did. Maybe she wasn't thinking straight—she was almost certain she wasn't—but this was Josh they were talking about. And although he had admitted he'd killed those girls, she was having trouble reconciling the sweet, charming boy she'd known for sixteen years with the abominable killer she'd read about. Having trouble believing there was no hope that he could change.

She wished she had more time to sort out her thoughts. To really think this through. But time wasn't a luxury they had right now.

"You'll be risking your future."

Alexa's eyes filled with tears. "But I don't have a future . . . not the way I'm going . . . and not without you guys."

Am I seriously considering this? she asked herself as she stared at her daughter, every inch of her skin prickling. "If they catch us—" she started.

"They won't."

"They could . . . and they might."

"They won't."

❖❖❖

AT ELEVEN O'CLOCK that night, just as the nurse left after giving Josh his medication and checking his head bandage, Diane and Alexa set their plan into motion.

Diane asked Rick if he would pick up her sleeping pills at the house so she could finally get some rest, knowing that the round trip would take him at least thirty minutes. He'd already brought her a bag with a couple of changes of fresh clothes.

"Anything else I can get you from the house?"

"I don't think so," she said, blood thrumming at her temples. She felt horrible for misleading him. She was going to miss him, but she couldn't let herself think about that now.

He turned to Alexa. "You need anything?"

She shook her head.

Rick kissed Diane on the cheek. "Okay. I'll get going. I'll be back as soon as I can. If you think of anything else, text me, okay?"

Adrenaline charged through Diane's bloodstream as she watched Rick leave. As soon as he was far enough down the hallway, she closed the door to Josh's hospital room and pulled the curtain around his bed.

They were going to have to work fast.

Diane opened the narrow closet next to the windows and grabbed a pair of nurse's scrubs she'd had Alexa pick up from a medical supply store in New Cambridge earlier in the day. As she changed, Alexa readied the wheelchair she had discreetly wheeled into the room that afternoon.

Earlier, Diane had wired money into Alexa's college account, and Alexa had gone to the bank and withdrawn the funds before heading to her mother's home to pack for everyone and pick up any medical supplies they were going to need. The only thing Alexa hadn't been able to get ahold of was antibiotics. That worried her.

Three hours after she'd talked with him, Lance had begun blowing up Diane's phone again. His latest text read:

LANCE: Urgent. We have to talk. Where are you? CALL ME.

Diane used the electronic control to lift Josh's bed. He opened his eyes, but they were glazed over. The sedatives he had received were in full effect.

She squeezed his hand and hoped beyond hope she was doing the right thing. "We're going to move you, and it might hurt a little."

Josh closed his eyes, and Diane turned to Alexa. "We have to do this quick, all right?"

Alexa nodded. She moved close to Josh, and Diane started removing the stickers from Josh's chest and stomach and sticking them to Alexa. Then she removed the cannula that was supplementing Josh's oxygen intake. Diane looked at Alexa, who nodded back. It was all or nothing now.

Diane and Alexa lifted Josh into the wheelchair, being careful that his IV stayed intact. He needed to keep that as long as he could. It would be the last dose of antibiotics he would be getting. At least for the foreseeable future.

She unhooked the medicine bag from the IV post and set it into the nylon pocket in the back of the wheelchair. Then she layered blankets on her son's lap and wheeled him to the door. She looked back at Alexa, who was getting herself situated in the hospital bed.

"Three minutes," Diane said, barely able to breathe. "Then get the hell out of here."

Alexa nodded. "Okay."

●●●

DIANE WHEELED HER son into the bright corridor. She took the long way around to avoid passing the nurses' station and in less than a minute made it to the elevator.

Waiting for the elevator seemed to take an eternity. She kept jabbing the down button with her index finger. She placed a hand on Josh's shoulder, and he reached up and touched it, which gave her more confidence to do this and do it right.

Finally the elevator arrived and she wheeled him inside.

When the elevator door opened to the first floor, she pushed him down the hallway toward the lobby entrance. Up ahead she saw a security guard walking the hallway, heading in her direction. Her heart pounded in her throat, but she tried to look as casual as possible. As she passed the guard, she smiled, hoping her nervousness wasn't apparent. The guard smiled back and continued on his way.

As the twin doors to the outside of the hospital opened up, she breathed in a sigh of relief and picked up her pace. Luckily it was late enough that there were few people around. She was able to easily wheel her son out of the hospital and toward the parking lot, where Alexa had left the minivan.

The cold air was still as she raced the wheelchair toward her minivan. She threw open the back hatch, and Biscuit, who was in a traveling crate in the very rear hatch, barked in greeting.

Diane strained to lift her son into the vehicle, but he was too heavy. She heard the hospital doors whoosh open behind her and looked up to see Alexa running toward them.

"We have to hurry!" Diane said as Alexa caught up to them. They both helped lift Josh into the backseat and buckled him in a supine position. Then Diane climbed in beside him and slammed the side door while Alexa got behind the wheel.

❀❀❀

DIANE HELD HER son's arm tightly as Alexa navigated her way out of the parking lot. She pulled out onto the street, tires squealing.

Diane thought about Rick and how he would feel when he returned with her medicine. She felt awful about lying to him, but she couldn't get him involved. Even though she had fallen in love with him, she could never choose him over her children. The overpowering need to protect them was in her blood.

They had been and always would be her priority.

She just had to push him out of her mind.

"Oh my God, that was terrifying," Alexa said. The minivan hit a bump in the road, and Josh grimaced. He made a congested sound. He was trying to cough.

"Oh, no. You didn't grab Josh's nebulizer from the house, did you?"

Alexa glanced back at her mother. "No! You didn't tell me to!"

"I forgot. We need to go back for it."

"Are you serious?" Alexa asked. "We can't."

"We have to," Diane insisted. She tried to calculate the trip in her head. They still should have enough time to swing by the house before anyone was able to get there. "Take a right up here and head to the house. But whatever you do, don't go over the speed limit."

Seven minutes later, they pulled off the highway. They were on Main Street, just four blocks from Diane's house, when a Fog Harbor police cruiser flew past.

"Oh, no! Do you think that's for us?" Alexa asked.

"Stay calm and just turn left here. We need to get back on the highway. We'll have to get a nebulizer some other way."

Alexa did as instructed, and not three minutes later they sped past a sign that read:

THANK YOU FOR VISITING FOG HARBOR
PLEASE COME BACK SOON

CHAPTER 41

FIVE MILES OUTSIDE of town, Alexa drove the minivan over an ocean inlet and watched as her mother threw their cell phones into it. They'd buy burner phones when they were far enough away.

Another fifteen miles out, they neared the entrance to the tollbooth for the interstate. Alexa pulled off the highway and into the dark parking lot of a skating rink. She sat trembling in the backseat with Josh as Diane replaced the car's license plate with one of the several from Josh's collection. They would change the plate again at the first exit after the tollbooth. Josh had over forty old plates in his collection, so they could keep changing them out.

They would also have to do something about the minivan before too long. But they'd cross that bridge later. Tears in her eyes, Alexa studied her sleeping brother. She still had a difficult time believing he was capable of the things he'd done. He just had so much good in him. She knew, because she'd lived with him most of her life.

"Mom and I . . . we're going to take really good care of you, Joshie," she said. "You're going to be just fine . . . and you'll never ever even want to do those terrible things you did again." She said even more quietly: "And if you do, we won't let you. Okay?"

She watched her brother as he slept and hoped to God that what she'd just told him was true.

She glanced to the back of the minivan, where her mother was screwing on the new license plate, and she knew she'd made the right decision. For once she was thinking about her family instead of herself. About her mother, who had always put Josh and her first. About her brother, who needed her . . . and at the moment, she felt better about herself than she could ever remember before feeling.

❖❖❖

FOUR HOURS LATER they pulled into a gas station outside of Burlington, Vermont, and Diane watched Alexa pull her hood up around her head and run toward the bathroom. Diane did the same with hers and crawled out of the minivan to fill up the tank.

As she pumped the gas, a vehicle drove up to the pump behind her, and she instinctively angled herself so that her back was to it. Biscuit started barking from the back of the minivan. As she shushed him, she heard the door to the vehicle behind her open and someone get out.

A moment later: "Diane?"

Her heart tumbled into her stomach.

What the—

Her mouth turned to sandpaper.

She whirled around to find Rick standing next to a Dodge Caravan. It had been one of the two spare vehicles that had been parked outside of his cabin.

"You could have told me," he said gently.

She clamored for words. "Oh my God, how did you find us?"

He held something in front of him. A device of some kind. "It's the receiver to the GPS locator I gave Josh for our hikes, so I could easily find him if we'd gotten separated. He could never remember to turn it off. It must be in his coat pocket."

Josh's coat. It was packed.

"Diane, I know what you're trying to do here, but—"

Diane interrupted him. "You really shouldn't have followed us, Rick. This doesn't concern you."

"Let me help."

Tears stung her eyes as they stared at one another, but Diane managed to fight them back. Yes, she wanted his help, and she wanted him with them, but she couldn't let him get involved. What they were doing was dangerous.

"You won't get far alone," Rick said.

Diane shook her head again. "You don't know what Josh has done. I can't—"

Rick walked up to her and placed a hand on her shoulder, and she felt herself weaken to his touch. "It's all over the news right now. The police are calling all three of you persons of interest."

The dam inside of her finally broke. She felt her face crumple. "It was him, Rick," she whispered. "The whole time. Right under my nose. I just . . . I still don't understand. I can't wrap my head—" Saying it out loud untethered all the emotions she had been trying to push down, compartmentalize.

Rick wrapped his arms around her. He held her tight for a long moment, then tilted her chin up so she was looking into his eyes. His gaze was warm, determined.

"Let me help. I know back roads. I can get us across the border. And the first thing we need to do is all get into my vehicle. It's not traceable."

She was incredulous. "I can't ask that of you."

"You don't have to."

She stared at him, her heart almost bursting with love for him at the thought of him risking himself for her and her children. But still she was unsure of what to say or do. It just wouldn't be right. Not that she was even close to certain anything she was doing tonight had been.

"I think he should come." Diane turned to see Alexa standing behind her.

"It looks like you're outvoted," Rick said.

Diane gazed at both of them, and she nodded through her tears. "Okay."

"There's a weigh station a mile north. Follow me there and we'll make the switch."

❖❖❖

THEY PARKED AT the far end of the weigh station's parking lot, and Rick effortlessly carried Josh and situated him in the back of the Dodge Caravan.

Diane and Alexa climbed in. Alexa sat in the passenger seat, and Diane sat in the back with Josh's head propped on a pillow in her lap. Biscuit lay in his crate in the vehicle's third row with the luggage.

Before getting into the driver's seat, Rick handed Diane a duffel bag.

"What's this?"

"A go bag. I have plenty of antibiotics and syringes in the back if he needs them. I have two types of pain meds and cannabis oil, too. It's one of the best treatments there is for seizures . . . in case he ends up getting them, which he probably will."

A minute later they were on the highway, speeding north again. Diane realized that in a blink of an eye she had gone from a law-abiding suburban widowed mother of two teenagers to the fugitive mother of a serial killer. She was also helping an admitted serial killer evade the law, something she never would have imagined in her wildest dreams ever doing.

She was going against everything she believed in. What she was doing certainly wasn't right, legally, morally, or ethically, but the serial killer she was sheltering was her son . . . a child she'd spent nearly her entire adult life caring for and trying to protect . . . and at this moment, right or wrong, her heart was speaking much more loudly than her brain. Her whole adult life had been about sacrificing for her children. And Ellie, who had been right about so much, had been wrong about this one thing: this wasn't the time to stop.

She looked down at her son and noticed his eyes were open. He was trying to say something.

She bent down so her ear was closer to his mouth. "My . . . fish," he whispered.

She teared up at the irony that he'd be worried about his fish after all that he'd done. "Alexa left him on the kitchen counter with a note for Mr. Davidson," she said. "Asking for him to adopt it. I'm sure he'll give it a good home."

He closed his eyes again.

She ran her hand gently over the rough adhesive of his bandages, then through his dark hair, and shuddered at the thought that Josh had really hurt those girls. Those animals. She was determined to get him the help he needed to recover: physically, mentally, and emotionally.

She had briefly read about promising research a British psychiatrist who had treated several serial killers recently conducted. The facts that Josh had shown remorse and had wanted help to stop what he was doing made her hopeful. When they found a safe place to land for a little while, she would research much more.

She also thought about what the neurologist had said. There might be personality changes. Did that mean it might be possible that he would no longer even have the urge to kill? She considered it, then a shiver crawled up her back at another thought. It *could* also mean he might have the urge to kill *more*.

One thing was for sure, though: she wouldn't let him hurt another soul. She'd die before that happened. And this time around, she wouldn't miss the signs. She'd watch him like a hawk.

She'd also find a way to help the families of the victims. She knew she could never make it up to them. That would be impossible. But she'd do something. She'd make Josh do something as well.

And as far as Alexa and herself went, it wasn't difficult to get new identification. They would get it, and they would start new lives. New lives with blank slates.

"Mom, look. It's the manager from the supermarket," Alexa said, and held out her iPad. A reporter was announcing that the Fog Harbor PD had obtained surveillance footage, and they were showing the grainy video of Josh in the store, his hood over his head. He'd been standing in an aisle not far from a girl who was shopping.

The report cut to a red-faced Wayne, who was being interviewed outside of Brookmart. "I know that boy . . . and I know his mom," he said. "They always seemed to be good people." He shook his head. "But I'm afraid you never know what people are capable of," Wayne continued. "You just don't know. Aside from that, I have no words. I guess I'm still in a state of shock."

When the news report was over, Alexa powered off the iPad, sat back in her seat, and closed her eyes. Diane studied her daughter and realized that she was carrying herself differently. She was no longer hunched over; she was sitting straight for once.

She reached for Alexa's hand with her right hand and Josh's with her left—and she squeezed both. It was the first time in years that she'd been so close—physically and emotionally—to both of them at the same time, and her heart swelled.

She thought about how her daughter had finally opened up and let her in. Admitted that she was suffering and wanted help. Diane knew exactly how to help her, and she *would* help her. She'd help them both.

Now that the adrenaline had run its course, Diane was exhausted. She lay back and closed her eyes, and her thoughts went back to Thanksgiving dinner. The red pill–blue pill conversation. Red pill: know the scary truth, or blue pill: live peacefully in ignorance, even though to do so, she was basically just buying into a big, fat lie.

It was a difficult question.

While she'd normally pick the red pill, right now the blue pill was looking awfully alluring.

She stared out the window. The weather had taken a turn for the worse, and now rain was coming down in sheets all around them. It beat against the sides of the vehicle and thrummed steadily against the windows. Rick eased off the accelerator and guided the vehicle more slowly through the inky night, toward what . . . she wasn't sure.

But despite not knowing, Diane felt a bizarre sense of calm. All her life she'd wanted nothing more than for her family to come together and feel whole. To feel as though they were all on the same team, the same side. And right now, no matter how motley and broken they all were, they finally did . . . and were.

ACKNOWLEDGMENTS

I have many people to thank for helping bring my fourth thriller, *The Stranger Inside*, to life.

First, a huge thank-you to Brian Jaynes for playing Mr. Mom for a good part of the year so that I could hole up for weeks at a time and write. Without your help, writing this book would have been close to impossible.

I'm grateful to my sons for sacrificing time with me and being reasonably understanding when Mommy had to work late and on weekends. I'll always remember Ryan getting irritated after a while and telling me, "Mommy, you should just give up writing that book." And Christopher for chastising me for writing scary books and telling me I ought to be writing funny ones instead.

Mom and Terry for understanding the many weeks I went off grid and couldn't be found. I am grateful to David Wilson for all the amazing support he's always given me. Mark Klein, a wonderful friend who continues to be one of my biggest cheerleaders and always an early reader. My awesome friend Charles Schreck for answering all of the questions I had about the profession and private life of a seasoned Marine sniper. Cindy Ward for opening up the doors to her "cabin in the woods" so I could have a quiet place to focus and write. Dana Koy for answering my crisis center questions. Roger Canaff for answering law enforcement questions and commenting on an early draft.

A huge thank-you to my beta readers: Izabela Jeremus, Ashley Previte, Laura Helseth, Amy Blair, and Kylie Eason.

I am thankful for Charlotte Herscher for her eagle eye during the development process. She always makes my books so much better. Jessica Tribble for excellent notes and being an all-around amazing editor and so much fun to work with. JoVon Sotak for also being a wonderful editor, and for buying this book!

I am thankful to Thomas & Mercer for being one of the very best publishers ever—and for getting my books in front of an incredible number of readers worldwide.

And I am *mostly* grateful to each and every one of my readers. Without you, I wouldn't be able to do what I do—and I absolutely love this work.

ABOUT THE AUTHOR

Photo © 2014 Alan Weisman

USA Today bestselling author Jennifer Jaynes has always had a passion for writing, even if it took her a while to turn her passion into a career. After graduating from Old Dominion University with a bachelor's degree in health sciences and a minor in management, she made her living as a content manager, webmaster, news publisher, editor, and copywriter. Then everything changed in 2014 when her first novel, *Never Smile at Strangers*, topped bestseller lists at *USA Today*, Amazon, and Barnes & Noble. At that point, there was no going back.

Since her debut, Jennifer has added two more novels to the Strangers Series and has released her first stand-alone. When she's not writing or spending time with her husband and twin sons, Jennifer loves reading, cooking, and studying nutrition. She and her family live in the Dallas area.